Olivier Bernard

Crossing Fates
Gay Love in Freedom Beyond Loss and Grief

Olivier Bernard

Crossing Fates

Gay Love in Freedom Beyond Loss and Grief

Historical Romance and War Fiction

Bibliografische Information der Deutschen Nationalbibliothek: Die
Deutsche Nationalbibliothek verzeichnet diese Publikation in der
Deutschen Nationalbibliografie; detaillierte bibliografische Daten sind
im Internet über http://dnb.dnb.de abrufbar.

Verlag: BoD · Books on Demand GmbH
         In de Tarpen 42, 22848 Norderstedt, bod@bod.de

Druck: Libri Plureos GmbH, Friedensallee 273, 22763 Hamburg

ISBN: 978-3-7693-1468-7

ONE

„Have you read the newspaper?", Paul asked Will... „No, not yet...
Why?" „... Here... Read the „Petit Parisien"...", Paul said, giving the
newspaper to Will... On the front page, in large prints, it said: „TOTAL
VICTORY OF JAPAN OVER PEARL HARBOUR" Under that title, the
„Petit Parisien" had reproduced the French translation of a text from the
White House, detailing the attack on the Hawaiian islands... A list of the
sunk ships had also been reproduced, and Will began to read it. He read
that the battleships USS Arizona and USS Oklahoma had been sunk, that
the battleships USS West Virginia, USS California and USS Nevada had
been sunk or very seriously damaged. The USS Pennsylvania was safe...
Other ships had also been sunk, such as the destroyer Cassin and the
destroyer Downes... The „Petit Parisien" also said two hundred planes
had been destroyed, and more than one hundred fifty had been badly
damaged... Will read the article to the end, then looked at Paul and said:
„But my poor, Paul: It's not a victory.... it's a total defeat for the Japanese...
They are probably crying their last tears in Tokyo by now..." „Huh? ... Are
you crazy, or what?", Paul answered, looking at Will... „...Look at the list
of the sunk ships over here... look..." „Yeah?" „...All you see on that list
are battleships, destroyers... and so on, right?" „....Yes..." „Do you see the
name of one single aircraft carrier on that list?" „...No. So what?" „Well,
aircraft carriers are certainly what the Japanese were looking for at Pearl
Harbor, not battleships..." – „But battleships are so big and so
powerful...", Paul answered... „Yeah... and so were the dinosaurs...
Battleships are a thing of the past! They have been replaced by aircraft
carriers..." „... What the hell are you talking about?", Paul asked... „Look
Paul, you remember last May, when the Bismark sank?" „Yes..." „...As
you know, the Bismark was our finest battleship... She was the world's

11

most feared warship... and she was known as the „terror of the sea"...,
huh?" „I do remember..." „Well, last May, she sank the Hood, Britain's
finest Battleship, then crippled the battleship „Prince of Wales"... but
later, she was attacked by a very small plane, a single plane, from the
British aircraft carrier „Ark Royal"... A torpedo from that small plane hit
its rudder and disabled the steering... As the Bismark was no longer able
to maneuver, she was attacked by other British ships, and she bravely
fought until her guns fell silent, her last munition spent. Then, our guys
sunk her, as she was in danger of falling into enemy's hands..." „Yeah?"
„...So, you see: A very small airplane from an aircraft carrier was capable
of disabling the world's most feared warship... Now, if I were the
Japanese, I would very much like to know where the American aircraft
carriers are.... Right now, they could be sailing to Tokyo, and Tokyo could
soon be bombed from hundreds of planes from those carriers..." „...I
wonder if the Japanese thought about that?" „Oh sure! That's why I say
it must have been a big, big disappointment to them when they didn't see
aircraft carriers at Pearl Harbor when they bombed that naval base..."
„What do you think is going to happen now?" „...In my view, the
Japanese have made a big mistake: It's a giant they have awaken... Thank
God, the Americans haven't declared war to Germany..."

But that was going to change... since on December 11, 1941, Hitler
declared war to the United-States... „...He's CRAZY!!! Totally insane...",
Will shouted out, when he heard the news... „...Calm down Will... Please!
Calm down...", Paul said to him... „Sure! Those clowns in Berlin are mad
as hell, and you ask me to calm down? Hitler must be crazy! To declare
war on the United-States, I mean..." „... What can you do? Please, Will: Sit
down!" „(...) I can't believe it! No, I can't! Not only are we at war with
England and Russia... but now, we'll have the Americans on our back..."
„(...) And I have another bad news...", Paul said, looking down at the
carpet... „What else?", Will answered. „(...) Well... Two weeks ago, I sent
a long letter to my parents in New York... telling them everything about
the two of us... you know... I was expecting a reply from them... But since
Hitler declared war to the United-States, my direct phone line to New
York has been cut... and I've been told it was no longer possible to send
or receive letters from the United-States..." „Huh? (...) But France is not at
war with America...", Will answered... „...I know that... But who do you
think has control over the phone lines and the postal services around

here, huh?" „(...)" „Yeah! ... That means I can't talk to my Dad and my family anymore... And I don't see how I could receive a reply from them, thanks to the Führer...", Paul answered, with a very sad face... „... I'm so sorry Paul... Really..." „I know Will... I know you are. All of this happens at the worst of times..." A few days later, they made a big Christmas tree at Paul's mansion, just like the year before... and although they tried, they didn't have much fun decorating it... „... Are we going to Berlin for Christmas? My Mum and Dad are expecting us...", Will asked Paul... „...Sure! Let's go... And I'm sure Ludwig is expecting us, too...", Paul answered, laughing... Then, looking at Lutz and Franz, Paul asked them: „Are you coming, guys?" „... I can't", Franz answered... I'm working..." „...And I won't leave him..." Lutz added... „Oh yes, you are... you're going to Berlin, I'm telling you!", Franz said to Lutz... Lutz took Franz's hands into his, and, looking straight into his lover's deep blue eyes, he said: „...Look Franz: I'm staying here with you... I won't leave you all alone... and there's nothing you can say to change my mind! I love you Franz, and that's it!" „But... I want you to go... to see your family...", Franz answered, with tears in his eyes... „...I know... But I'm not going. Period.", Lutz answered. Franz turned to Paul, and told him: „Say something... I want him to go to Berlin..." „... I think I understand how he feels... and if I were in his shoes, I would make the same decision... I would never leave Will alone...", Paul answered... „...And neither would I...", Will added... „See... and don't worry Franz... I'll see my family later...", Lutz answered, giving Franz a light kiss on his lips...

Two days before Will and Paul were about to leave for Berlin, Franz came to see Paul... „(...) We received a long message at the embassy from New York... Since it was coded, I had to decipher it... (...) It's from your mother... Please Paul, sit down..." Franz said to his friend, as he was giving the message to him... Paul sat, then took the long message, and started to read it... Franz kept silent and sat beside his friend... As Paul read the message, he turned white, and tears came to his eyes... When he had finish reading the message, he slowly put it down on the coffee table in front of him and stared at the oil painting of his parents over the large fireplace... Franz looked at Paul and took his hands into his... „(...) I'm so sorry, Paul..." Paul turned to look at Franz. His eyes were full of tears. But he was silent... „(...) What can I say, Paul... what can I say?", Franz said... „Nothing", Paul answered... „I just can't believe she wrote that..." „...(...)

I know..." After a long moment of silence, Paul looked at Franz and said: „...Now... not a word to Will about that message... Promise me! It's almost Christmas, and I don't want this message to ruin his fun!" „But..." „Not a word! Promise me..." „I swear...", Franz answered. „Thanks. I'll tell him later... after Christmas...", Paul answered. After Franz had left, Paul went to his bedroom, and cried all the tears he had... Thank God he was alone, and thank God Will was at work... He cried for a long time, then fell asleep...

When Will got back from work that night, he found Paul on his bed, still sleeping... He sat on the bed, gave his lover a kiss... When Paul woke up, he looked at will, and smiled... „How come you're sleeping at this time of day...", Will asked, smiling at his lover... „Oh... I wonder if I haven't caught a cold... It's nothing, really... I already feel better...", Paul answered, smiling... „We won't go to Berlin if you're not feeling well...", Will said... „That's out of the question! A good night's rest, and everything will be alright, I tell you!", Paul answered, with a grin on his face... „...We'll see about that...", Will said... „Come on: Let's go downstairs, and have supper... I'm feeling better, I swear to you..." Paul put a big smile on his face, and nothing was said about the message he had received from New York... Two days later, Will and Paul flew to Berlin, where Will's father as well as Ludwig were waiting for them at Tempelhof Airport... „I'm so glad to see you, both...", Ludwig said, as he hugged them... „And so do I...", Will's Dad said, as he hugged them too... „Let's go home...", he added... On Christmas Eve, they had a big party, and Lutz's parents were there, too... Lutz had explained to them he couldn't make it to Berlin this time, since he had to work on some important papers in Paris... They sang Christmas carols, and had a lot of fun... At least, Paul was acting as if he was having lots of fun... but in fact, his heart was bleeding... „... At least, this year, you didn't have to go to a Christmas party at the New Chancellery...", Will's Mum said, laughing... „Thank God! I guess they are too busy with the war in Russia to throw a party! (...) But do you know what? Last year, a few weeks after that party, the German embassy in Paris sent me a framed picture of me with the Führer... shaking hands...", Paul said, laughing... „... What did you do with that picture?", Will's father asked... „...Oh, it's in my study, locked in a drawer... Do you believe me, if I tell you I'm not running around, showing that picture?", Paul answered, laughing... „...I can understand...", Lutz's Mum said, laughing her heart out... „Yeah! So, as I said... with the war in Russia... There was no party this year...", Paul said... „...I saw my brother the other day...", Will's Dad started to say... „The Field Marshal?", Lutz's Dad asked... „Yes...", Will's Dad answered. „He had a heart attack last month, and when he strongly opposed continuing the advance into the Soviet Union because it's winter now, Hitler refused to call a halt. Since his views were rejected, he asked to be replaced... and the Führer granted his request..." „Did he say how things are going on, on the front...", Will asked... „...He said our soldiers are freezing to death, right in front of Moscow..." „Thank God, Hans is not there... According to his last letter, they took Rostov at the end of last month... He said it's not so bad over there...", Lutz's father said... „... I wonder if this madness will stop one day...", Lutz's mother said, with tears in her eyes... „Oh it will, Madam... It's just we don't know when...", Will answered... The day after Christmas, as Ludwig was out with a few friends, Will and Paul showed Will's parents the military deferment papers they had received from the Wehrmacht... „...Thank God!", Will's mother said... „How can we thank you, Paul!" – „...We want Ludwig to come to Paris in June, at the end of school...", Will said... „...It's not easy for us to let him go, you know...", Will's Dad said... „...I know, Dad! But he'll be with us... and I swear to you, I will take good care of him! I just want to see him out of the Reich...", Will answered with tears in his eyes... „And I wish you wouldn't stay in Berlin..." „...Where would we go?", his Dad asked... „We're perfectly safe here... but we want to keep Ludwig away from the army for as long as we can... So, your mother and I have talked a lot about that, and we've decided Ludwig will go with you... as long as you two swear you'll take good care of him..." „...Herr von Rundstedt... I love Will more than anything in the world... and I love Ludwig as much as I love my own brother! So, today, I solemnly swear to you... and to you too, Mrs. von Rundstedt... That I'll do all I can... and that I'll use all the means at my disposal to protect your two sons! And I swear to you I'll take good care of them...", Paul said, with tears in his eyes... „We know you will, Paul! We know you will, son... and we love you... We love you more than you can think...", Will's Mum answered... „You don't know how much that means to me, hearing you say that...", Paul said, crying... „And I swear to you, Mum and Dad, that I will take good care of my baby-brother... I swear!", Will added... „...Oh, we know you will, Will... that's why your mother and I have decided Ludwig will go with you...", his Dad answered, hugging his son...

Of course, when Ludwig got back, he was totally ecstatic about the fact he was going back to Paris nest summer, to stay there, with Will and Paul... „Yeah bro...", Will said, grinning... „But don't forget: I'll be the one who will check your school's results... and let me tell you, mister: They better be food, cause if not, it's going to be hell for you, I swear!" „And you're going to have to obey to what Will and Paul say to you... Otherwise, you'll be back to Berlin before you know it! Is that clear, son? Is that clear?", Will's Dad said... „Yes Dad! I hear you loud and clear...", Ludwig answered... „I swear to you and to Mum I will obey them... I swear..." – „Fine!", Will's Mum answered, smiling... As Will and Paul were about to leave for Tempelhof, Will's Mum took Paul apart, and she said to him: „...Here, son... Take this letter... Should something happen to us, I want you to give it to Will. Can I count on you?", she asked, with tears in her eyes... Paul looked at her, and answered: „...Nothing will happen to you..." „Maybe... but swear to me that, should something happen... you will give that letter to Will..." Paul took the letter and, looking Will's Mum straight in the eyes: „You know, Madam, I love you... so count on me... I will give it to him, should something happen to you..." – „I love you too, Paul... And I trust you...", she answered, before kissing him on both cheeks... „Now go, son..." Will and Paul flew back to Paris, and one night, after supper, Paul looked at Will and said: „... Before we left for Berlin, I got a message... from my mother... It came through the Swiss embassy..." – „Oh... But why didn't you tell me..." „(...) I couldn't...", Paul answered... „(...)" „But why?" „Wait for me..." Paul walked over to his study, took the message... and walked back to the drawing-room, then sat beside Will... „Here: Read it. You will understand!" Will took the message, and started reading it... After he had read it, he looked at Paul, his eyes full of tears... „(...) I... I can't believe...", Will started to say...

„... I can't believe your mother wrote you a letter like that...", Will said, stunned...The letter said they had received Paul's letter, in which he was explaining to his parents he was gay and in love with Will, a German officer but not a Nazi... In her reply, his mother said she was devastated; that, as a devout Catholic, she could no longer recognize him as her son; that he was living in sins; that he was depraved... She went on, saying

16

homosexuality was condemned by the Bible and by the Pope, and that she was ashamed to have given birth to a pervert! She further wrote that he was a traitor, not only to his religion, but to France as well, being „in love" with a German officer... Last, she wrote that, not only was she breaking all relations with her son, but that she had forbidden Paul's sister and brother to come into contact with him! Period! Will read the letter for a second time... Obviously, Paul's Mum had carefully chosen each word as to hurt her son in what he loved the most: His country, his love for Will and his ties to his family... Will raised his eyes and looked at Paul, who was silently crying... „.... I... I don't know what to say, Paul... all I know is that I love you... and whatever she says, I know we're not depraved, nor are we perverts..." „.... She's my mother, Will! My own mother, for God's sake!" – „(...)" „.... I don't know, Will... I don't know what to think, really: I don't."

For the first time, it struck Will that they were right in the middle of a big crisis... He suddenly realized his happiness was seriously threatened, and there was absolutely nothing he could do to chase the clouds away: The storm was right there, right over their heads... and he didn't know how to navigate through it... After a long moment of silence, Will said: „....Do you want me to leave? (...) I could move to an army camp..." „....Not over my dead body! You're not going anywhere...", Paul shouted out, with tears in his eyes... Will remained silent. Tears were running down his cheeks. He was totally lost! After another long moment of silence, Paul said: „.... May I ask you something, Will?" „Huh?" „.... Would you mind if I'd took a few days, and go to Bagatelle... alone... you know... to sort things out a bit?" Hearing that, Will started to cry like a baby! He felt he was losing Paul... He felt helpless... All he knew was he couldn't live without Paul! Now, Paul was about to leave... „....Hey! Don't get me wrong...", Paul said, seeing Will was desperate... „ ...Just a few days: That's all I ask!" – „.... But... I don't want you to leave...", Will said, sobbing like a child... „... I must go, Will! I need some time all by myself..." „.... I love you, Paul! That's all I can say! I love you!!!" „So do I...", Paul answered, with a very sad smile on his face...

The morning after, Paul was gone... Will told Lutz and Franz about the message from New York... and the fact that Paul had left. He felt sick, and had difficulty breathing... „Did you know about that message?", Lutz asked Franz... „Yes. We received it at the embassy, and since it was coded,

17

I had to decipher it...", Franz sadly answered. „And you didn't tell me about it?", Lutz asked... „I'm sorry Lutz... It was private, and I was under strict orders to give it to Paul, and to no one else, and to keep my mouth shut!" „(...)" „Now, he's all alone at Bagatelle... and I don't even know when I'll see him again...", Will sadly said... „Don't worry Will: Paul is a strong guy... He's stronger than any of us here... and I know he loves you... Give him time...", Lutz said, giving Will a big hug... „Lutz is right, Will!", Franz added... „Paul is my best friend, and he never failed me... I know he will be back to you, cause he loves you!" „...Sure!", Lutz said... „But this mother of his is a real bitch, if you want to know what I think! She doesn't deserve to have a son like Paul! I hope she will rot in hell one day!" „...Oh, I'm sure she will", Franz said... „And she will be in good company there, since her Pope will be rotting there, along with her!" „...I'm not a Catholic... so I don't give a damn about that Pope...", Will said, grinning.... „...At least, it makes you smile, thinking he will be rotting in hell...", Lutz answered, laughing... „Yeah!", Will replied, laughing... „It's good to see you laugh...", Franz said. „And like the British like to say: If you're going through a storm, pull your hat over your eyes, and charge into it..." „They have been doing that pretty well, for the last two years, haven't they?", Will said... „Yup! And they are still there, fighting against all odds...", Franz answered, grinning... „I'll do that!", Will said. „Anyway, what else can I do?"

At Bagatelle, a few days later: „Monsieur de Brion", the governess said to Paul... „Monsieur le Curé est arrivé..." „Oh yes... Thanks! Please, show him in...", Paul answered. „Ah monsieur Paul: Comment allez-vous? Heureux de vous revoir... et merci pour l'invitation à souper...", the Vicar said, with a big smile on his face „My pleasure...", Paul said... „Please, do sit down... May I offer you an aperitif?" „Oh, ... would you still have some of the Grand Marnier your grandmother used to have?", the Vicar asked, with a crooked smile on his face... Paul burst out laughing, and said: „...But of course, Father! I just didn't think a man of the cloth like you would be drinking Grand Marnier..." – „Oh? But why not? It's not because I'm a priest that it means I'm not living in the same world as you..." „...Yes... I suppose so..." A bit later, and as they were savoring their aperitif, Paul said: „...Father... I have something here... that I would like you to read..." „But of course... What is it?" „It's a letter I've recently received from my mother in New York!" „Oh?" „... Please: Read it!" As the Vicar was reading the letter, Paul kept staring at him, to see any sign on his face... any trace of... disgust! He didn't see anything like that on the Vicar's face, to his relief... Then, the Vicar gave back the letter to Paul and, looking at him straight in the eyes, he said: „...Those are very harsh words! I'll have to pray for your mother..." „...And what about me? Am I going to eternally rot in hell?" „...What about that German officer she's speaking about?" „...It's true, Father! He's German! But he's not a Nazi... Not at all! He hates Hitler as much as I do... And I'm not a traitor, just because I love someone who happens to be German! All Germans are not Nazis, and all Germans are not bad... just a few of them... And Will is not one of those! He's a fine man! And I love my country: I would give my life to save it, I swear to God!" The Vicar smiled, and said: „...Now... calm down, son... I believe you! And you're quite right: All Germans are not bad... And no... you will not rot in hell because of your homosexuality..." „... But the Bible says so... and so does the Pope!" The Vicar raised his eyes, and looked at Paul straight in the eyes, then asked him: „Have you ever read the Bible?" „...No!" „You should!", the Vicar answered, grinning... „(...)" „You see, son, contrary to what most people believe, the Bible is not „ONE" book... it contains seventy-two different books... Forty-five of these books are called the „Old Testament", while twenty-seven of them constitute what we call the „New Testament... Now, the term „Old Testament" refers to all versions and translations of the Old Hebrew Bible... Who wrote what? and When? And who translated what, and when? We don't know... And when you, or your mother, say homosexuality is condemned by the Bible, you're wrong! It's condemned in ONE passage of ONE of these seventy-two old books... As I said, these books were written long before the birth of Jesus... and if you read them... or at least most of them... you'll be disgusted! They speak about war... about so many battles, I've lost count of them! Blood is flowing like rivers... people are slaughtered... It's one massacre after another... And according to these books, it's perfectly normal for a man to have as many wives as he wants... and he can repudiate them, if he wants to... No problem! He can sell them... he can kill them or have them pelt with stones... OH! And slavery is perfectly normal... And indeed, all of those who, until recently, were in favor of slavery, used to quote the Old Testament to make their point! Now, do you think slavery is okay?" „...Of course not!", Paul answered... „...See? (...) We have to be very, very careful when we read these old books... I read them... I even spent years, studying them, and I tell you: I'm staying as far away from them as I can! And I would never, ever quote them to make a point! And most certainly, I didn't become a priest, because of the Old Testament! „Oh?" „If you really want to read something useful, read the New Testament... Read what Jesus said and preached... The only thing he talked about was LOVE! He never condemned anyone... And in fact, when a crowd wanted to lapidate a poor woman, because she had committed adultery, he stopped them from doing so. He simply looked at the crowd and said: „He who has never sinned, may cast the first stone..." And of course, they all left... But by doing what he did, Jesus went against what is written in the Old Testament, since that form of punishment is clearly authorized by the old books... No! I tell you, son: I became a priest because of what Jesus taught us: Love! And Jesus doesn't condemn you for what you are... He loves you! He created you the way you are! How could he hate you? And if some people say it isn't so, let them say whatever they want: They are bigots! And remember son: Never argue with bigots... they are not worth it..." „Nevertheless, the Pope condemns me..." – „No! He condemns homosexuality... not you!" – „What's the difference? I mean..." „Oh, but there is a big difference, son! The Pope also condemns... say... gluttony... but that doesn't mean you'll be excommunicated, just because you ate too much..." the Vicar said, laughing... „Of course, son... I'm a member to the Church, and I won't speak against Rome! But remember: Years ago, Rome condemned Galileo, because he had said Earth was round... (...) You're laughing, now?" „Well... I mean..." „Yes, But I'm telling you: At the time, Galileo wasn't laughing..." – „No, I can imagine...", Paul answered, grinning... „So, you see... The church is not perfect, because we, human beings, are not perfect... we are only perfectible... So, when you go to sleep tonight, don't worry about hell! Only Hitler will go there... and I'm not even sure of that, for God is so merciful! (...) Now, I don't know about you... but I'm starving...", the Vicar said, laughing... Paul burst out laughing and, together, they walked over to the dining-room, where they ate plenty... „...Some wine, Father?", Paul asked the Vicar... „...I thought you'd never ask!", the vicar answered, laughing... That night, after the Vicar had left, Paul gave Will a call, to let him know everything was fine... „...I'm so glad to hear your voice, Paul... I love you so much! When are you coming back?" „...I don't know yet... In a day or two, maybe...I have a few things to do here, before I leave..." „You should come back as soon as possible... Franz has another message for you... It's from your father!" – „Shit!" „No, no... Although he refused to tell me what it was, Franz said you would like it..." „... Do you have that message with you?" „No. Franz kept it. He said he's under strict orders not to give it to anyone else but you..." Paul grinned, thinking that Franz was indeed a very good friend... Then he said: „I'll be back tomorrow... and Will?" „Yes?" „I love you..." „I love you, too... so much!" „See you tomorrow... Night Will!" „Night Paul!"

The day after, when Paul got back home, Will was waiting for him... When Paul opened the door, Will took him into his arms, and the two lovers started crying, then kissing... „...I've missed you so much...", Will said... „I've missed you, too... but I had to go, do you understand?" „...As long as you're back, I'm not asking myself that kind of questions..." Will answered, smiling... Then, Paul told him everything about the discussion he had had with the Vicar... „...He's a wise man!", Will said... „He's wrong about one thing, though..." „What?" „...Hitler will rot in hell!" They burst out laughing and, after a while, Paul said to Will: „...Let's give Franz a call: I want to read my father's message..." Later that night, Franz came with the message and, as he was about to leave, Paul told him: „Where the hell do you think you're going like that?" „...I wanted to leave you two alone..." „Sit right there, mister! You're my friend... I want you here with us... We have nothing to hide from you..." Franz sat, then waited for Paul to read the long message from his father. Will was sitting right next to Paul, but he was not trying to read the message over Paul's shoulder. He was just nervously hoping for the best! As Will and Franz were watching Paul, they saw tears in his eyes... Then, Paul raised his head and gave the long message to Will: „Here... read it!", was all he could say... Will took the message and started reading it... Paul's father was explaining he had just learned about his wife's message to Paul. He had not known about it, much less read it... He said he loved his wife dearly, but that he also loved Paul... his dear son! For the first time in his life, he had to disagree with her on something important: He didn't share her views, and it was with a broken heart he had learned what she had said to Paul... „Mon fils, je ne te juge pas! Tu es mon fils, et tu le resteras toujours. Quelque soient tes choix, je serai toujours avec toi! Et je suis fière de porter ton nom! Je t'aime, mon fils... Et je serai toujours là pour toi! Toujours!" At the end of his letter, Paul's father was asking him to forgive his mother... „That's a beautiful letter... beautiful...", Will said, with tears in his eyes... „I love him so much! (...) I needed that message...", Paul answered... „...I guess he's expecting a reply...", Franz said... „Yes! I'll write it right now, so you can send it to him as soon as possible...

„Cher père: J'ai bien reçu ton message: Merci! Du fond de mon coeur... Je t'aime également... Pour ce qui est de mère, et puisque tu me le demandes, je lui pardonne... mais je ne puis pas oublier... Je le regrette, mais c'est ainsi! De ton fils qui t'aime..."

Paul gave his reply to Will, who read it. He didn't say anything. He just nodded, to let Paul know he agreed with it... Then, Will gave the message to Franz... Franz looked at it, then said: „I understand. It will be sent first thing, tomorrow morning..." „Thanks Franz! You're a pal!", Paul answered... That night, after Franz had left, Will didn't know what to do... He wanted so much to make love to Paul... But he was afraid to make the first move... Paul sensed it, and said to him: „Come here, you fool! You belong to me, and no one will ever take you away from me!"

Within moments, their clothes were off... Paul ran his hands all over Will's beautifully defined and hairless body... and their mouth joined, their cocks rigid, hard pressed against each other's stomachs... Paul squeezed Will's heavily laden balls, then his throbbing dick... Will sighed, then he pushed Paul to his knees: „Oh please... suck my cock, Paul... I need it so much..." Will held back of Paul's head, while he was giving his lover the best blowjob of his life... Will was gripping Paul's hair, forcing his dick further inside his lover's mouth. As Paul mouth fucked him, Will looked down on Paul's beautiful face working on him, and said: „Ohhhhh... it feels so good... I love you so much Paul... so much!" – „Un-huh!", Paul answered... Will pulled Paul up and cupped his face in his hands. He opened his mouth, and his tongue wandered out at him. Paul did the same, and their tongues met outside their mouths, and it was incredible! They were sucking on each other's tongues and kissed passionately. They were enjoying the closeness of their hot bodies... Then Will decided he wanted Paul to ride him, and so he stopped kissing his lover and laid down on the bed... „Come on, my love: Why don't you sit on me?", Will asked... „Yeah!", Paul answered, giving his lover a very sexy smile... He went to Will, and laid down over his beautiful lover... He

kissed him tenderly, then started nibbling on his ear... „I love you, Will...“
Paul rose and then, straddling Will, he pushed down his butt against
Will's crotch. He started making grinding movements, and Will's dick
responded quickly, oozing so much and growing harder as Paul rubbed
his butt against it... „Shit, you're good... I swear: You're the best“, Will
said, grinning... „Just wait...“ Paul's hands found their way up Will's
chest, and over his hard stomach... „You're so perfect, Will... I love your
body...“ „...And I'm all yours...“ Paul's hands slowly made their way
down on Will's hairless stomach... Finally, he felt Will's hard dick in his
hands... Paul moved his body down a bit and sat over Will's legs. He
leaned on his lover's crotch, and guided his oozing dick to his lips... First,
he just kissed it... But after a while, he couldn't resist anymore, and he
took it in his mouth... „Ahhhhhhh....“, Was all Will could say... Will's hard
dick filled Paul's warm and velvety mouth, and he played around with it
with his tongue... After a while doing that, Paul sensed it wouldn't take
long for Will to cum, so he pulled back, looked up at Will, then said: „Are
you ready to go to heaven?“, he asked his lover... „...With you... I'm ready
to go anywhere...“, Will answered, grinning... Paul sat over Will's very
well lubed dick... As he lowered his butt down, Will's hard cock parted
his buttocks, and slowly entered him... „Ohhhhh... That feels so good“,
Paul shouted out, as he felt Will's mushroom cap enter his ass ring.... In
one swift movement, Paul impaled himself completely on Will's hard
shaft, and he moaned, when he felt the mushroom cap hard pressed
against his prostate... „Oh shit! Oh shit... That's good...“, Paul cried out...
Paul swiveled his butt, and loved the feeling of having his bum screwed
by Will's oozing dick... „Oh my God...“, Will said... „I'm almost there
already... but I don't want to cum yet: Don't move for a minute or two,
okay?“ Paul grinned, but stayed still for a while... „...Okay...“, Will said...
„You can ride me now...“ Since Paul was sitting over Will with his legs
bent, Will was able to thrust up into him, as well as he to drive himself
down onto him... The squelching sensation of so much juicy ooze and the
sloppy wet noise it made added a complete animal feeling to the whole
deliciously hard fuck they were now having... Paul started to move faster
and harder, up and down Will's hard cock... It was incredible... Will felt
his hard dick racing in and out of Paul's tight arse, and they were both
moaning with passion as they fucked. Paul leaned over Will and, before
their lips touched, Paul said: „Harder! I want all of you deep inside me...“

Will put his arms around Paul, and they started kissing passionately, as Paul remained still over Will's dick, and Will started fucking him, thrusting his hips forward, then downward... It was not long before they neared cumming. Paul's oozing dick was rubbing against Will's smooth and very wet stomach with each movement... He couldn't keep it any longer and soon, he was cumming all over his lover's stomach... „...Oh shit, Will... I'm cumming... Ohhhhhhh...." As he felt his dick squeezed by Paul's ass muscle, Will shouted out and started cumming deep inside his lover's tight ass... „Here I cum... Ohhhhh... I'm cumming Paul...", Will cried out, moments before he drained himself, finally emptying his load into Paul's insides. His body shook with the feeling of complete release and utter pleasure at the act... They went on kissing for a while, then their lips parted, and Paul said: „That was good Will... That was sooooooo good!" „Yeah!", Will answered, laughing... „That was just incredible... But now, it's your turn..." „Huh?" „... Your turn to fuck me...", Will answered, grinning... „Oh, you...", Paul answered, laughing... And fuck his lover, he did! Slowly and lovingly at first, then with all the passion and power of youth... Oh yes... It was a long, a very long night! A night of pure love! And that night, before he went to sleep, Will said to himself: „Yeah! The crisis is over... The storm is over, thank God!" And he was right! Their love had been stronger than that storm! And it was a good omen, since other storms were in store for them in a not too far future...

T W O

The winter of 1942 was a very cold season, and in April, everybody was very happy to see spring was back once again, with warmer temperatures... „Maudit hiver!", Paul said to Will, as he was folding some winter clothing... „Yeah!... I guess if we were living in Martinique, we would not need those...", Will answered, smiling... „...I hope we will one day!", Paul answered. Early in May, Lutz told Paul and Will he had received a letter from his brother Hans, telling him they were on the offensive again on the Russian front, and that now, they were fighting in the Crimea and would soon be at Sevastopol's doors... „...They said last winter was the coldest winter they had seen in Leningrad since over a hundred years... can you imagine? No fuel, no food... nothing... They must be all starving to death...", Lutz added... „...This is totally inhuman...", Paul answered...

A few weeks later, they had a perfect example of how inhuman war can be, when Will came home one night and told Paul: „I guess it's „pay back" time for us..." „What do you mean?" „...Last night, Köln was bombed... and they say it was terrible... the biggest air raid we've ever seen over Germany... I've heard that more than one thousand British planes bombed the city and reduced it to rubbles..." „Shit! ... Was Berlin bombed?", Paul asked... „No!" „Thank God! I'm glad we'll soon be taking Ludwig away from the Reich... Things will only get worst over there..." „I wish my father would agree to leave Berlin... but he keeps saying he can't leave his clinic and his patients...", Will said... „Anyway, I don't believe they are in danger in Charlottenburg... it's so residential over there... no industries... no plants... Why would the Allies want to bomb Charlottenburg?", Paul asked... Will looked at his lover with a sorrow face and answered: „...That never bothered the Luftwaffe, you know...

when they bombed British cities: Whole residential areas were erased from the map in London... even though there were no industries over there..." „...The Allies are not savages, you know...", Paul replied. „Maybe!", Will answered, unconvinced.

At the end of June 1942, Paul flew to Berlin and had a few meetings with his German business partners... As usual, he was staying at Will's house and needless to say Ludwig had already packed his luggage... „I'm ready...", he stated, beaming... „...I can see you are...", Paul answered, laughing... „Now, behave yourself, young man!", Will's father said... „I will, Dad... I will...", Ludwig answered. That day, when they all got to Tempelhof, they were all crying... and as Ludwig kissed his Mum and Dad goodbye, he told them: „I love you so much... Thanks for letting me go..." – „We love you, son... Take good care...", they answered. „...And I love you too, Karin", Ludwig said, looking at his sister... „I'll miss our fights... but I want you to know that I really love you... really...", Ludwig said to her, hugging her and kissing her on the cheeks... „You won't believe me, Ludwig... but I'm going to miss you too... a lot... I love you bro, I swear...", she answered, crying... They didn't know it yet, but they were all turning a page in their lives... It was the end of an era, and they didn't know it yet! That was the last time Ludwig saw his parents and his sister alive. Later, he would not regret having taken the time to tell them he loved them!

Minutes later, as Ludwig and Paul were sitting aboard the airplane and were waiting for take off, Ludwig said: „YES! ... Paris, here I come!!!" Paul burst out laughing, then said: „Yeah... The Rabbit is back!" „What?", Ludwig asked... „The „Rabbit"... You're like a rabbit... a real sex maniac...", Paul answered, laughing... Ludwig burst out laughing, and then he started to rapidly tap the door with his foot, impersonating a hot rabbit... and he said: „Yeah! Here I come... Hold on to your hats, ladies..." „Oh my God! (...) We better buy a lot of rubbers...", Paul answered, laughing too... „You bet!" When they landed at the Bourget Airport, Will, Lutz and Franz were there to meet them... and they all burst out laughing when Paul told them: „I brought the Rabbit back with me: God bless all of us!"

Since they had decided they would spend the summer at Bagatelle, Paul and Ludwig moved over there as soon as they came back from Berlin. It had been agreed that Will would join them there every weekend, and that Lutz and Franz would come as often as they could... Ludwig went back to work at the greenhouse and was more than happy to find out that Marie-Hélène was still working there... Yup! The Rabbit was back, and it didn't take long before the two of them were... well... you know!!! That summer, Paul had decided to resume his swim training: He had developed a good swimming workout plan to help maintain and even develop his swimming technique and to get fitter, and had convinced Ludwig to train with him, since Ludwig liked to swim... At seven o'clock every morning, he would wake Ludwig up, and soon after, they would be in the lake, for an hour of daily training... Of course, the training was physically exhausting, but as they were getting stronger, they were also getting fitter... and it didn't take long for the results to show on Ludwig's body. At seventeen, he now had a well toned body, with nice pecs and he was rather proud of his rippling stomach... Of course, the swim training was helping a lot, and his shoulders were getting stronger as the training was progressing... „Do you think I have stopped growing?", Ludwig asked Paul one morning, after their daily training was over... „Oh... At seventeen? Probably not... you're what? 1.85 m ... I wouldn't be surprised if you grow another five cm before you stop growing..." „Hey! That would be cool...", Ludwig answered, beaming... Paul was smiling, thinking to himself that Ludwig was still very much a kid, but into a man's body... And what a body! With his blond hair and beautiful blue eyes, Ludwig was a typical example of the Aryan race Hitler was so found of, however stupid that notion was... Nevertheless, Ludwig had turned into a very good-looking hunk, Paul thought, and he had no doubt women would soon be chasing after him... He and Will would have to keep a very close eye on that young guy, otherwise he would wreak havoc in Paris... and Marie-Hélène would only be his first victim...

Paul never gave a thought about the fact Ludwig could also wreak havoc among men, too! He should have... That summer, a farmer from around the village had asked Paul's manager if his young son could have a job on the estate, since the family badly needed some extra money... So, one day, the young man came to see the manager, and introduced himself: „Good morning, Sir... I'm François... I think my father told you about me! I'm looking for a job..." – „Oh yes... I remember...", the manager answered, smiling... „How old are you?" – „Sixteen..." The manager looked at the young man, and was pleased to see he was quite muscular for a guy his age... Obviously, hard work on his father's farm had help him to develop a strong body, and that was what the manager needed on the estate: Strong arms to do some hard work... „...When can you start?", the manager asked... „Right now...", the young man answered, beaming... „Fine. You're going to be working at the greenhouse, since we're making extensive repairs on that building. I'm sure the guys over there will be glad if you can give them a hand..." „Sure can...", François answered, smiling... The manager and François walked over to the greenhouse, and the manager introduced him to the other guys working there... „Welcome dude!", Ludwig said to him... „Take a hammer and come with me..." The manager was glad to see Ludwig and François working together since they were about the same age, and the other guys were all older men. That way, the manager thought, François would not be pushed around by the others... As the days went on, Ludwig and François became good friends, and had a lot of fun, working together... But work at the greenhouse was not easy, and as it was very hot in there, most of the guys were only wearing pants or shorts, sweating like hell while working long hours... François wasn't shy about showing his body though, since for a sixteen-year-old kid, he had quite a well toned body. But what interested him most was to glance at Ludwig's very nice body... and more than once did he feel his dick twitch in his shorts, looking at his friend's strong shoulders and bare rippled stomach! François knew he was gay, but never would he say anything about that, knowing perfectly well he had to hide it: In the countryside where he was living, gays were not accepted, and were seen as sick and devious people... If he wanted to stay alive, he had to act as if he was straight, and he knew he had to act accordingly... And of course, it didn't take long before François learned about the „special relation" that existed between Ludwig and Marie-Hélène, as Ludwig never missed a chance to tell him about her „hot and tight slut", and her „big tits"... Each time, François would tell Ludwig how much he was envying him, and how much he was hoping he would soon find a girl like her... One night, Ludwig asked Paul if he could invite François at La Vacherie, so they could go swimming and have some fun... Paul wasn't too keen about the idea of having another person from the village at La Vacherie, since he wanted to keep the place a secret! On the other hand, Paul knew Ludwig was fond of his new friend, and it was only normal for him to be around a guy his age for once, instead of older guys like Will, Lutz and Franz...So Paul reluctantly gave Ludwig permission to invite François at La Vacherie, but under one condition: François would have to swear he would never, ever tell anything about the secret place to anyone. And Paul made sure François understood! Before Ludwig had a chance to talk to François about La Vacherie, Paul walked over to the greenhouse and took François apart. He told him Ludwig wanted to invite him over there, explained everything (or almost...) to him about the place, and made him solemnly swear he would keep the place a secret. François swore he would!

That weekend, Ludwig went to fetch François, and when they arrived at La Vacherie, François was stunned to see Will, Lutz, Franz and Paul, going around the place, stark naked! „...Oh! I forgot to tell you about that...", Ludwig told his friend, as if it was no big deal, and nobody cared... But for François, it was a big deal! How the hell was he going to hide the sizeable bulge he already had in his pants, just looking at those naked guys all around him! „I'm lost!", François thought to himself! Minutes later, he was even more stunned when he saw Lutz and Franz, kissing... „...They are gays...", Ludwig nonchalantly said to him... and he said that as if it was the most normal thing in the world... „And so are Will and Paul: They are lovers!" „...Are you, too?", François asked Ludwig, looking at his friend straight in the eyes... „No. I'm not.", Ludwig answered, grinning... „But it's their business... and I couldn't care less about that. Do you?" – „No, no... it doesn't bother me at all... I mean..." „Good!", Ludwig answered... „Now, let's go inside and get undressed, then, let's go for a swim... What do you think?" – „Sure", François answered, not knowing what else to say or do... He followed Ludwig inside the pavilion, and, in no time, Ludwig was stark naked right in front of him, waiting for him to get undressed... „...Ludwig... I don't know if I can... I mean..." „Are you shy?", Ludwig asked his friend... „It's not that... I don't know how to explain... I mean..." „What?" „...Ah shit! I have a hardon, that's why!", François answered... Ludwig looked down at his friend's pants and saw that, indeed, his friend had quite a bulge in his pants... „Nah! Who cares... It's not as if we're not used to see hardons around here...", Ludwig said, laughing... „Come on dude: Get undressed, and let's go for a swim... you'll see... the water will cool you down..." „...You think?", a very uneasy François asked... „Sure!" Reluctantly,

François slowly got undressed and when he took his underpants off, Ludwig said: „Hey dude! You really have a hardon…" François blushed to the roots of his hair and tears came to his eyes when he said: „…I told you so… What am I going to do… I'm so embarrassed… I can't go outside like that… and I suppose you will no longer want to be my friend…" „What? Just because you have a hardon? Do you think I care? Even if you were going to tell me you're gay, I wouldn't care…", Ludwig answered, laughing… François didn't answer, but felt relieved to hear Ludwig say that… „…Listen, pal: I have an idea, if you want to get rid of that hardon!" „Huh?", François answered… „Follow me into the kitchen: We'll get a bucket full of cold water… you'll put your dick into it, and I'm sure in no time, your dick will shrink…", Ludwig explained, laughing… „That might work…", François answered, grinning… And indeed, it worked! „Thanks, pal… I owe you one…" „Hey, no sweat! I get hardons all the time…", Ludwig answered, laughing… Maybe, François thought to himself… but you don't get a hardon like me, just looking at nude guys… But François' ordeals were not over: He almost went unconscious when he learned he would have to share a bunk with Ludwig later that night, since all the other beds were already taken… The rest of the day went well though, as François tried his best not to look at the other guys, and as he kept thinking about very bad things, each time he felt his dick was starting to get hard… Later, as all the others were going to bed, Ludwig said to his friend: „…Give me a hand, will you? We'll move our bunk over to the veranda… it's too crowded in there and besides, those clowns over there snore like bears…" „Sure, no problem…", François answered, grinning… As they went to bed, François said to his friend: „…Night pal! Sweet dreams…" „…You, too…", Ludwig answered. François couldn't believe he was laying there, right next to his nude friend… Obviously, Ludwig was totally oblivious of the fact his friend had fallen in love with him, and was doing his best not to show it… François made sure he was laying as far away as he could from Ludwig, but that was not so easy to do in such a small bunk…

Later during the night, he was awakened by Ludwig's moans… He didn't open his eyes… and started listening… Oh my God! He thought to himself… Is it possible? And of course, he was right: Right next to him, Ludwig was wanking… doing his best not to awake him! But François was already wide awake, and was very much enjoying the situation…

„...Taking care of a need?", François whispered to Ludwig, grinning...
„...Didn't know you were awake...", Ludwig answered, silently laughing... „Sorry if I woke you up, pal... but you know how it is... I had one of those urges..." „Yeah! I know what you mean, man... I'm hard as a flagpole myself..." „Hey! You gotta do what you gotta do, man... And I don't care if you want to take care of your urges... just don't cum on me...", Ludwig answered, grinning... François couldn't believe it: And before he could even give his friend an answer, Ludwig had removed the sheets, revealing his very hard and oozing dick to his friend laying right next to him... „...Might as well make ourselves comfy... and that way, we won't stain the sheets...", Ludwig whispered, looking at François with a grin on his face... „Wow!", François whispered... „It's quite a big dick you have there, man... Mine is not so big..." Ludwig looked down at his friend's hard dick and answered... „...Not as big as mine... but nothing to be ashamed of, dude..." „...I've never done that before with another guy...", François said... „Who cares... It's not as if I was jacking you off... or giving you head..." „Right!", François answered, thinking he would gladly put his friend's big dick into his mouth, and give him the best blow job of his life... „Hey!" Ludwig said, looking at François who had started wanking... „Not like that... spit into your hand... it's much better when your dick is slippery..." François couldn't believe his ears: The most beautiful guy in the world was laying right next to him, wanking, and giving him tips about how to jerk-off... „...Here... give me your hand...", Ludwig said to François... As François gave Ludwig his hand, Ludwig spat out a big gob of saliva onto it, then said: „...Now: Go for it, pal..." François was in heaven: He began slowly wanking his dick with Ludwig's saliva... loving it... loving him! „...Better?", Ludwig asked... „Shit, yeah!", François answered... „Much better..." Of course, François did his best not to stare at Ludwig's big dick all the time... but as it was quite dark outside and as Ludwig's eyes were closed... he did give it a few glances... No doubt, he was living the best night of his young life...

Then, he saw Ludwig do something his eyes couldn't believe: His friend put his index finger into his mouth, lubed it well, slightly raised his legs... then started to play around his asshole, with the tip of his finger... „...What are you doing?", François whispered... „What do you think I'm doing? Don't you play with your hole when you wank?", Ludwig answered... „...Never done that...", François answered, stunned...

„...You should! Marie-Hélène does that to me all the time... It's fantastic!"
Hearing that, François slightly raised his legs, lubed his index finger, then
started to play with his asshole... „...That's it, man... but don't stop
wanking... and then, slowly push your finger inside your rosebud...",
Ludwig explained... „What?" „Come on... do as I say... you'll love it...",
Ludwig answered, grinning... So, François did as Ludwig had said, and
he quivered when his fingertip came into contact with his love spot...
„Ohhhhh shit!", he said... „That feels good..." „Have you found your love
spot?", Ludwig asked, grinning... „Hell! I don't know what I've found...
but I love the feeling...", François answered, moaning... „Keep rubbing
it... you'll love the result!" It didn't take long before the two friends were
groaning and moaning... and as their hard dicks were oozing so much,
their hands started to bob faster and faster on their hard pricks... „Shit",
François whispered... „That's my best hand-job ever! I swear..." „Yeah!...
Feels good, doesn't it?", Ludwig answered, grinning... „But keep your
voice down, will you?" „I'm doing my best... but... Oh shit!... I'm going to
cum..." „....Me too...", Ludwig answered... The two friends orgasmed at
the same time, and started to shoot wads after wads of hot young teen
cum all over their muscular bodies...

„...Told you, you would love it...", Ludwig said, as he dipped a finger
into his cum, then took it to his mouth, tasting it... „....You eat your cum?",
François asked, stunned... „...Don't you eat yours?", Ludwig asked...
„...Never tried..." „Try it..." François did as told, and a bit later, he said:
„Yeah! It does taste good..." „Told you...", Ludwig answered, grinning...
„Do you know many other tricks like that?", François asked... „Yeah! I've
heard about a few others... but... you know... since we're straight, they are
not for us..." – „Oh?" „Yeah...", Ludwig answered... François wished he
could ask Ludwig all about those other „tricks"... But he refrained from
doing so, not wanting his friend to learn he was gay! François was certain
Ludwig would never wank with him again, if he knew he was gay... and
he wanted so much to repeat the experience again. It was much better to
keep his secret all to himself, he decided! As the weekend came to a close
and as Will, Lutz and Franz were packing, Will said to François: „Hey
dude! Want a lift? On our way, we could drop you off at your home, if
you wish..." „Sure!... Thanks!", François answered... Later, as Will and
Paul were alone, Will said to Paul, talking about François: „He's a nice
kid!" „Yeah! And I'm sure he's gay!", Paul answered, grinning... Will

grinned and answered: „...I was wondering if you had felt it, too..." „...Not that he's effeminate... quite the contrary... but I can feel it... I can't explain why..." „Same for me!", Will said... „Do you think Ludwig knows?" „...I don't think so... Not the way he's acting... To him, François is just another straight friend, that's all..." – „Yeah! And I suggest we don't say a word to him about that... If François is gay, as we think... and if he wants to tell Ludwig... it's his business, not ours..." „Right!", Paul answered, giving Will a tender kiss... „I'm going to miss you this week...", Will said... „Oh but you won't be alone all week long... I have to go to Paris on Thursday... so I'll sleep there that night, and Friday night, we could come back here together... I could ask Franz do drive my car back..." „Good idea...", Will answered... „But we would leave Ludwig here, all alone?" „Well, he's seventeen now... and he's working all day long at the greenhouse... I don't think he needs a babysitter for one night, do you?" „...You're right. A little leeway won't hurt, I guess..." „I love you!", Paul answered... „And I you...", Will replied! That Thursday morning, right after their usual swim training, Paul had a serious talk with Ludwig. He explained to him he had to go to Paris and would not be back before Friday night. Then he said: „...Now Ludwig, I want you to promise me that, while I'm away, you won't bring Marie-Hélène here... I don't want to have her father on my back again, like last year... do you understand?" „Yes, Paul... I promise I won't, trust me! (...) But would you mind if I ask François to stay with me at La Vacherie, while your gone... He could keep me company..." „Sure. No problem. But just the two of you, you hear?" „I swear!" So Paul left for Paris, confident that Ludwig would be true to his word... and he was! But was it wise to leave Ludwig alone with François? That question never crossed Paul's mind!

THREE

„Hey man: We have the place all to ourselves...", Ludwig said to François, beaming... „Where's Paul?", François asked... „In Paris! Won't be back till tomorrow night... Care for a dip into the lake?", Ludwig asked his friend, as he was getting undressed... „Sure... Why not! It's so hot tonight..." It was always so hard for François to get undressed in front of Ludwig... But his efforts were rewarded, and once again, he succeeded to do so without sporting a hardon... In fact, to avoid such an embarrassment, François had imagined a very good stratagem: Each time he felt his dick was going to get hard, he would start thinking that Marie-Hélène, Ludwig's girl friend, was going after him instead and that she wanted him to fuck her! He hated the girl! What a disgusting idea, he thought! He would never agree to fuck that girl... Never! And that would do the trick to his dick... Oh yes! So, as he was getting undressed, he started to think about Marie-Hélène going after him, and he was so disgusted by the idea, his dick did not even twitch... They ran into the lake and had fun there, like two kids in a candy store... Later that night, they had supper on the veranda... just the two of them... Ludwig had opened a bottle of wine, and the two of them had fun, talking, laughing at Ludwig's jokes... François couldn't stop thinking about how lucky he was to be able to spend such a beautiful night, all alone with the guy of his dreams... Ludwig is so beautiful, he thought, and the guy does not even realize it! After supper, Ludwig went inside the pavilion and a few minutes later, he was back with a bottle of rum! „Hey... Go easy with that...", François warned him: „That's not like wine, you know... My Dad drinks that kind of stuff, and it's strong..." „Oh come on dude...", Ludwig answered, laughing... He took two small glasses and filled them up to the rim with rum. He gave François one glass, took his, then raised it and said: „Santé!" Ludwig took his glass to his lips, opened his mouth, then swallowed all of its content in one big gulp! „Wow!", he said... „That's strong man!", he said, laughing... François grinned and took one small sip from his glass... „Oh boy... That's good stuff, you know...", François answered... Then François saw Ludwig fill his glass again, and he drank it all in a swig... „...Shit man... take it easy...", François said... „Don't drink so fast..." Ludwig had drunk wine on many occasions since he was in France, and he had drunk a few beers... but this was his first time with spirit and, like all first-time drinkers, he just didn't know how to drink... After the second shot came a third, than a fourth... and then a fifth... all swallowed in one gulp... „...I'm telling you pal: You're going to have a big hangover tomorrow...", François told him, laughing... „Nah!", Ludwig answered, filling his glass for the sixth time... François took a sip from his glass... and felt the warm stuff go down his throat, with a burning sensation: He could feel the glow of warmth deep down in his stomach, and wondered how Ludwig could drink so fast... Ludwig was laughing his heart out and at one point, when he tried to raise from his chair, he just fell right back onto it... A few minutes later, and even though he was trying hard to concentrate, he was not able to put two intelligible words one after the other... „...I'mmmmm dro.... drunk...", He succeeded saying, laughing... „...I'm going to get you some water...", François said to him...

He went inside to fetch a glass of water and when he came back, he found Ludwig passed out, with his head resting on the table... François tried to wake him up... and all Ludwig said was that he wanted to go for a dip into the lake... „Oh no pal!", François said... „You're so drunk, you would drown yourself... The only place you're going to go is to your bed, silly..." Ludwig was too drunk to answer... „Come on pal... Enough for tonight... Let's go to bed, you fool!", François said, laughing at his drunk friend... Since Ludwig was no longer able to do anything on his own, François helped him get off from his chair and all he understood was that Ludwig needed to take a piss... „Okay, okay pal... Come with me..." François put his arm around Ludwig's waist to help him walk over to the edge of the veranda... „Okay... you can piss now...", he said to his friend... After a few seconds, François realized Ludwig was pissing not only all over the veranda, but also on his feet... „Hey! Stop that!", François said... Since François was standing right behind Ludwig, holding his friend so he wouldn't fall... he put one arm around Ludwig's waist and with his other hand, he took hold of his friend's dick, telling him: „...Okay now... you can piss... come on Ludwig: I can't do it for you...", François said, laughing... „Piss straight... over the edge, not all over the veranda... and not on your feet... can you do that?" „Yerrr", Ludwig tried to answer... Ludwig started to relieve himself: He began to piss and this time, his piss gushed below, on the ground... and not all over his feet... „Ahhhh", Ludwig said... too happy to empty his full bladder... Ludwig was leaning hard on François, his back hard pressed against his friend's rippled chest... François couldn't believe he was holding Ludwig like that; his dick was hard pressed against his friend's very cute bubble butt, and it didn't take long for him to get a hardon...

This time though, François didn't think about having to fuck Marie-Hélène to make his hard cock go down... He didn't have to, since Ludwig was too drunk to see or remember anything... As Ludwig was still pissing, François kept his grip around his friend's big dick and felt it was getting hard in his hand. God! Ludwig's dick felt so hot! François couldn't resist the temptation, and he started to tenderly kiss Ludwig's neck, still holding him tightly with one arm, is other hand holding his friend's semi-hard dick... At some point, Ludwig finished pissing, and François gave his dick a few tugs... Ludwig moaned... „Now pal... let's go to bed... and help me, will you: I can't carry you over there, you're too heavy..." Indeed, at 1.85 m, and at 80 kg, Ludwig was quite a big guy, and was no match for François, who was doing his best not to let his friend slip out of his arms and fall to the ground... „...Put your arm around my shoulder...", François told his friend. Ludwig slowly complied and put his right arm around his friend's strong shoulder... They turned as to go inside the pavilion and again, François put one arm around Ludwig's waist. Then he said: „Okay dude! Now, let's walk inside..." As they were slowly walking, François could see his very hard dick swinging from side to side... He looked down at Ludwig's semi-hard dick and smiled: Ludwig's cock was about 17 cm, and not even hard yet! Wow... François thought... He really has a big one...

Finally, both friends made it to a bed, and François help Ludwig lay down on his back... Although there was only one candle burning to light up the room, the dim lightning was good enough for François to clearly see Ludwig's well toned body laying there, in all its glory, right before his eyes! God! This guy is beautiful! François thought... He is nothing short of magnificent! Obviously, Ludwig was completely wasted. And now, he was passed out sleeping like a baby... François took all his time to admire his beautiful friend... He looked at his blond hair, at his very sensual lips... Ludwig looked like some huge Nordic god, François thought... Then his eyes went down on Ludwig's smooth abs... François was mesmerized by his friend's beauty and his own dick was so hard, he couldn't believe it! And it was oozing so much... He went on to look at Ludwig's dick: It was limp now on its back pointing towards his head... even limp, it was quite big... Then François looked at Ludwig's nice, hairless balls... and started jacking himself... He couldn't help it: He was so horny, just looking at his gorgeous friend... but when he felt he was about to squirt, he stopped wanking... not wanting to cum... at least not yet! He went to the kitchen where he found a washcloth. Then he walked back to the bed and began to wash Ludwig's piss-soaked feet. He washed them thoroughly... then went back to the kitchen to rinse the washcloth... When he came back to Ludwig, he sat on the bed near his friend, and started to wash Ludwig's dick and balls... First, François washed Ludwig's blond pubes, and when he began washing his friend's dick, Ludwig stirred a little... François realized his boner had died quickly, thinking Ludwig had caught him touching his dick while he was sleeping... Luckily, Ludwig didn't say anything so François stayed right there on the bed, not moving, and he stayed like that until he was sure his friend was sleeping again... He heard Ludwig's breathing get steady again... Knowing it was safe to resume his ministrations, François began washing Ludwig's big balls... Ludwig let out a moan... and François smiled to himself, seeing Ludwig's dick was getting hard under his touch... Obviously, his friend was writhing in need under his hand, and François loved it! He finished washing Ludwig's privates, put away the washcloth, then laid down beside his friend. His dick started to get hard immediately... Slowly, he moved his hand to Ludwig's inner thigh, then to his smooth balls, and he heard his friend sigh. François grinned... He waited a couple of seconds and listened to see how Ludwig was breathing. He was breathing steadily and since François knew how much rum his friend had drank, he was sure he was sleeping soundly...

Then François decided to take Ludwig's semi-hard dick into his hand, and he started to jack him off, even though the angle was weird... It didn't take long before he felt Ludwig getting hard in his hand: His dick was so big... so beautiful... so hot! François started jacking himself with his free hand and suddenly, he felt Ludwig's right hand dropped down and lay directly on top of the hand he was using to wank... He stopped jacking, let go of his dick, turned Ludwig's hand a little and put his huge boner inside it! François closed Ludwig's fingers on his oozing dick and started to pump with his dick, as if he was masturbating himself... He naturally started to bend over with the motion and then crouched himself closer to Ludwig's hard dick...

Was he going to do it? Was he going to give his best friend a blowjob? What if Ludwig woke up! (...) Nah! He was too drunk... So, François grabbed his friend's dick and let it sit in his mouth for a while... It was so big and so hard! François heard Ludwig moan... Ludwig's dick was probably 25 cm long, François thought... and pretty damn thick! He loved the feeling of having it all in his warm mouth. It felt sooooooo good! Then, he started to suck him hard. Ludwig didn't wake up but moaned again... Ludwig's dick was now oozing a lot into his friend's velvety mouth and François tasted each and every drop... and he loved the taste! He couldn't believe he had Ludwig's big hot dick deep inside his mouth! As he was only 30 seconds from an orgasm, François took away Ludwig's hand from his throbbing dick, and let it rest for a while... Then he went back to suck on his beautiful friend's dick and with his mouth, he began to bob faster on Ludwig's hard and oozing prick... When François heard him shudder, he stopped, and looked up at Ludwig... to make sure he was still sleeping... Although Ludwig breathing was heavier than normal, his eyes were still closed, and François was sure he was sleeping soundly...

But he was wrong! François should have known that even if a guy is drunk, you don't play with his dick without him noticing it... He has to be really really drunk for not noticing it, and in such a case, he wouldn't get hard at all! But Ludwig was hard! Oh yes, he was! So, François should have known his friend was not completely wasted, as he thought he was. But he didn't know that! When Ludwig woke up, he felt something warm and very wet on his hard dick. At first, he thought he was dreaming but then, he realized someone was giving him head, and it felt incredibly good... Where was he? How come he was in bed with Marie-Hélène? Those were the first questions that went through his mind... He slightly opened his eyes, and, after a while, he remembered he was at La Vacherie... then, he looked down and was stunned to see it wasn't Marie-

Hélène, giving him a blowjob, but his best pal François! First, Ludwig smiled to himself: He should have known from the start it wasn't Marie-Hélène giving head to him, since she was not „THAT" good at it... But then, he fully realized another guy had his dick in his mouth, and he paralyzed... The feeling was good, though... Very good! What am I going to do? He asked to himself...

He closed his eyes and continued to pretend he was still sound asleep... He found his emotions were too mixed together to analyze at the moment: François was gay? That possibility had never crossed his mind! Nah! he thought... But then, why was he giving him the best blowjob of his life, huh? Then, he started to think he should wake up, push François out of the bed and ask him to get the hell out of here... But then, François was his best friend, and he liked him a lot. He couldn't do that, he thought. And again, François was doing a hell of a good job, and what he felt was incredibly pleasurable... Shit! Ludwig thought to himself... But I'm not gay! I know I'm not! What the hell am I to do? Then he began to think he was just an unwilling participant in this whole affair! Obviously, François was under the impression he was completely passed out... It was him who was giving him head, not the opposite... Besides, he thought: What is gay, and what is not? Is giving head to a friend a queer thing to do? Not really... Heck! What are friends for... just helping a friend with his urges, I mean... And anyway, for the moment, he was not „participating" in the act: He was just receiving! Heck, why not! Ludwig smiled to himself, and started to relax... He decided he wouldn't move nor do anything, except continue to pretend he was still sleeping, as long as François was not trying to fuck him! No way! If he wasn't sure about other things, he knew being fucked by a guy was queer! Should François try to fuck him... then I'm going to „wake up", he said to himself, and I'm going to tell him I don't want that. Hell no! He's not going to push his dick into my hole! Never, Ludwig thought. As he had decided not to „wake" up, Ludwig felt François swallowing his dick deep into his mouth... He couldn't help it and moaned softly... Then he shuddered when François started to tongue bath his balls and began kissing and nibbling on his inner thighs... God! The guy was talented! Obviously, François was giving a lot of attention to the job he was doing on his friend's crotch... Is that queer? Ludwig was not sure about that... But to him, the „line" had not been crossed, yet... Then François stopped! What the hell is he doing? Ludwig asked himself... Why did he stop? And of course, he couldn't open his eyes to see what was going on... He felt very frustrated!

François slowly parted Ludwig's big muscular legs, and went down on his knees between them... He put his middle finger in his mouth, and when it was totally wet, he leaned a bit over Ludwig's crotch and pushed his hand back under his friend and found his hole... What the hell is he doing? Ludwig asked to himself... But then, he moaned when he felt the tip of his friend's wet finger playing around his asshole. It felt so good! With his other hand, François grabbed Ludwig's oozing dick. He leaned down a bit more and took it into his warm mouth! Ludwig wanted to cry out in total ecstasy, but he couldn't... He was supposed to be completely passed out... As François started to deep-throat his very hard dick, Ludwig became more and more verbal... François looked at him... but saw his friend was still sound asleep. Good, he thought! That's when he decided to put his middle finger in his friend's asshole! He went slowly, as he was so afraid Ludwig could wake up! But no... No... Ludwig didn't do anything to stop his friend... after all, Franz had done the same thing to him, to show him where his „love spot" was... and to him, that wasn't queer. Just fun! François slowly eased his finger in up to the first knuckle... he paused for a second... then moved his hand in a little more and put his finger in up to the second knuckle. He could feel Ludwig's warm insides on his finger and moved it around a little... After a while, he let his finger slip in Ludwig's hot asshole a centimeter past the big knuckle...and then, he started to pump his finger in and out of his friend's asshole... Of course, Ludwig groaned and gasped! François looked at him and was happy to see he wasn't waking up! So, he started to suck him hard, and he softly moaned, tasting Ludwig's precum that was now flowing generously... When Ludwig felt his friend's finger hit his love spot, he just couldn't help it, and he groaned again! It felt sooooo good!

But when François sealed his wet lips, gripping Ludwig's cock shaft, going up and down on it with his hot mouth, Ludwig couldn't take it anymore... His cock jolted twice, then he erupted his hot teen cum deep inside his best friend's mouth, while his prostate was being stimulated by his friend's finger... Ludwig went through the best orgasm of his life: He couldn't believe it... and he orgasmed for what seemed like hours... As Ludwig erupted deep inside his mouth, François quickly gulped every time Ludwig shot another wad. Ludwig's cock was pulsating... Tenderly,

François began sucking Ludwig's knob, before his lips tightened around his hard cock rod again. His head moved back and forth, and he pulled his head off Ludwig's cock only after he had made sure he had swallowed his final trapped wad! Shit! That tasted good, François thought to himself! Ludwig felt totally exhausted, but he had no doubt François had given him the best experience of his life! Although his eyes were still closed, he began to hear a very familiar sound, as François was now furiously wanking his oozing dick. Sure enough, Ludwig heard his friend groan and moan... François bobbed faster and harder on his hard prick... Then, Ludwig heard him gasping with lust when he started to fire torrents of cum... „Ahhhhhhh", François softly cried out, as his orgasm reached its peak... Ludwig smiled to himself, hearing that... and he thought his friend had earned his pleasure, after the very good blow-job he had given him...

Then, everything felt silent... Minutes later, Ludwig realized François was going off the bed... He heard him walk over to the kitchen, then he heard the water running... Seconds later, François was back with the washcloth, and he began washing Ludwig's privates all over again... How considerate of him, Ludwig thought to himself... But of course, he's only trying to erase all the traces of his mischief...Poor François, Ludwig thought: If only he knew... When he felt François had finished his cleaning job, Ludwig rustled and turned his body over onto his right side... François got rid of the washcloth, blow the candle off, then laid himself down right next to his friend. He sighed... He was totally exhausted... Exhausted, but so happy! Poor Ludwig, he thought: He's really passed out... How could he get drunk like that! He's going to have a terrible hangover tomorrow... And that was his last thought, as he quickly fell asleep... It didn't take long for Ludwig to really fall asleep, too... and this time, he wasn't faking...

Hours later, when Ludwig woke up, he really had a hangover... He looked at François, who was still sleeping soundly... Ludwig slowly moved out of their bed, and walked over to the veranda... It was a beautiful warm day, he thought... He went for a dip into the lake, and that helped him regain some vigor... There's nothing like cold water to help a guy in my condition, he thought to himself, grinning... Later, he walked back to the pavilion, then to the kitchen where he quietly started to make coffee... Of course, the odor of freshly brewed coffee eventually reached François, and before long, he was on his feet. He walked over to the kitchen and, seeing Ludwig there, he said: „... Hummmm... it smells delicious..." Ludwig turned, and looked at his smiling friend... „...Yeah! It does... Hope coffee will help me get over my hangover... Sorry pal! I guess I drank too much too fast last night..." „Yeah! I guess you did! Next time, go easy with that stuff..." „... I suppose I made a fool of myself...", Ludwig asked... „...No... But I had a problem stopping you from going to the lake and have a dip..." „Oh..." „...And I had a bigger problem when you decided you wanted to piss, but couldn't stand on your two feet on your own..." „I don't remember that at all...", Ludwig answered, feeling a bit embarrassed...

And it was true: He couldn't remember anything, up to the moment he had felt his friend's warm mouth going down on his hard dick... But the rest, he did remember! „What happened?", Ludwig asked, out of curiosity... „...I had no choice but to help you... I mean..." „Oh..." „...Only problem is, you pissed all over your crotch and all over your feet..." „...Did I?" „Yeah!", François answered, laughing... „And then, I brought you to bed, and I had to wash you... so if you find a used washcloth somewhere inside, smelling like piss... don't ask why, pal..." „...I guess I was completely wasted... Thanks, dude... for what you did..." – „Sure. No problem..." „... I tell you... I slept like a baby... I even had a fantastic dream...", Ludwig said, grinning and watching his friend's reaction from the corner of his eye... „(...)" „...Yeah", Ludwig continued... „I dreamed I was having the best blow-job of my life, really! I hope I didn't cum all over you, though..." „...Over me? No! Not over me...", François answered, blushing scarlet red... „Good!", Ludwig answered, laughing... „I guess we're going to take it easy today... If you see what I mean..." Poor François, he didn't know what Ludwig meant by that... Did he remember what he had done to him last night? „.... You know... take it easy... I guess I'm going to stay away from booze for a while...", Ludwig added, laughing, knowing perfectly well what François was going through in his mind... „...Oh yes!", François answered, with a smile on his face! „I'd do the same, if I were you...", he added, relieved... „Yeah... When I think I don't even remember what happened last night..." „...It's no big deal...", François answered, grinning... „...Let's have breakfast... then, let's clean up the place. What do you think?", Ludwig asked his friend... „Fine with me", François answered, beaming...

That day, they had a lot of fun... and Ludwig didn't say a word to his friend about what had happened the night before! He knew that, at some point, he would have to talk to François about that... but he was not ready yet... He wanted to have time to ponder a few things before... For now, let's just have some fun, Ludwig thought to himself...

In Paris, Paul was far from having fun, though! In fact, he was going through one of the worst crises of his young life, and for once, he didn't know what to do...

FOUR

July 15, 1942, was a beautiful summer day. When Paul arrived on Avenue Foch from La Vacherie, Will had already left for work so Paul went to his study, and started reading a few reports... His business partners in Germany had suggested to invest some money, a lot of money in fact, in some kind of industries in Germany and Poland and now, Paul was studying the deal as well as the balance sheets... and he just didn't know what to think of them... First, he couldn't really tell what those industries were producing... Second, from the documents he had, he could see that others were already holding a large stake in those industries, but he couldn't tell who they were, since the title-deeds were not clear... But most of all, Paul's attention was drawn by the fact that, going over the balance-sheets, he could see hundreds of people were working in those industries, but... were not paid! That doesn't make sense, Paul thought to himself! Normally, salaries constitute a big part of the expenditures... but according to the balance-sheets he had in front of him, no such expenditures existed in those industries. Paul was puzzled and the only answer he could come up with was that the balance-sheets were false! He decided to give a call to one of his business partners in Berlin, in order to obtain some explanations... The only explanations he got were laughs! No, he was told... the balance-sheets were right: There were no such expenditures as salaries in those industries... since the workers over there were... well... „furnished" at no cost! How was that possible? Who were they? Furnished by whom? The guy in Berlin wouldn't say. „... Better not to ask too many questions about that, my friend", he told Paul! When Paul hung up the phone, he didn't know what to think about the whole thing: It just didn't make sense at all... So, he decided that, for the moment, he would put aside the proposition so later, he would have time to think about it... He looked at his watch and realized Will was about to get back from work. He went upstairs, took a quick shower, changed, then came back just in time to see Will come through the door...

„Hi! How was your day?", Paul asked him, with a big smile on his face... But before Will had time to answer his question, Paul realized there was something wrong with Will... „Hey... What's wrong?" At first, Will didn't answer. They slowly made their way to the drawing-room, then sat. Paul was looking at Will. „Something big is going on...", Will answered, with a worried look on his face... „What do you mean by „something big"... „... That's the problem: I don't really know! At the office, we heard rumors about a big operation called „Vent printanier" – „(...)" „I asked Oberstleutnant Koch about that operation, and he said he doesn't know much about it, since the Wehrmacht is not involved: According to what he heard, only the Gestapo and French policemen are involved..." „The Gestapo? (...) And French policemen? What the hell are you talking about?" „...I don't know, Paul! (...) And I've also heard that, a few days ago, hundreds of vehicles had been requisitioned..." „Huh?" „...Yeah!" „What does that mean?", Paul asked... „...That lots of people will soon get arrested, what else?" „Shit! But why?" „If the Gestapo is involved, as they say... I'm sure we're talking about Jews..." „...Jews? But..." „...I've heard about these operations... It happened in the past, all over Germany! Policemen come without warning, usually during the middle of the night, and all the Jews in a borough or a city are arrested..." „Where are they taken to?" „...We don't know! (...) Like our Jewish neighbors in Berlin that have vanished one night... you know... I've told you that story... and as I told you, we never heard from them again", Will answered, looking down at the carpet... „...What you're telling me now makes no sense..." „That's what I used to think. Rumors... That's what I used to think. But tell me, Paul: Why the hell have our Jewish neighbors totally disappeared? One night, they were there... and the morning after, they were gone! And not just one Jewish family: All the Jews living on our street! They had suddenly left their homes, with all the furniture in! They had abandoned all their belongings? Suddenly? Just like that? I've seen it with my own eyes, Paul! So, we're not talking about rumors here..." „That's beyond me..." „Well, get back on earth, will you?" „(...)" „What about your next-door neighbors? Have you thought about them?"

„(...) Mrs. & Mr. Bloomfield? What about them?" „You told me they are Jewish..." „...Well... Yes. But they are French citizens: Pétain would never allow French citizens to be arrested like that..." „My poor Paul: The old man has no control over the situation. He's not even his own man! He's just a puppet... Besides, how do you know for sure your neighbors are French citizens?" „...I've known them since I was a child... As far as I know, they have always been our neighbors and my father's tenants. Hey! I've been to school with their son, and I used to play with him in our back-yard..." „...So? That doesn't prove they are French citizens: Only that they've been around for a while... If I were you, I'll walk over to their home and ask them!" „Are you crazy or what? ... I would walk over there like that... knock on their door, and out of nowhere, I would ask them: „Hi! Are you French citizens?" Get serious, Will!" „...As you wish... But I'm telling you: If they ever „vanish" into the night, don't blame me..." – „...We're in Paris, here! Not in Berlin! That will never happen! Never!" After that, the two lovers changed the subject and made small talk about trivial matters...

Suddenly, Paul rose up and, as he was walking out of the drawing-room, Will asked him: „...Where the hell are you going like that, in the middle of our discussion... What's the matter?" Paul turned to look back at Will and said: „...I'm going to pay a visit to... my next-door neighbors..." „What are you going to tell them?" „...I have four minutes to think about it!" An hour and a half later, Paul was back and Will looked at him: He was as white as a ghost, and his hands were shaking. He sat down and said: „...They were born in Brussels! Their son is a French citizen, since he was born in Paris... But they are not! They said they never bothered themselves with such details..." „Shit! What are they going to ..." „They are packing a few things... jewels, mostly..." „Where are they going?" „...They are coming over here..." „Huh?" „...Where the hell do you want them to go? They have no place to go... They are no longer young... „ – „...What about their son?" Paul raised his head and looked at Will straight in the eyes: „...They don't know where he is. He's with the résistance... All they know is that he's with the Front National* (...)" (*Not to be confused with a far-right political party that actually exists in France today...) „That's the group founded by the French communist party, isn't it?", Will asked, stunned... „Yes... And I don't care!" „...We're talking about the résistance, here... These guys shoot at us!" „...I don't think we have time now to think about that, do we? Remember: We're talking about my Jewish neighbors... not their son!" „...Right. (...) But even if they come over here... They can't stay here... Sooner or later, they would get arrested, and we would be in big troubles, you and me!" „What else can we do? We must help them...", Paul said. Will started thinking that, indeed, what they were about to do could lead them into big troubles... He was a German officer... helping Jews... and worst: Hiding them! He preferred not to think about the consequences for him, should the Gestapo ever find out! „Yes..." Will answered... „We must help them... that's the right thing to do, so let's do it!" Paul looked at Will and, with a big smile on his face, he said: „...I knew that's what you were going to say! And I love you Will..."

An hour later, Mrs. & Mr. Bloomfield were knocking on the door, and as Paul opened it, they quickly made their way inside... They all went to Paul's study and closed the doors behind them: Paul didn't want any of the servants to see Mrs. & Mr. Bloomfield, so if later they were questioned by the police, they could swear they had not seen them... „I can't believe this is happening to us...", Mrs. Bloomfield said, with tears in her eyes... „...We don't know for sure Paul is right, dear", Mr. Bloomfield said to his wife... „But I think it's better for us not to take any chance..." „But... We can't leave everything behind us like that... Our home... Why? We have not done anything wrong! Why us?", the old lady asked... „...As long as we are alive, the rest doesn't count, dear...", Mr. Bloomfield answered, showing a very resigned face... „You're right, Mr. Bloomfield: There are questions we can not answer for the moment... For now, let's make sure you're in no danger... Later, we'll have time to think..." „What are we going to do now?", Mr. Bloomfield asked... They all turned to look at Paul for an answer! Like if I had the answer to that question, Paul thought to himself! What the hell are we going to do now, he thought... „What about a cognac?", he asked... Everyone agreed, and while he was serving cognac to his guests, he was thinking. And thinking fast! „I can't hide them in the attic... Nor can I hide them in the cellar... They are no longer young, and anyway, the mansion could be searched", he thought to himself. „I could take them to Bagatelle... or to La Vacherie... but... before long, the servants over there would become suspicious... They would start asking questions... We're not sure we can count on them to keep such a secret... They could be scared and run to the police... No! That's not the solution...", he thought... While he was serving cognac, Paul knew very well all the eyes were on him... They were all expecting an answer from him... Then, it hit him in the face! „YES!", he shouted out... Everybody looked at him, stunned by his sudden reaction... „We are all going for a car ride...", he said, with a big smile on his face... Then he rose up, went to his desk, took the phone and made a call. „Thank you for taking my call" he said to his interlocutor... „No... I'm in Paris... I can't explain to you right now... but we're going to pay you a visit tonight. I have a big, a very big favor to ask you... Yes... No: I can't explain over the phone, sorry! But don't go to bed until we get there... And please: Don't say a word about our visit... You'll understand later. Yes... And thanks ... a lot... see you later tonight!"

He hung up, then turned and said to Will: „Come with me for a minute: I need to talk to you... Please, excuse us, Mrs. & Mr. Bloomfield... it won't take long..." Will and Paul walked over to the drawing-room, and Paul said to Will: „Call Lutz... We need him! Tell him to come over here as quick as possible... and tell him to bring your uniforms! Tell him it's urgent! Don't tell him anything over the phone..." „... What the hell is going on? Why do we need Lutz?", Will asked, flabbergasted... „We need a second driver... No time to explain... stay near the front door, and as soon as he gets here, bring him here and let me know... I'll then explain everything to both of you..." „I hope you know what you're doing...", Will answered. „...Do you trust me?", Paul asked... „With my life!", Will answered. „Fine! Call Lutz..." Paul left Will and walked back to his study. He sat down near Mrs. & Mr. Bloomfield, looked at them straight in the eyes, caught his breath, then explained his plan to them... „... Do you think you can make it?", Paul asked his neighbors... „That's the only way out..." – „It's risky... all the roads are closely guarded...", Mr. Bloomfield answered... „Yes, I know. But I've minimized the risks... and in a few minutes, don't be scared when you see my cousin and one of my friends in German uniforms... That's part of my plan..." „Are you the devil?", Mrs. Bloomfield asked, smiling... „No... but almost!", Paul answered, grinning... As soon as Lutz got there, Will came to fetch Paul and they walked back to the drawing-room, where Paul explained his plan... „You don't have to accept, Lutz... If you don't, I'll understand... I know what I'm asking you is very dangerous... And you don't even know my neighbors..." Lutz grinned and said: „I'm in with you! When do we leave?" Paul smiled to his friend and said: „...As soon as the servants are all gone to bed. Just bring your car inside the underground garage... Will will go with you... then, put on your uniforms..." – „Fine!", Lutz and Will answered.

Later that night, Paul made sure all the servants had gone to bed, then he led Mrs. & Mr. Bloomfield to the underground garage. As soon as they got there, they looked at Will and Lutz in their German uniforms, and Paul said: „Perfect! We could swear you are German officers... Oh... but that's not all..." Paul took something out of his pocket and walked over to his father's official car: On the hood, there was a small flag stick where a French flag used to stand, as his father used to be a minister with the French cabinet... All the others could see was Paul's back... and they had no idea about what he was doing... Then he turned to face them and, with a big smile on his face, he said: „Voilà!" They all looked at the car and saw a... Nazi flag... soundly attached to the flag stick... „Thank God your father is not here to see that...", Mr. Bloomfield said, stunned! „He would be doing the same...", Paul proudly answered... „Now, let's go... and sorry for the inconveniences..." Paul opened the trunk of his father's car, and Mrs. Bloomfield slowly laid down inside of it... Then, Lutz opened the trunk of his car... and Mr. Bloomfield did the same... „All set?", Paul asked... „Let's go", Lutz answered. At one o'clock that night, they made their way out of Paris. Will was first, driving the big black Citroen... with the Nazi flag on the hood... Paul was sitting on the back seat, as all „important" people do! Lutz was driving his car right behind them... An hour later, they had to slow down... and then, they saw German soldiers on the road, checking each and every car... As they were waiting to be checked, Paul leaned to the front seat, put a hand on Will's shoulder and said: „Stay calm, Will... Stick to our story... and don't worry: God is with us! Nothing can happen..." Their hearts were beating fast... and as Will felt he was almost out of breath, he pulled his side window down... The soldiers were now checking the car right in front of them... They were next! When Paul saw the soldiers were about to walk over to their car, he said to Will: „Do you know what, Will? When they get over here, I'll stick my dick up your ass... and I'll fuck you... right in front of them... what do you think?" „What?", Will asked, stunned... „Yeah! I'm going to fuck you real hard, right in front of them... Do you think they would like our show?" Will couldn't help it, and he burst out laughing... So, when a soldier walked over to their car, what he saw was a German officer, laughing his heart out... He looked at Will's uniform and at the car... Then, he leaned over a bit and, with a grin on his face, he said: „Guten Abend, Unterfeldwebel..." „Guten Abend, Kollege", Will answered, still laughing... The soldier was now smiling at Will, and he politely asked: „Ausweise und Zulassungspapiere, bitte!" The soldier checked the papers, as well as Paul's papers... Will answered his questions, and explained they were on their way to join a party thrown by German officers at Chartres... They were already late, Will explained... and were in a hurry! What kind of party? Oh! The kind their wives back in Germany would not appreciate, if you see what I mean...

Being a simple soldier, the young man thought to himself it was better for him not to make too many troubles... After all,... the guy driving the car was a German officer... „And the officer driving the car right behind us is also coming to the same party...", Will said to the soldier... The soldier walked over to Lutz's car, checked his papers, then walked back to Paul's car... He gave Will back his papers, smiled, then he looked at the other soldiers who were blocking the road and shouted at them: „Alles klar, in Ordnung..." Then, the soldier looked back at Will and said: „Bitte vorwärts... Auf Wiedersehen, und viel Vergnügen!" „Vielen Dank ... und gute Nacht...", Will said as he raised his side window and began to slowly drive right pass the other soldiers... He saluted them, and they all smiled back at him... Will looked in his rearview mirror, and saw Lutz's car was following him... A few minutes later, they were driving at full speed, and back on their way... „Thank God!", Will sighed... „All I had in mind was the firing squad... and your dick up my ass!" – „Which one would you prefer?", Paul asked, grinning... „Do I really have to answer that?", Will said, laughing... „Fucking me in front of them... Were you crazy or what?" „It did the trick, didn't it? Instead of looking at a nervous wreck, all the soldiers saw was a German officer, laughing his heart out...", Paul answered...

„Cela ne fait pas très distingué, cependant...", they heard Mrs. Bloomfield say, from the trunk where she was hiding... Will looked back at Paul and they burst out laughing: They had totally forgotten Mrs. Bloomfield could hear them perfectly well from where she was hiding... „Are you alright in there, Mrs. Bloomfield?" „... Fortunately, your father has a big car... It's not too bad in here... But I worry for my husband...", she answered. „Oh, don't worry Ma'am... We're almost there...", Paul answered. As they neared the place where they were going, both drivers shut down their headlights... and they slowly made their way to a house... Paul got out of the car and went to a door. He knocked and waited. A man opened the door, smiled at Paul and said: „Ah! Monsieur de Brion... Je vous attendais... „... Any danger?", Paul asked, looking around... „None!", the man answered. „I have a surprise... A big surprise for you!", Paul said! He walked over to his car, opened the trunk, and helped Mrs. Bloomfield make her way out of it... As Will and Lutz got off their cars, the man was a bit... puzzled... to see two German officers... Then Lutz opened the trunk of his car and helped Mr. Bloomfield out of it... „Quick!", Paul said... „Get inside..." As they all went inside the house, Paul looked at the man and said: „Monsieur le Curé, je vous présente madame et monsieur Bloomfield... Ils sont juifs... ... And this is Will, and the other officer is Lutz... I've already told you about Will, if you remember...", Paul said, looking the Vicar straight in the eyes... „Oh yes... He's... your mother was talking about him in her last letter, if my memory serves me well...", the Vicar answered, smiling at Paul... „Precisely...", Paul answered, grinning... „Well... Welcome all to the Presbytery... Please, do sit down...", the Vicar said, with a big smile on his face. They sat down and then, Paul explained everything to the Vicar... „... Your church is the safest place I could think of...", Paul concluded.... „...And you were right!", the Vicar answered.... „The Gestapo will never come in here...". And, turning to Mrs. & Mr. Bloomfield, the Vicar said: „And you are most welcome here... My church is one of the best hiding places in France... It was built more than four centuries ago, and underneath the structure, there are hiding places no one could find... During the Revolution, a few noble-men hid there, and they were never found by the revolutionaries... We shall hide you there, and we'll wait to see what's going on in Paris..." „How can we thank you all...", Mrs. Bloomfield said... „We don't know what to say..." „Nonsense! You would do the same for us...", the Vicar answered... „I understand you have a son?", he then asked... „Yes", Mrs. Bloomfield answered... Obviously, she felt uneasy, talking about her son in front of a priest... „Can I tell him?", Paul asked Mrs. Bloomfield... „... Yes, please, do!", she answered...

„Monsieur le Curé..." Paul started to explain to the Vicar... „I've known their son Robert since childhood... He's a fine young man! He's with the

Résistance... He's a member of the Front National..." „Oh... Is that why you were a bit embarrassed... because he's a communist?", the Vicar asked Mrs. Bloomfield, laughing... „Well, you're a priest...", Mrs. Bloomfield answered... „No need to be embarrassed, Madame: You should be proud to have a son with the Résistance... And it so happens that I personally know of a few guys who are members of the Front National... So perhaps, I can try to pass the information to them, so that your son knows you are here, well and safe...", the Vicar answered, with a smile on his face... „Now Father, you will excuse us... But we have to go back to Paris right away...", Paul said... „I understand!", the Vicar answered, grinning... Paul walked over to Mrs. & Mr. Bloomfield and kissed them both on the cheeks... „Don't worry... I'm taking care of everything... You'll see me soon again...", Paul said to them... „We love you Paul... You're like a son to us...", they both answered... „And thanks to you too...", Mr. Bloomfield said to Will and Lutz... „God bless you all for what you did tonight..." As he was leaving the Presbytery, Paul turned, looked at the Vicar, smiled to him and said: „I knew I could count on you, monsieur le Curé! Vous êtes un saint homme! „Oh! No! I'm only a poor Vicar, trying to do what's right in life..." „Here, Father!", Paul said, as he gave the Vicar a thick envelope... „You'll find enough money inside to cover all the expenses and all of their needs... Don't spare, please... I'll be in touch with you as soon as I can..." „Your grandmother would be proud of you, son... May God be with you!", the Vicar answered. „Thanks, Father!"

On the way back to Paris, everything went fine... the soldiers were no longer there, and they had no problem getting back to Paul's mansion. „...It's five o'clock... It's been a long night! Let's go to bed! I'll try to get some sleep, before I go to work!", Will said... Later, they were awakened by someone knocking on their bedroom door... Paul went to the door, opened it, and saw madame Louise, standing there in the corridor... „Oh... Good morning, Madame Louise", Paul said... „I'm sorry, Sir... to wake you up like that... but... we have two gentlemen downstairs... and they insist... they want to talk to you... they even questioned me..." „Who are they?" „I don't know, Sir... Germans, I think..." „Oh? And why did they question you?" „I don't know, really... They asked me a few questions concerning our neighbors..." „Our neighbors? Which ones?" „Mrs. & Mr. Bloomfield..." „Oh? I wonder why?... And what did you tell them?"

„...Nothing! I told them I had not seen them recently... and that I didn't know where they were...“ „Oh, well... I guess I will have to get dressed, then see these gentlemen... Please, show them to my study... I shall meet them there in a few minutes...“ Paul closed the door, turned and looked at Will... „The Gestapo!“, Will said... „They know...“ Obviously, Will was frightened... „What are we going to do?“, he asked Paul, with a quivering voice... „You go back to sleep! I'm going to take care of these bastards...“, Paul said, with a very calm voice... „...I think you don't realize who they are...“, Will answered... „Oh yes, I do! Perfectly well! Now, stay calm... And stay here!“

Paul got dressed, then went downstairs... He walked over to his study, opened the doors and saw two Gestapo officers, dressed in trench coat and hat, one of them sitting at his desk as if he was the owner of the place... Paul walked in, looked at the officer sitting at his desk, then said to him: „This is my desk you're sitting at... Get the hell out of that chair!“ The Gestapo officer sitting at the desk looked up at Paul and frowned... He was not used to be addressed to like that... with such... arrogance... Of course, he was mad! But then, he started considering the fact he had barged into this mansion... A very expensive one... and he started thinking that the people living here had to be very rich... He considered Paul for a few seconds... The guy was young, and very well dressed. But what intrigued him the most about Paul was the fact he was speaking German perfectly well... „Be cautious“, he said to himself... „... You don't seem to realize, young man, who we are...“, the Gestapo officer said to Paul... with a stupid little smile on his face. „Oh, but you're wrong: I know perfectly well you two are Gestapo officers... Now, don't make me repeat myself, and get the hell out of my chair! Paul answered, slowly walking over to his desk, with a threatening face... Even though Paul was a young man, the Gestapo officer could see the guy in front of him had a very tough personality, and that he wouldn't compromise... Obviously, this young man wasn't impressed nor scared... The other Gestapo officer was stunned to see his superior rise from the chair and walk away from the desk... Paul went to his chair then sat down at his desk... „That's better“, he said... „Now gentlemen... why are you violating the privacy of my house? he calmly asked... „Don't play that game with us, young man! You know perfectly well why we are here: Where are your neighbors? They are gone, and someone saw two cars leave your house late last night!“

„First", Paul began to say... „Don't you ever speak to me with that tone of voice... you could regret it dearly! Second... the fact that I went with friends to a party last night has nothing to do with my neighbors! Why are you looking for them? And by the way... I'm not their guardian, you know! Why should I know where they are? When they're going somewhere, they don't usually tell me where they are going, you know... It's none of my business! Are you crazy or what?" „Who the hell do you think you are?", the Gestapo officer barked... „I know perfectly well who I am... The problem is: I think you don't know to whom you're talking to. My name is Paul de Brion and..." „I don't give a damn about your name or about who you are... All I know is that your neighbors are gone missing... and that last night, you've been seen going out at a very late hour! Where did you take them to?" „I don't know what you're talking about... And as I told you... I don't know where our neighbors are... I haven't seen them..." „... I think you know very well where they are... And if you don't tell us... instead of them, it's you we'll take with us, instead of them... And I'm tell you: You won't like that! We know how to deal with people like you..." Paul burst out laughing, then said: „Before you do so, may I show you something?" Paul slowly opened one of his drawers and took a framed picture out of it, then gave it to the Gestapo officer he was talking to... The Gestapo officer looked at the picture and was stunned to see Paul standing there with... the Führer, shaking hands with him! The picture had been taken a while ago, during that Christmas party at the Reichskanzlei in Berlin Paul had been invited to... The Gestapo officer just kept staring at the picture... He didn't know what to think nor what to do! The Führer... with that guy in front of him! Who the hell is that guy? After a long moment, he raised his eyes from the picture and looked at Paul... „... Before you arrest me", Paul said to him... „may I suggest you call Herr Abetz at the embassy... you know... just to make sure you're not making a big mistake... Or perhaps, you would prefer to give a call to Berlin, and speak to Herr Funk, the Reich Minister of Economic Affairs... He's a good friend of mine! Anyway, here are the phone numbers... And I have a direct phone line to Berlin, should you decide to call Herr Funk instead of Herr Abetz... Do as you wish..." Paul gave the numbers to the Gestapo officer, then said to him: „Please, call..."

The Gestapo officer was not smiling anymore, and when he took the phone, Paul could see his right hand was slightly shaking... At the

German embassy, the officer explained why he was calling, and asked to speak to ambassador Abetz... While he was waiting on the line, he kept looking at Paul... When ambassador Abetz came on the line, the Gestapo officer explained to him why he was calling and, obviously, he was interrupted by his interlocutor because, out of nowhere he said to his interlocutor: „... Yes, Sir!... (...) We didn't know, Sir! I'm sorry that... Yes, of course, Sir! Yes, I understand, Sir! We will, Sir! Heil Hitler!... One moment, Sir..." Holding the phone, the Gestapo officer said to Paul: „The ambassador would like to have a word with you, Sir!" Paul smiled then took the phone: „Good morning Herr Abetz: How are you?, he asked the ambassador... Paul looked up at the Gestapo officer standing right in front of his desk and saw beads of sweat on his forehead... Paul smiled to himself! „...No, no, Sir... No harm done, really..." he said to the ambassador... „It seems they are looking for my neighbors, I don't know why... but really, I don't know where they are! (...) I beg you pardon? If I want to press charges against these officers? (...) Oh no, Sir... That won't be necessary! I suppose they are doing their jobs... Yes... As I said Herr Abetz, no harm was done, really! (...) Thank you, Sir! (...)You too: Have a nice day!" Paul hung up the phone and looked at the two Gestapo officers... „...We are truly sorry, Sir..." the officer standing in front of the desk said... „We didn't know..." „Yes, I understand...", Paul answered. Paul refrained from smiling! He thought about what his father used to say: „We always have too many enemies in life!"... Bearing that in mind, he decided not to further humiliate the two Gestapo officers... „... And thank you, Sir... for not pressing charges against us..." „Yes. (...) Now gentlemen, may I go back to bed? I came back very late last night from a party, and now I'm paying for it with a very bad headache, if you see what I mean..." „...But of course, Sir! We're leaving you right now... Again, Sir: Please, excuse us..."

Paul rang Madame Louise, and when she knocked on the door, Paul said: „Ah Madame Louise... Would you please show these gentlemen their way out: They are leaving..." – „Bien sûr, monsieur..." „Heil Hitler!", the two Gestapo officers shouted, as they were leaving... „Yes, yes... to you too...", Paul answered! „Bastards", he thought to himself! While Madame Louise was showing them to the door, one of the officers looked at her and said: „He's a gentleman..." She looked back at him and answered: „Yes... a real gentleman! A rare breed nowadays... don't you think?" The officer didn't answer!

As soon as the two Gestapo officers had left, Paul ran upstairs to his bedroom, and when he opened the door, he saw Will sitting there... staring at him... pale as death and looking sick! Paul burst out laughing, looking at his beautiful lover..."... Only thing for you to do is to call your office, and tell them you're sick today... No way you're going to go to work today the way you look..." „... Are they gone?" „Yup!" „(...)" „Don't look at me like that: You scare me!", Paul said, laughing... „... What happened?" Paul sat next to Will and told him exactly what had happened... „...You didn't...", Will said, totally incredulous... „Yup! I swear! When I think I wanted to throw away that goddamn picture... And the best part is that today, without even knowing it, the Führer helped me save two Jews... If he knew about that, he would have a heart-attack!", Paul said, laughing... (...) „But you were right, Will: During the night, thousands of Jews were arrested in Paris... According to what Madame Louise heard on the radio, the operation began at four o'clock this morning... and it's still going on! She said thousands of Jews... men, women... children... old-aged people... were taken away during the night and many of them have been sent to the Vel d'Hiv." „What's that?" „It's a covered stadium... on rue Netalon... It's called the „Vélodrome d'Hiver", or the „Vel d'Hiv"... (cycle racing- track...) „Did they say where those poor people will be taken to?" „No... We don't know. But at least, Mrs. & Mr. Bloomfield are not amongst them..." – „...Thanks to you, Paul..." „No. Not only me! It's thanks to you and Lutz, too... You've proven Germans have a heart! Last night, you took big risks... And you knew about it! But you and Lutz didn't back off... I'm so proud of you...", Paul said, as he gave his lover a sweet kiss... „Now, call your office... then come back to bed: I'm exhausted!"

A few days later, a meeting had been arranged by the Vicar... and so Will and Paul went to the presbytery... where they met with Mrs. & Mr. Bloomfield... „You were right, Monsieur Paul... And thanks to you, your cousin and your friend, we are still alive and free...", Mrs. Bloomfield said... „And I have a surprise for you...", the Vicar said to Paul... The Vicar went to a door, knocked on it... then said: „You can come out now..." The door opened, and a tall young man walked in... „Robert!", Paul shouted out... „Come here, you fool... and give me a big hug!", the man said to

Paul, laughing... „Will... This is Robert Bloomfield...", Paul said to Will... Will looked at Mrs. & Mr. Bloomfield and asked: „....Your son?" „Yes...", Mr. Bloomfield answered, with a big smile on his face... Will walked over to the tall young man and, shaking his hand, he said to him: „Nice to meet you..." Will knew perfectly well this guy was with the Résistance... They were mortal enemies! Not because they wanted to, but because of that stupid war! And Will knew perfectly well that, tomorrow, this guy could very well be the one to shoot him down, somewhere in Paris... „If I'm gunned down, let's hope it's not by him...", he thought to himself... After a while... Robert looked Will straight in the eyes and asked: „Sorry to ask... but you have a slight accent: Are you German?" „Yes", Will calmly answered... „I'm in the Wehrmacht... but don't worry, I'm not a Nazi... and I hate Hitler as much as you do..." Mrs. & Mr. Bloomfield were stupefied... „... But... We thought... he was your cousin...", Mrs. Bloomfield said, looking at Paul... „No. He's my lover!", Paul calmly answered, looking at Mrs. & Mr. Bloomfield... „I think we should all sit down, shouldn't we?", the Vicar said, grinning...

After a long moment of silence, Paul explained everything to his neighbors. To say the least... they were stunned! „It's your life, Paul..." Robert said... „You're my friend, and you and Will saved my parents: Who am I to judge you... In fact, I don't give a damn..." „Thanks Robert: I appreciate!", Paul answered... „... I don't know what's worst: Us, being Jews... or you and Will, being homosexuals! From what I've heard, your kind is not treated better than we are by the Nazis!", Robert said, with a very sad smile on his face... „And what about your other friend?", Mr. Bloomfield asked... „Lutz? He's in the Wehrmacht too... He's a translator, just like me. And he hates Hitler just as much as I do...", Will answered... „So, he's German?", Mrs. Bloomfield said... „...He's a human being, just like you Mrs. Bloomfield... and the other night, he risked his life to save you both...", Paul answered... „He's right, dear...", Mr. Bloomfield said to his wife... „If they had been caught, both of them would have been brought before a firing squad..." Mrs. Bloomfield rose up and walked over to Will. She took him into her arms, and she kissed him on the cheeks, saying: „Thank you, Will: I'll pray for you..." „Thanks Ma'am... That means a lot to me...", Will answered... Mr. Bloomfield hugged Will and said: „...Yes! You're a good man, Will! And I know not all Germans are Nazis..." „Most of us are not, you know...", Will answered, with tears in his eyes... „Well... That calls for a celebration, don't you think?", the Vicar said... He walked over to a cabinet... there was a sign over it that said: „Vin de messe" ... He opened a door and took out a wine bottle from the cabinet and said: „Let's have a drink..." Of course, they all laughed... „Vin de messe, huh?", Paul said to the Vicar, laughing... „Sure! The best! ...And don't worry Mrs. & Mr. Bloomfield: The wine has not been consecrated yet..." „We wouldn't care...", Mrs. Bloomfield answered... „After all, we all believe in the same God, don't we... Whatever the name we give to him..." „You're so right!", the Vicar answered, laughing... Later that night, Robert explained his parents would soon be taken out of France, to a place where they would be safe. He couldn't say how... nor where... but soon, they would be safe... „I'm relieved to hear you say that...", Paul said... As they were about to leave, Will and Paul kissed Mrs. & Mr. Bloomfield... „God bless you...", Will said to them... „And God bless you, too, young man... We'll never forget what you did for us...", Mrs. & Mr. Bloomfield said to him... As Will and Paul were about to leave, Robert took Paul apart, and said to his friend: „I can't thank you enough for what you did..." „It's only natural Robert... But please, keep your guys away from the Palais Bourbon: That's where Will and Lutz work... and remember... they are only translators..." „I'll do my best... I promise! And Paul?" „Yes?" „(...) Listen... We may need your help in the future... Can we count on you?" „...You mean... the Résistance?" „Yes, Paul... I'm not a communist... I'm not a capitalist: I'm just a patriot! Should we need your help, can we count on you?" „... If I can help, I will... I swear to you... you can count on me!" They hugged, then Paul and Will left... That was the last time Paul saw Mrs. & Mr. Bloomfield...

He later learned from Robert that his parents had made it out of France... and had been taken to a place where they were safe. Where? Paul didn't know. And from then on, from time to time, Paul would receive a call from Robert asking for Paul's help to hide Allied pilots that had been shut down by the Germans over France... With Paul's help, all were taken to the Vicar's presbytery... then hidden somewhere under his church where no one was ever found! All Paul knew was that, at one point or another, all had made their way out of France, thanks to the Résistance. How? He had no idea... He understood he was only a small link of a much bigger chain... and that the less he knew, the better it was... for if arrested by the Gestapo, he couldn't tell much... Fortunately he never got arrested!

And no German soldier was ever gunned down by the Résistance near the Palais Bourbon in Paris!

F I V E

A few months later, Paul was having breakfast with Will and Ludwig when madame Louise, the governess, came in to tell him he had a call... Paul went to his study and took the call there... „Oh bonjour Monsieur le Curé, comment allez-vous?" „....Not too good, I'm afraid... Tragic events occurred here last night... and quite frankly... I didn't know who else to call but you..." „Oh?" „....Yes. Last night, a young man from the village was severely beaten... He's one of your employees, and works for you at Bagatelle... I thought I should give you a call..." „Who is he?" „François Dubois..." „François?... But... What happened?" „... I can't tell you over the phone... but... he was the victim of a gay bashing..." – „(...) How is he? Where is he?" „He's here, at the presbytery... the doctor is here, too... and... François is in pretty bad shape, I'm afraid. The doctor says he needs an operation, and it's urgent that he goes to the hospital... But that's the problem: His family has no money for that and, anyway... his father is not very... cooperative, due to the circumstances..." „Could he travel to Paris?" „The doctor thinks he could make it, but he has lost a lot of blood... It's a question of time..." „Father, I'll be there as soon as I can... I'm leaving Paris right now! And I'll take François back to Paris with me. Don't worry! But I want to see his father... Is he there with you?" „...No..." „Make sure he's at the presbytery when I get there..." „Yes. Count on me for that..." „I'm leaving right now..." „Fine..." Paul went back to Will and Ludwig... explained everything to them and, looking at Ludwig he said: „...You're coming with me... Let's go!"

They left Paris in a hurry and on their way to the village, nothing much was said. They didn't know what to expect and quite frankly, they didn't understand what had happened... As soon as they got to the presbytery, the Vicar explained to them: „...Last night, François and his friend Jacques

61

were caught while they were... well... they were engaged in a sexual relation, if you see what I mean... From what François could tell us, they were caught „in the act" by Marcel Foucarde and four of his friends... Now, François is a strong young man, so at first, he was able to fight them... and it gave Jacques enough time to flee... But then, François was alone against five guys... So, in the end, he was overcome, and he was badly beaten. „...According to the doctor", the Vicar continued to explain... „they used an object to sodomize him... something like a baseball bat... and François bled a lot. But the worst wounds were caused to his sexual organs... The doctor said they must have hit him there very hard and repeatedly. According to the doctor, he urgently needs an operation, or he will die." „...But this is savagery... Have the gendarmes been called?" „Yes! They spoke to Marcel Foucarde and his friends... But they all deny having been involved in the beating. And from what I understand, the gendarmes do not intend to press charges, due to the nature of the activities François and his friend were engaged in, when the attack took place", the Vicar answered, with a sad look on his face. „But that's horrible...", Paul shouted... „Yes, it's shocking...", the Vicar said... „And there is not much we can do, except take care of François." „Where is he?" „He's upstairs with the doctor. His parents are also there. His mother is deeply troubled, of course... As for his father... well... obviously, he doesn't accept the fact his son is... gay!", the Vicar answered. „I see..." „Can we go see François?", Ludwig asked... „Yes. Come with me...", the Vicar replied. They went upstairs and when they saw François, Ludwig said: „Shit! Why the hell did they do that to him?" „Don't worry... For the moment, he doesn't suffer. I've given him a very strong sedative", the doctor explained. Ludwig took a chair and sat right beside his friend's bed... „...My poor François..." Ludwig said to his best friend... „What have they done to you..." Of course François, being under sedation, could not hear nor answer that question...

Paul looked at the doctor and at Mrs. & Mr. Dubois and said to them: „... May I talk to you in another room?" „Of course", they answered. The Vicar led them to another room where they sat. Paul looked at the doctor and asked: „How is he?" „In a very bad shape. He lost a lot of blood. I've stopped the bleeding for now... but he needs an operation, and it's urgent!" „I don't have the means to pay for that...", François' father bluntly said... „He should have known that that's what happens to a sissy like him! My own son! When I think..." He didn't have time to finish his sentence, since Paul looked at him and said: „... We're talking here about your son's life, may I remind you! Not his sexual orientation..." „Well... If it was not for his „sexual orientation", as you say, he wouldn't..." „ENOUGH!", Paul said, looking Mr. Dubois straight in the eyes. Mrs. Dubois was sitting there, not saying a word, sobbing... Obviously, she was fearful of her husband, and her opinion probably didn't count for much, Paul thought... „Now", Paul said... „We're going to take François to the hospital! We're going back to Paris with him, and don't worry Mr. Dubois: I'll pay the bills. François is one of my employees... and he's Ludwig's best friend. We'll take care of him..." Then Paul turned to the doctor and asked him: „...Can you come with us to Paris, just in case something goes wrong during our trip?" – „Yes..." „As soon as we get there, I'll ask someone to drive you back here, don't worry..." Paul looked at Mrs. & Mr. Dubois and asked them: „Do you want to come?" „It's out of the question...", Mr. Dubois dryly answered. „I have work to do on the farm... and my wife has to take care of our other children back at the farm..." „Very well", Paul answered. „But you'll have to sign a paper authorizing me to take the necessary decisions at the hospital and sign all the documents on your behalf. François is still a minor, so he can't give his consent..." „No problem... as long as it doesn't cost me anything..." – „IT WON'T", Paul sharply answered...

Paul wrote a general authorization giving him power over François, and Mr. Dubois signed it. The Vicar also signed it, as a witness... „Fine", Paul said. „Now, let's go..." As François was being carried to Paul's car, Mrs. Dubois took Paul apart and told him: „Please... Please, Sir! Take good care of my son. Please! I love him so much! (...) My husband is not a bad man, you know... It's just that..." „Don't worry Madame Dubois: Your son is in good hands. I'll do all I can to save his life, and nothing will be spared, I swear to you..." Madame Dubois was silently crying. She raised her eyes and said to Paul: „I don't know how to thank you Monsieur de Brion! You're a good man... I trust you fully..." „... Do you have a phone at the farm?", Paul asked her... „Of course not!"

„... Don't worry, through the Vicar, I'll keep you informed..." „Yes... And since every morning, I come to Mass..." „Fine!" Later that same day, as they arrived at the Hôtel-Dieu Hospital in Paris, the village doctor explained everything to one of his colleagues there... Then Paul met with the surgeon... Paul introduced himself to the surgeon, who looked at him and said, with a smile on his face: „Monsieur de Brion? Of course... I know your father well..." „Please doctor, do the best you can. I'll take care of the bills, so don't worry about that! I want the best for him, do you understand me?" „Yes, Monsieur de Brion. I'll do my best!", the surgeon answered... „Now, we must take him over to surgery..." – „We will stay and wait...", Paul answered. While they were waiting, Paul signed all the forms. He took a private room for François, and went there with Ludwig to wait... Later, he gave Will a call, and explained everything to him... And of course, it didn't take long before Will, Lutz and Franz got to the hospital... They were all waiting... „....I can't believe it!", Will said, after he had heard the complete story... „And the gendarmes will do nothing?", Franz asked... „No!", Paul answered, with a very sad look on his face. „We must do something... This guy (...) What's his name again?", Will asked... „... Marcel Foucarde", Ludwig answered. „I've seen him once or twice last summer. He's a scamp..." „Well... Promise me you won't do anything against that guy...", Paul said, looking at Will... „It's bad enough the gendarmes won't press charges against him... I don't want them to press charges against us, for something we would have done to him in retaliation... And you too, Ludwig: Promise me!" „(...) Yeah yeah, I promise...", Will reluctantly said... „Me too...", Ludwig said... „I promise... but..." „No „but"... You've promised. That's it!", Paul answered, satisfied... The only problem was, Paul forgot to make Lutz promise the same... And when Ludwig raised his eyes to look at Lutz, he saw a grin on his friend's face...

They waited for another three hours ... Then, the surgeon came to the room and sat down, exhausted. „... I did my best!", he said, looking down at the floor... „How is he?", Ludwig anxiously asked... „....Well... I guess, he'll never get married..." „I beg you pardon?", Paul asked, stunned by the doctor's answer... „(...) He'll survive... but I had no choice... The damages caused to his sexual organs were extensive. I had to proceed to the removal of the scrotum and testes..." – „(...)" „....That's why I say he'll never get married. As for the other wounds, they will heal. Your friend is young, strong and healthy! He's going to need lots of rest, but he will heal..." After a long moment of silence, Paul looked at the surgeon and asked him: „(...) But... What about his sexual life?" „....Of course, no woman will ever want to marry him... I mean... He will never be able to reproduce..." „That's not what I'm asking you, doctor...", Paul said... „Well, from the moment a man can't reproduce...", the doctor started to say... Paul looked at him. He had no doubt the surgeon was a very competent one but, obviously, he was not a very imaginative person! In the good doctor's mind, outside procreation, sexual relations did not exist! „... Just so I understand, doctor...", Paul slowly said... „Let's say... and I understand that it is highly hypothetical, but let's say François meets a widow who has already had children... And let's say all she wants is to find a husband, who can bring back home a paycheck each week... and that all she wants is to find a father to her orphan children... Do you follow me?"... „...Yes", the doctor said, looking at Paul... „...And let's say this woman doesn't want to have any other children...", Paul continued to explain... „would François be able to... how could I say... to „honor" her?" „You mean... sexual intercourse?", the doctor asked... „Yes!" „Oh well, yes! You see, his penis was not removed. It was intact... So yes, he will be able to get erections... It would have been quite different if all this had happened before puberty... But at his age, yes, he would be able to honor her..." „... And... What about orgasmic potential?", Paul asked... „... His capacity for sexual pleasure remains intact. But of course, his libido could be weaker... He will even be able to ejaculate! After all, his prostate is intact... but the liquid he will ejaculate will contain no sperm and as I explained to you, he will never be able to reproduce..." „...But he will experience sexual pleasure?", Will asked the doctor... „Oh yes! (...) Now you must also understand that, apart from the fact he will never be able to reproduce, there are other small inconveniences he will have to get used to... The growth of hair will quit him... Before long, he will lose his body hair... The hair on his head will not be affected, though... Also, he will have to watch his weight... Men that have been castrated have a tendency to gain weight! Oh, and don't worry: He's voice will not change, since his castration has occurred after puberty... So, I guess... well... that's all I can say..." „(...) Thank you very much, doctor... Now we understand... And... how long will he have to stay in here?", Paul asked... „...A week or two... If he recuperates as fast as I think he will, I'd say he'll be out of here in about ten days..." – „Can we see him now?", Ludwig asked..."In an hour or two, he will be moved in here from recovery... You'll be able to see him but please, let him sleep. Wait until tomorrow if you want to speak with him..." „We will, Doctor. And thanks for all you

did...", Paul answered. „... I did my best! Poor guy... I'm really sorry..."
„We understand...", Will answered.

Later, François was moved to his private room where his friends were
waiting for him... He was peacefully sleeping... „I'll stay and spend the
night in here... just in case...", Ludwig said. „Now, go home, and have
some rest..." he said to the others... „Yes", Paul answered. „I'll give the
Vicar a call, to let him know about the operation... and tomorrow
morning, I'll come back..." „Fine", Ludwig answered, with a sad smile on
his face. The morning after, when François opened his eyes, he saw
Ludwig sleeping in a chair, right next to his bed... He didn't know where
he was... but could remember all the events that had led to his beating.
He started to silently cry... When Ludwig finally woke up, he rose his
head and saw François was looking at him... „How do you feel dude?"
„...Like if I had been run over by a train, I guess..." „At least, you're
alive!", Ludwig answered, smiling at his friend... „I was scared like hell..."
– „Have they found Jacques?", François asked, worried... „Not yet! The
Vicar said he's hiding somewhere... But he wasn't beaten..." „I'm sorry for
what I did...", François slowly said, with tears in his eyes... „What?",
Ludwig exclaimed... „You did nothing wrong François, nothing..." „... I
guess I can no longer hide from you the fact that I'm gay..." „... Why didn't
you tell me before?" „I was afraid I would lose you as my best friend..."
„Shit! (...) But François: You are my best friend! I would never let you
down, just because you're gay! What the hell were you thinking? I love
you François... as much as I love my brother Will... I'll always be your
friend François..." „Thanks, pal! (...) Then, looking at his body under the
sheet, he asked Ludwig: „What have they done to me?" „(...) I... Paul will
be here later... he will explain to you. I'm afraid I'm not too good with
medical explanations, you see. (...) Are you hungry?" „...Like hell, I am...",
François answered, grinning... „Good! I'll go see what I can find..." „Oh
Ludwig?" „Yes?" „Where the hell am I?" „...In Paris. At the Hôtel-Dieu
Hospital..." „...In Paris?" „Yes... Wait for me: I'll be back with something
to eat..." „Like if I was about to go somewhere...", François answered,
smiling to his friend... „Yeah... Well, don't move!" „I won't. Each time I
move, it hurts!"

As he had said, Paul got to the Hospital that morning, and he sat down
near his young friend's bed. „What have they done to me?", François
asked him... „(...) Give me your hand, François... and look at me, straight

in the eyes...", Paul slowly answered. Then, Paul began to explain to François the nature of the wounds he had suffered... and the nature of the surgery performed on him... François screamed, when he learned what the surgeon had done, in order to save his life... "Scream, François! Scream all you can! You have the right to...", Paul said, holding his young friend's hand. Later, when François had calmed down a bit, Paul told him all what the surgeon had explained to him the day before. Then, Ludwig sat on the bed and looked at his friend... "... It's bad. It's terrible, I know. (...) But it could be worse! You could be dead! (...) You're alive... And at least, you still have your dick... and you haven't lost your capacity for sexual pleasure! I suppose you were not planning on getting married and on having children..." "...Not really, I guess..." "See? (...) And don't worry: Soon, you and I will have fun again, wanking..." François began smiling at that thought. But after a while he said: "...I don't want to go back to the village..." "...You're not going back there...", Paul calmly said... "...What am I going to do? Where can I go?" "First, as soon as you are discharged from the Hospital, you're coming with us to our home... and you will stay with us... Don't worry François... We all love you, and we won't let you down! Count on me! (...) Later, when you're better... we'll talk about your future... But tell me: Do you like school?" "...I loved school... and I had good marks... But then, I had to quit... My Dad needed me on the farm, so..." – "When did you quit school?" "Two years ago..." "...Would you like to go back to school?" – "I'd love to... but... that's not possible..." "Oh yes, it is! Believe me: It is!", Paul answered, grinning... "As I said, you get better... We'll have time to talk about that later..."

As the doctor had said, ten days later, François was discharged from the Hospital and went to Paul's mansion... François couldn't believe his eyes! "A palace", he exclaimed, when he was shown around the mansion... "...This is the bedroom you will share with Ludwig...", Paul explained to him, as he showed him a large and very nice bedroom with two beds in it... "Why are you doing this for me?", François suddenly asked Paul... "You're a fine young man, François! And I know how hard it is to be gay. I know how it feels to be rejected by one of our parents. Believe me: I know! (...) So... I'm going to help you, my friend! Whether you like it or not, you're stuck with us!", Paul said, laughing... "... Stuck with you? Hey... That's the best thing that has happened to me in a long, long time! Do you see me complain? (...) But I don't think my father will agree... He will want me back on the farm..." „Oh, don't worry about that: I have a plan... Just trust me!" Indeed, Paul had a plan...

A few days later, he met Mrs. & Mr. Dubois at the presbytery. The Vicar was present. Paul explained to them he wanted François to go back to school, and that he was going to pay for it. François would stay with them in Paris, free of charge. Furthermore, Paul was ready to pay Mr. Dubois the salary François used to bring back home each week, when working for him at Bagatelle... and he would do so for as long as Mr. Dubois would agree to let François go to school in Paris... Of course, Mr. Dubois was too happy to agree! He was embarrassed to have a gay son, and was too happy to think he would no longer have to tolerate that faggot around him anymore. Also, he would no longer have to feed him... and would continue to cash his paycheck! What a deal, he thought... Before he left, and while they were alone for a minute, Paul talked to Mrs. Dubois... and it was agreed with her that, every Monday morning, before Mass, she would come to the presbytery where François would call her... That would be the only way to maintain contact between the two of them, since Mrs. Dubois didn't know how to read, so of course, François couldn't write to her... Hearing about the „deal" Paul had made with his father, François was ecstatic! But now, François had to get used to his new life... And Ludwig had to get used to the fact he was now sharing his bedroom with his friend! No more „privacy"! That wouldn't be easy... and both friends would have to find ways... to manage that problem! Can we do that? That was the big question François had on his mind! The answer to that question was not obvious, due to the circumstances... After all, François was gay... and Ludwig was not! „I'll have to talk to him...", François thought to himself! „Problem is: I don't know what the hell I'm going to say to him..."

That day, on their way to Bagatelle, Paul and Will stopped by the presbytery, to pay the Vicar a visit. When the Vicar opened the door and saw them standing there, he looked at them and said: „Ah, there you are!!! I wanted to talk to you... Come in!" Obviously, the Vicar was not in a very good mood... Will didn't have time to close the door behind him that the Vicar was asking them: „....What did you do to him?", he asked Paul... „To whom?" „....Marcel Foucarde! The guy who gave François a beating..." „What do you mean? (...) We have done nothing...", Paul answered, with a very sincere look on his face... „Why do you ask?" „... Early in the morning, two days ago... He was found stark naked, shaved all over his body, tied to a tree in the village square! No one touched him before noon... and from what I've been told, he had been whipped...", the Vicar answered... „Wait, wait, wait...", Paul said... „I don't understand... What do you mean by „whipped"? And how come nobody untied him before noon?" The Vicar gave Paul an angry look and said: „...There was a sign at his feet..." „A sign?", Paul said, stunned... „Yes! A big sign! And it said something like: „I have beaten a guy, just because he is a homosexual. I have been punished for my act. Just look at me... And if anybody does what I did, he will receive the same punishment like me! Don't untie me before noon, because if you do... you'll be punished!" „I still don't understand...", Paul said... „It's obvious, isn't it? Those who did it wanted to make an example... and they wanted the whole village to see him... and they succeeded...", the Vicar answered. „Father, I swear to you I have nothing to do with it... I swear to you on my grandmother's grave! I know nothing about it...", Paul said. Then the Vicar turned to Will and looked at him... „...No no... I swear to you... I have nothing to do with it... Paul made us swear we wouldn't exact revenge... and we did not! I swear!" Will told the Vicar. „...I believe you... both of you. But I wonder who did it..." „...I have no idea, Father! I swear!" Paul answered with a very honest face. „...Neither do I", Will added... „Alright... (...) I know what Foucarde did to François was very wrong, but it is not for us to render justice...", said the Vicar. „Have the gendarmes (policemen) been called?", Paul asked... „No! He refuses to talk... and he refused to call them. I don't know why...", The Vicar answered.

Later, Paul and Will went to Bagatelle, then to La Vacherie, where Lutz, Franz, Ludwig and François joined them... After Paul had told them what had happened to Marcel Foucarde, Ludwig said:

„... I didn't do it! I swear to you... I have nothing to do with it..." „Oh stop looking around for the guilty ones... I know who did it...", Lutz answered, grinning... „What?", Paul shouted... „You never made me swear anything, remember? (...) But I didn't do it myself..." „Who did?" „...Ah... well... You remember the guy from Berlin I told you about... He's in the SS, and works at the SS Headquarter in Paris... A few times, he asked me to do him favors... and I've translated a few documents for him...." „...Yeah? What about him?", Paul asked... „...Well I called him... and I told him about what Marcel Foucarde had done to François... and I asked him if he thought he could teach him a lesson..." „...Is this SS guy a gay?", Will asked... „No, no... He's just a bit... sadistic, shall I say!", Lutz answered, laughing... „I wrote the sign they found near Foucarde, that's all I did!" „(...)" „Look Paul..." Lutz began to explain... „I told this SS guy about Foucarde... where he could find him... and I told him he needed a good lesson! But I told him not to kill Foucarde, and that I didn't want the guy to be permanently maimed... Except for that, he had free rein..." „Oh my God!", Paul exclaimed... „What did you do that for?" „Foucarde and his friends are not only scums... They are also dangerous!" Lutz said... „François was not the first to be beaten like he was... And I thought about Jacques, his friend... He escaped, but he's still in hiding..." „That's true, Paul: We don't know where he is...", François said... „Now, Jacques can come back to the village, knowing Foucarde and his friends will not try to beat him", Lutz continued to explain... „They are all too scared for that now... And if François wants to visit his mother, he has no reason to be afraid anymore: Foucarde and his alikes will stay away from him! (...) The gendarmes refused to do anything after François was beaten... I couldn't tolerate that! That's why I acted the way I did..." „...He's right, Paul... The gendarmes did nothing... nothing at all! And why? Because François is gay, that's why!", Will said... „...Well... Under the circumstances...", Paul started to say... „...Look Paul: I would never have done what I did if the gendarmes had press charges against those scums... and if they had been brought to justice...", Lutz explained. „...As I was saying... under the circumstances, I guess I understand", Paul slowly said. „But why does Foucarde refuse to call the gendarmes? And what did this SS guy did to him? Do you know?" Now, Lutz had a big smile on his face, and he said: „...Foucarde doesn't want to call the gendarmes, because he thinks the beating was done by the gendarmes..." – „Huh?", Will exclaimed... „Yes, yes...", Lutz said, laughing... „The SS guy I'm telling you about... well... He, along with three of his SS friends... were wearing gendarmes' uniforms when they did it..." – „I don't believe you...", Paul said... „...Well, that's what he told me yesterday...", Lutz said, laughing... „They even had a car with the insignia of the Gendarmerie on it... So now you understand why Foucarde doesn't want to call the gendarmes, don't you?" Paul couldn't help it and grinned... „Yeah! But that doesn't tell me what they did to him..." „Well, I didn't ask too many questions, you know! All I know is that Foucarde... well... Let's say he will have some problems walking for the next few weeks..." "What do you mean?", Ludwig asked... "Well, Foucarde knows by now how it feels to have more than one dick in his ass at the same time... and... well... he also knows how it feels to have a... fist... up there, too", Lutz answered, laughing his heart out... "You're kidding!", François said... "No, no... I swear...", Lutz replied, laughing... "But not only was he shaved... He was also whipped... At least, that's what the Vicar told us...", Paul said... "Oh yes!", Lutz said, grinning... "He was shaved all over, including his head, just so he would be humiliated in front to the whole village... I like the idea... But of course, his hair will grow back. But the whipping will leave permanent marks on his body... He will have them till the last day of his miserable life. And that will serve as a... reminder, you know... What Foucarde and his friends did to François was horribly wrong..." Of course, they all looked at François, who had remained silent most of the time while Lutz was speaking. All they saw were tears running down his cheeks... "...Okay! Now guys, not a word about it, do we agree?", Paul strenuously asked... "We saw nothing... We heard nothing... We know nothing...", Ludwig answered, laughing... "Yes...", the others answered...

Later during that weekend, Ludwig went to Lutz and said: "...Um, Lutz... I'd like to ask you something..." "What?" "...Let's take a walk... just you and me..." "Sure", Lutz answered, a bit puzzled... So, they went for a walk into the woods... and after a while, Ludwig said to him: "Now Lutz... You know François is my best friend... I'm so proud of you, for what you did... I would have done it myself if I had not given my word to Paul..." "I know Ludwig..." "Yeah. (...) Nevertheless, I'd like to know what those SS guys really did to Foucarde..." – "You sure?" "Yes. I want to know..." "...Okay... But swear to me you will never tell..." "I swear", Ludwig answered. "Okay! There it goes...

This is what the SS guy from Berlin told me: "Lutz... We've done the "job"... and I swear Foucarde will never beat a gay guy again..." – "...What did you do to him? (...) He's not dead, huh?" "No, no Lutz... Do you want to know what we did to him?" "...Yeah..." "Well... I spoke to three of my "friends", you know... They are members of the SS, just like me... But I'm not sure they are very... how should I put it... "sane"... (...) Yeah! Let's say I'm not really sure they are sane... Anyway... We found your guy! At first, he wasn't too frightened... since we were all wearing gendarmes' uniforms... We told him we knew about the gay bashing... we laughed a lot with him about it... and after a while, he started to brag about it... So, we knew then we had the right guy! We all had a few beers with him... then we told him we had a little surprise for him, and he followed us to our car... We drove a few kilometers... away from the village... Then, we took him out of the car, and we stripped him... I tell you Lutz... He was stunned! And he started to put some resistance! Of course, I had to beat him, and tell him he had to be very polite with us... I told him why we were there, and then... I tell you Lutz... I saw fear in his eyes! Oh, but I told him we would not kill him... no, no... but that he would suffer for what he had done to your young friend... That's when I think I saw piss running down his legs... Oh well, anyway... First, we shaved him... I mean... all over! The poor guy was sobbing! And he got very nervous when we started shaving around his dick and balls... you know... My friends are not barbers: They are butchers! So, I guess they left him with a few cuts down there, if you follow my drift... Anyway... We were all laughing a lot... But not him! Oh no! I looked at him and asked him: „Tell me you like what we're doing to you... I don't know why Lutz... but he didn't answer me... I don't like it, when someone doesn't answer me! So, I punched him a few times in the stomach, and explained to him it would be better for him to answer me and to address me as „Sir"... It didn't take long for him to understand, I swear... Then I told him: „So I hear you like to put things up some other guy's ass, don't you." Can you believe he didn't answer my question? I had to punch him again... a few times...and finally he said: „....Yes!" „Yes what?" „....Yes, Sir!" „Ah... Now we're going somewhere with you", I told him... „Would you like to have a big dick up your cute ass?" – „(...)" Of course, I had to punch him again... „Yes, Sir!", he finally answered. „Good... Cause my friend here would very much like to fuck you... Look at him, Foucarde: He has a big dick! Don't you like it?" „....Yes, Sir", he answered, with a disgusted look on his face... „Ohhhhhhh no... That's not the way to answer me... Tell me you like his big dick... Tell me you really want it up your ass... Tell me... „(...) Yes, Sir! (...) I do... I love his big dick... I want it up my ass..." „Good!" Then, I turned to Ernst... one of my friends... and said to him: „Ernst: He's all yours..." Now... my friend Ernst... well... he really has a big dick... And I think he would fuck anything with two legs... even with four legs, you see? Anyway... Ernst is not... how could I say... he's not very „delicate", if you see what I mean... We roughly pushed Foucarde over the car trunk, face down... and while two of my friends were holding him there by his arms... Ernst shove his big dick in his ass... right up to the hilt... I don't know why, Lutz... but Foucarde screamed... And I think I saw tears in his eyes... Can you believe that? Anyway... Ernst is a special specimen... He likes it rough... He fucked Foucarde hard and fast... and it didn't take long before he shut his jizz deep inside Foucarde's tight ass... Of course, I asked Foucarde: „Did you like that, bastard?" – „...Yes, Sir!" „Yes what?" „I loved it, Sir!" „Do you want some more?" „(...)" „Do you?" „...Please, Sir: Stop it!", he pleaded... „It's a bit late to plead for mercy, bastard! Did you stop beating Dubois when he pleaded for mercy? I don't think so... So! Answer my question: Do you want some more?" „....Yes, Sir... More..." „Ahhhhh! Good! Cause I have another friend here who's waiting for his turn..." „(...)" I turned to Karl and said to him: „Your turn, Karl..." Now Karl... I don't know what's wrong with him... really... It didn't take half a second before Karl had driven all of his dick up Foucarde's ass! Of course, Foucarde shouted out... With pleasure, I'm certain... I don't understand why he had tears in his eyes, though... Karl went under Foucarde with his right hand, and grabbed his balls... Then squeezed them a little. Okay, okay... he squeezed them hard! Anyway... He fucked Foucarde for a while, squeezing his balls... and do you know what Lutz? Foucarde had a hardon! Yup!... A hardon... Of course, we couldn't believe it! But I swear... he had one... „Ohhhhh You're a sissy, aren't you?" I asked Foucarde... „(...) Yes, Sir", he reluctantly answered... Of course... Karl shot his cum deep inside Foucarde's ass... But do you know what he did after that? He turned Foucarde around over the trunk so he would lay there on his back, and Karl started to masturbate the guy! Yeah! After a while... Karl looked at us and said: „Just wait, guys... you'll see..." Karl was grinning... So, he kept jacking-off Foucarde and, of course, the guy eventually shot his load. He was so ashamed... Problem is: Karl kept jacking him off, even after he had cum. Poor Foucarde! It didn't take long before he started screaming... He just couldn't take it anymore... And all the time, Karl just kept jacking him off... Laughing... Anyway... It was Joachim's turn now to fuck Foucarde! Now Joachim has a very, very big dick... That's the reason why we had decided to keep him for dessert, you know... That's when Ernst decided to lay down on his back over the trunk... My friends forced Foucarde to lay down over him, on his back... so his back was now hard pressed against Ernst's stomach... Ernst entered him from behind... then... Karl decided Foucarde needed a second dick up his ass... So, he forced his dick inside his ass, right along Ernst's big dick... Oh! They loved the feeling... I had to ask Foucarde: „Do you like to be double-fucked?" Believe me or not... he didn't answer me... „... Do you want a third dick up there?", I had to ask him... „No, no, no... I mean... It's perfect right now, Sir!", he finally said... „... Is it? Do you love the feeling?", I asked him... „Oh, yes, Sir! I love it..." „...Do you want my friends to go faster... deeper?" – „...Yes...Sir! Faster! Deeper!", he answered... „Say please!" „Yes, Sir. Please, Sir!" I don't know why... but something tells me Foucarde did not really enjoy the ride... But since he had asked for a faster and deeper fuck, we had to comply... And so, Ernst and Karl did their best to fully satisfy Foucarde... you know... My friends are just like that: So, kind... This time... It took longer for Ernst and Karl to cum... But after quite a while... They did. A lot... And all the time... Joachim was still waiting... So, when Ernst and Karl had finished fucking Foucarde, I told Joachim: „I guess it's your turn... but you have such a big dick... I wonder if he can take it..." „Wait, wait...," Ernest then said: „I don't think his ass is ready to accommodate Joachim's big dick... but maybe... with a little „preparation" „Oh?", I asked Ernst... „And what do you have in mind?" „...Well I wonder if he would like to feel my fist up his ass! I've heard gays love that... and after that, I guess his ass would be slack enough to accommodate Joachim..." „...Hey, Foucarde", I asked him... „Would you like to have a fist up your ass? „(...)" „...I'm sure you would love it, wouldn't you? „I had to give his balls a few twists... then he said: „Yeah, yeah... I would love it, Sir!" „Love what?" „...To have a fist shoven up my ass...Sir!" „Well... Since you ask... „We didn't have any lube with us... But my friends had shot so much cum in there... you know... „Well Ernst, let's see what you can do", I told my friend... „So, Ernst, laughing his heart out, started to put three of his fingers into Foucarde's asshole... No problem! Then, Ernst added a fourth finger... soon to be followed by his thumb. No problem! I guess Foucarde was already a bit slack down there... Anyway... Ernst started to push his fist inside his ass... and... I wonder why... Foucarde began to scream! Why? Hell, I really don't know... really... But when I saw Ernst fist disappear inside Foucarde's ass, I asked him if it felt good... „Answer me, you scum!", I shouted... „...Yes, Yes... Yes, Sir! I love it..." „Do you want him to go deeper inside you?" „(...)" „Is that a yes?" „Yes, Sir! Yes..." „Come on, Ernst: Give it to him! He loves it!" „Now my friend Ernst is always eager to please everyone... He's like that! But at one point, I had to stop him... cause his fist and arm were pretty deep inside Foucarde's ass... and I didn't want to see Foucarde loose consciousness... I wanted him to be fully aware of what was happening to him... You know how I am...Yeah! I wanted him to experience all the pleasures we were giving him... „Come on Ernst... Take your arm out of him... I think he's slack enough, now..." „So Ernst did as I had asked... Okay, okay... He didn't remove his arm slowly... but I guess... He didn't know better! Then, it was Joachim's turn... I mean... The poor guy had been waiting for so long... I looked at Foucarde and asked him: „So bastard... look at my friend here... you like his big dick? Huh? Want it up your ass?" „(...)" „...Tell me you would love that... Or... perhaps you would prefer to have Ernst's fist back in your ass? „No, no, no... His dick... I'd love to have his dick... Sir!" „Good!" „So that's when my friend Joachim fucked him good with his big dick... But poor Joachim... He found that Foucarde's ass was a bit too slack by now... and although he did cum big, deep

inside him, he was not totally satisfied... I felt sorry for Joachim... After all, he had waited so long for his turn! So, I said to Foucarde: „Hey bastard: How about you gave my friend a good blow-job? You know... he's not really satisfied with the fuck you gave him... You're too slack..." „(...)" „What did you say?" I had to asked Foucarde again... „...Yes... I would like it very much, Sir!" „That's nice!" Of course, Foucarde was forced to give Joachim a blow-job... It took some time for him to learn how to do it... and Joachim is so big... but he learned... I swear... After he had shut his cum deep down Foucarde's throat, Joachim told me he had experienced his best blow-job ever! Foucarde is talented, you know... And with a little help, he learns fast. Anyway... After that... We tied Foucarde between two trees... I mean... It was my turn to have some fun! You know... So, I whipped him good... I'm very talented with that, you know! I've learned a lot, being with the SS... But I'm not sure Foucarde appreciated my talents! Oh, well... First, I whipped him all over his back... Then I turned to face him... and I started to whip his chest good... „Tell me you love it...", I asked him... „(...)" „Answer me!", I had to shout... „PLEASE.... STOP.... PLEASE!!!", he answered... „Tell me you love it, bastard... I won't stop before you tell me how much you enjoy it...", I told him... „Of course, I hit his dick and balls a few times... you know... so I guess it's going to take a while before he can wank again... Perhaps in a few months... Who knows? „... I love it! I love it, Sir...", Foucarde finally answered... „Well... I had to stop, since I had promised you I wouldn't kill him... you know... So, we took him back to the village, tied him between two trees... and placed your sign at his feet. That's all we did! Really! Not much, as you can see...

Hearing what had been done to Foucarde, Ludwig just stared at Lutz... and after a while, he said: „...You're kidding me!" „Oh no... I'm telling you the truth! That's what they did to him..." „...I can't believe it... (...) I guess Foucarde got his lesson, didn't he?", Ludwig asked... „Yeah", Lutz answered, with a grin on his face... „But let's keep it a secret between you and me, okay?" „Yes! I don't think Paul would like to hear about that..." „NO!!!", Lutz answered, laughing... „I don't think so. Now, let's go back to our friends, shall we?" „Yes...", Ludwig said... „And Lutz... Thanks again for what you did. It will not bring back my friend's balls... But at least, Foucarde paid dearly for what he did to François... Thanks!" „Yeah!", Lutz answered, grinning... „He paid his due!"

„Hey, Paul... Do you remember... the last time we were at Bagatelle, we were wondering where Foucarde was?", François asked... „Yeah?" „... Well... I've just called my Mum, and she said that, indeed, they don't know where Foucarde is! It seems he's nowhere to be found... Anyway... She said she doesn't feel sorry for him, and that the village is no longer terrorized by him and his gang of thugs..." „I'm glad to hear she doesn't pity him!" „She doesn't... Nevertheless... I still wonder what those SS guys really did to him..." „All we know is that he was whipped...", Paul answered... „...Not just that! My Mum heard rumors about other things... But she said it's too terrifying to talk about it...", François said, a bit puzzled... „...Well... Whatever they did to him... at least, we know he's still alive, isn't he?" – „Right!" Now that François was back to school, and as he was recovering nicely, things were going back to normal on Avenue Foch... Except that Ludwig had a problem on his hands! „...François?", Ludwig asked his friend one night... „Yes?" „...You know... I'm glad you're living here have our bedroom all to myself... Oh, I don't mind sharing it with you... no... That's no big deal..." „What's wrong then?", François asked, a bit anxious... „(...) Well, when I had the room all to myself... I had my „privacy", if you see what I mean..." „Huh?" „...Well...

and don't laugh..." „I won't Ludwig... I swear..." „It's just that... well... it is the only place where I can jerk-off in peace..." „Ahhhhh, so that's it, huh?" „.... You know, when we're in Paris, Marie-Hélène isn't here to take care of my „needs"... So, I have to take care of them myself... and I do it... a lot!", Ludwig answered, laughing... „I see dude! (...) And no need to sweat... I mean, I'm here, I know... and I can't make myself disappear... but... listen to me Ludwig: I don't care if you wank in your bed all night long, you know... I know it's not easy for you, having me here in your bedroom... But I don't want you to feel uneasy because I'm sleeping in a bed right next to yours... Please Ludwig, don't make me feel bad!" „No no... I don't want to make you feel bad... not at all... but... Um, can I ask you a question François?" – „Sure!" „(...) Tell me François: Are you in love with me?" Since Ludwig was sitting on his own bed, François walked over to him and sat on his bed, facing his friend... „...Look Ludwig: You're a terrific guy... and you're gorgeous... no, no... that's true... And yes... I was in love with you at one point! But then, I've realized you're not gay, and that you would never fall in love with me... Then, I met Jacques... As you know, he's gay, and we had a lot of fun together... Now he doesn't want to see me anymore, but that's another story! The point is that, when I met Jacques, I realized I was losing my time loving you... I don't know what's going to happen with Jacques... I sent him a few letters... Anyway, all this is to say that, at one point, I've stopped loving you! (...) I mean... I still love you, but like I love my brothers and my sisters... So, if today you ask me if I'm in love with you, I can tell you „NO". „ „....Thanks for being honest with me, François! I appreciate! Now that I know you're no longer in love with me, it makes me feel a lot comfier to jerk-off while you're in the room... But... Um... I have another question for you though?" „What is it you want to know this time", François answered, laughing... „Um... well it's not easy for me to ask..." „Come on Ludwig: What's on your mind?" „I don't want to hurt you, if I ask..." „Oh shit, Ludwig: You're my best friend... Why the hell would you want to hurt me? Come on..." „Okay... (...) I was wondering... since the „accident"... how have things been going on for you „down there"?" François burst out laughing... and then asked Ludwig: „You mean... if I can have an erection?" „Sort of..." „Sure! (...) I don't get hard as easily as I used to do, but I can, if that's what you want to know...", François answered, still laughing... „Good! (...) Cause I don't want to be wanking right next to you, knowing you feel bad about it..." – „No, no... Don't worry about that..." „Um... Have you... Have you wanked since..." „No... I haven't tried yet... It's still a little bit painful „down there" as you say... But I'm thinking about it... A lot! It's just that... like... as if I was afraid to... You know... (...) But I can see you're curious, huh? I suppose you wonder how I look „down there" now... Want to see?" „I don't want to make you feel bad..." „No no... In fact, it will make feel more comfortable! If I show you, perhaps I will stop trying to hide myself from you each night, when we get undressed! Here... Take a look..." François took his shorts off, and Ludwig looked at his friend's crotch... His dick was there... but his balls were gone! All Ludwig could see was a pink scar, where his friend's balls used to hang... „What do you think?", François asked his friend... „Be honest with me..." „...The surgeon did a fine job!", Ludwig said... „Yeah! (...) He told me I was in a pretty bad shape, when I got to the hospital..." „Do you remember what they did to you? I mean... Foucarde and his thugs..." „...Yes! The others didn't touch me... They just held me there, while Foucarde kept hitting me... I couldn't defend myself... Fortunately, at one point, I lost consciousness..." „I wish I could kill him..." „Nah! I think he got a good lesson from those SS guys...", François answered, grinning... „...Oh yes, he did!", Ludwig said, laughing... „I swear to you: He did!" Eventually, both friends went to bed, and the lights were turned off. „Night, Ludwig..." – „Yeah! Night, François..." But later that night, certain sounds woke François up... He started to listen... and heard... slurping sounds... followed by moans coming from Ludwig's bed... „...Taking care of your „needs" pal?", he whispered, grinning... „...What else?", Ludwig answered, smiling in the dark... „Feels good?" „...Try for yourself, and tell me..." „...I can't get a hardon as easily as I used to...", François answered. „Here pal: Let me give you a hand with that...", Ludwig said, as he got up from his bed and walked over to his friend's bed... „...Spread your legs a bit, so I can kneel down between your legs..." „Are you kidding or what?" „No no... What are friends for, huh? Trust me, pal... You'll see you're going to get hard!" Ludwig hopped on his friend's bed, and knelt down between his parted legs... Then he took his friend's limp dick into his already slippery hand, and started to play with it... „What are you doing?", François whispered, a bit puzzled by Ludwig's move... „I told you: I'm giving you a hand with your problem! And it's not as if I was fucking you, huh? Now, that would be gay! But jerking-off a friend?

Nah!" Ludwig started to rub his fingers all around his friend's mushroom cap... He spat into his hand and smeared his warm saliva all over his friend's knob... François gasped: The sensation was unbelievable, since his knob was very sensitive to touch... „Oh shit! That feels sooooooo good, pal! I swear...", François moaned... As his dick started to swell into Ludwig's expert hand, François said: „Don't stop... I'm getting hard..." „I can see that... I can feel your dick growing into my hand", Ludwig answered, grinning... François felt his dick come to full attention, as Ludwig tugged at it gently. His breathing was deeper now... Soon, Ludwig's hand was stroking up and down on his friend's hard cock... Very proud of the good job he had done on his best friend's dick, Ludwig grabbed his own cock with his fist, and began stroking it... François enjoyed every sensation running through his body while lying outstretched on the bed: His cock was clearly hungry for attention, and Ludwig's ministrations were doing the trick for him... „....Hey", Ludwig whispered... „You're oozing, pal!" „Thank God!", François answered, relieved to see he was still able to produce precum... At the Hospital, the doctor had told him he would be able to do so, but at the time... he didn't believe him! Now, he had the proof... François started to relax... and he began to really enjoy the pleasures Ludwig was giving to him... „You're a real pal, mate!", François whispered to Ludwig... „Thanks, for what you're doing for me..." Hearing that, Ludwig smiled to himself... and after a few seconds, he said to himself: „Oh... what the heck! Why not give him a blow-job..." He leaned onto his friend's crotch, and, with his left hand, he guided his friend's very hard dick to his lips... François couldn't believe what was going on... "Was Ludwig about to give him a blow-job?" he asked to himself... Of course, he kept his mouth shut, and waited to see what Ludwig was about to do... And YES! Ludwig was about to give his friend a blow-job... At first, Ludwig just kissed his friend's dick... „...Not so bad...", he whispered... Then, he took it into his mouth... François moaned and groaned, tossing his head back, arching his back... driving his cock deeper inside Ludwig's warm velvety mouth... It didn't take long for his very hard dick to fill Ludwig's mouth and then, Ludwig began playing around it with his tongue! Ludwig looked up at François, and he realized he was sucking on his friend's dick with him looking down on him... Ludwig smiled to himself... and of course, François became hornier and hornier... „I thought I would never have such feelings again...",

François softly said, shuddering... Ludwig pulled his head off his friend's dick and asked: „...So pal: How does it feel?" „FANTASTIC! I wish I could do the same to you, though..." „... I wouldn't mind...", Ludwig answered... „You know... It's not as if you have never given me a blow-job before..." „Huh?", François answered, stunned... „Un-huh!... I was drunk that night, at La Vacherie... But not THAT drunk... I don't remember every detail... but I remember how you made my dick feel... And it felt damn good!" „... I thought you were totally passed out..." „No... I wasn't TOTALLY passed out..." „And you didn't punch me in the face?" „Hey dude: You were doing such a great job, so...", Ludwig answered, grinning... „You know Ludwig... You're the hottest looking hunk... with chiseled features any sculptor would handsomely pay to sculp... but don't worry: I swear to you I'm no longer in love with you... so what you're doing to my cock doesn't mean anything to me... except that you're doing a hell of a good job... It's as if you'd been doing this all of your life..." „I'm not sure it's a compliment, but if it is... Thanks dude!" „...It was meant as a compliment... And now that you know I'm no longer in love with you... will you really let me „service" your dick, so you have as much fun as I do?" „Hell, yes..." „Let's do a 69 then..." „Huh? (...) What's that?" „Ahhhhhh... you see? I've gained a little experience with Jacques... It seems to me I know a few tricks you know nothing about... yet!", François said, laughing... „Huh?" „Stop saying HUH and turn around... Let's lay on our sides... I'll rest my head between your legs, and you will do the same in reverse... That way, I'll be able to take good care of your dick, and at the same time, you'll be able to take good care of mine..." Ludwig moved his body as told... then he said to François: „(...) like that?" „Yup! Now, start working, pal...", François said, grinning... François didn't lose time and began kissing Ludwig's big, smooth balls... And he heard his best friend moan when he began giving his balls a very good tongue bath... „...You like it?" „SHIT!", Ludwig answered... For his part, Ludwig went back on sucking his best friend's dick... He knew from experience he loved the taste of his own precum... But he was a bit surprised to discover his friend's clear nectar tasted sweeter than his own... Slowly, Ludwig and François began licking and kissing one another's swollen knobs... Then, and at the same time, they both decided to go for it... They both began to give one another a real, good blow-job! After a few seconds, Ludwig began to hump his friend's face... and he moaned, when his knob entered his friend's throat... „SHIT", he thought to himself... „That feels sooooooo good..." Of course, Ludwig wanted to return the favor to François... He gagged a few times, trying to do so... but finally, he managed to relax... and then... François felt his dick slide deep into his friend's tight throat: The feeling was incredible! After a few minutes... and as Ludwig felt he was about to cum... he pulled his head off his friend's jolting prick and told him: „... If you continue... I'm going to cum! I'm telling you... I can't take it anymore... it's too good..." Hearing that, François smiled to himself! He sealed his lips around Ludwig's dick, and began to bob faster and faster on it with his hot mouth... Ludwig grinned, and quickly resumed sucking his friend's dick... But of course, before long, Ludwig was moaning and groaning again... „Ahhhhhhh" Ludwig grunted, as his cock jolted twice... Then, he erupted his hot teen cum deep inside his friend's mouth... François grinned to himself, and started to gulp every time Ludwig shot another wad... Ludwig's dick was pulsating.... After swallowing Ludwig's final trapped wad, François pulled his head off his dick and cried out: „Shit... I'm going to shoot..." Yes! He's capacity for sexual pleasure was intact, as was his orgasmic potential... He was not shooting cum, of course, but his precum flowed generously into Ludwig's hot mouth... That fitted Ludwig perfectly well, for he had no problem gulping his friend's precum, but he would never have swallowed his cum! Never! In Ludwig's mind, there was a fine line not to be crossed... between what was O.K. between good friends... and what was queer... Kissing a guy on the mouth was a NO-NO... While jerking him off or giving him head was O.K.... Fucking him... or letting him fuck you was queer! And he would never agree to that... But if a friend wanted to put a finger or two up his ass? Or him, putting a finger or two up a friend's ass? Nah! That wasn't queer... After all... doctors do that all the time, don't they? After his friend's orgasm had subsided, Ludwig turned around in bed, and looked at François: „....So? How was it"... „HELL... I'm so happy... I can't even start explaining...", François answered, laughing... „How's that possible?", Ludwig asked, intrigued... „Well... I mean... It's just like the doctor said to me... You know: When we were young, we used to have dry orgasm, didn't we?" „....Yes...", Ludwig slowly said..."Well... I guess... it's a bit like that, only better... since my prostate works just fine..." „So... you've enjoyed the experience?" „....A lot! Only thing though: I'll never be able to taste my own cum again..." „Heck!

You can have mine, for what I care...", Ludwig answered, laughing...
„...Yours tastes good..." „I know: I'm the best..." „... Hey: Don't get carried
away! Don't exaggerate..." „Okay, okay", Ludwig replied, laughing...
„Yeah! (...) Anyway Ludwig... If you ever wake up in the middle of the
night, and you have „urges"... Don't hesitate to wake me up: I'm always
a willing partner..." „Agreed", Ludwig answered, still laughing... Ludwig
walked back to his bed, happy to see his problem was solved! Not only
could he wank as much and as often as he used to in the past, but he had
gained a wanking partner! „Not bad", he thought to himself, grinning...
„Not bad at all!"

During the fall of 1942, they all went to La Vacherie, to spend a
weekend or two over there... One weekend, François decided to go to the
village, to see his mother... She was so happy to see him... and to see with
her own eyes her son was in good shape... She kissed him all over his
face... „Oh come on, Mum!", François said to her, laughing... „Stop that!
I'm no longer a kid, you know..." – „To me, you'll always be my kid...",
she answered, smiling at her son... They talked for a while... about
nothing and everything... Then, François asked his Mum: „...Where is
Dad?" „In the barn, working there... Why?"

„Well... I think I'm going to pay him a little visit..." „Oh! Do you think
it's a good idea?", she nervously asked... „...Don't worry, Mum. And if I
don't pay him a visit, we'll never know..." „Oh my God", were her last
words, before François left for the barn... François walked over to the
barn, and he found his Dad working there... „Good afternoon, Dad...",
François said to his father, smiling... His Dad raised his eyes, stared at his
son, then went back to his work without saying a word... „...Can I help
you with that?", François asked him... „Don't need your help!", his Dad
dryly answered... „Why do you treat me like that, dad?" „...When I think
I gave you life! (...) That night, I should have stained the sheets, instead of
making your Mum pregnant with you..." „(...) Yeah!", François answered
to his Dad... „You gave me life... and made me the way I am... I didn't
choose the way I am, you know... It's all thanks to your genes..." „...Get
the hell out of here... I don't want to see you again..." „(...) I'm beginning
to wonder if, after all, I'm not glad they removed my balls from me: That
way, at least, I'm sure I won't transmit your genes...", François dryly
answered. His dad turned around and, with a very angry look on his face,
he answered: „...Scram! You sissy..." „...Yeah! I'm leaving... Don't worry...

I've heard enough..." And as he was leaving the barn, François turned to look at his dad one last time... and he said to him: „Oh and Dad: Don't forget to cash my pay-checks..." There was nothing his dad could answer to that... so he remained silent! ... Furious..., but silent! Ludwig felt sorry for François, when he heard what his dad had said to him... „...I can't change him...", François answered, with a sad look on his face... „Anyway... I think he never liked me, so... (...) But I feel sorry for my mum... She's his slave! That's what she is... and I know she's miserable..." „Shit... That's bad...", Ludwig answered... „One day, I hope I'll be able to take her away for him... so she can have a decent life..." „Yeah!"

„Oh... but that's not all...", François added... „What else?" „...I went to see Jacques..." „Yeah?" „Well... He doesn't want to see me anymore..." „Did he tell you why?" „No! Just said he doesn't want to see me anymore, that's it!" „I'm so sorry François... Really! You didn't need that! Shit! That's not fair..." „Oh... That's the way things are... What can I do? (...) You know... I've been through a lot recently, and I've decided I had to go on with my life, whatever people say or think. I don't give a damn!" „Right" „...At least, you've got Marie-Hélène... You are lucky!" Ludwig burst out laughing, hearing that... Then, he said to his friend: „Are you kidding? She's a slut! Do you think I don't know every guy in the village has fucked her? Hey... I have sex with her, but that's all! And that's the way she looks at it, too... She doesn't expect anything from me, except a good fuck now and then..." „(...) I know she's not a Saint...", François answered, grinning... „Nope! Let's just say her portrait will never hang on a wall at Notre-Dame... And neither will mine, for that matter..." – „...And don't expect to see mine hanging in there either...", François answered, laughing... „Anyway... Today wasn't a very good day for you... And I want you to know I'm really sorry for you...", Ludwig finally said... „Thanks, buddy..."

Eventually, they all went back to Paris, and on with their lives... „Something else will happen", François said to himself... „Life is just too good right now..." And he was right! When life is too good, something bad always happen! Followed by something good... Not always... But sometimes!

SIX

Now that things were getting back to normal on Avenue Foch, with François getting used his new life in Paris, Will and Paul were breathing easier... François and Ludwig had developed the good habit of „helping" one another with their „needs"... and their agreement in the sex department was working just fine. After a few weeks in college, François had begun making new friends, and finally, life seemed to be good for him! But now that he was going to college in Paris, he didn't have much time left to visit with his friend Jacques, back at the village... Of course, he was writing letters to him... but Jacques had problems with writing, and so his letters to François were scarce... As time flew, François realized his last letters to his lover had remained unanswered. One weekend, and as they were all staying at Bagatelle, François went to see Jacques, too make sure he wasn't sick or something... Jacques was important to François, since he had been his first lover... and it was to protect him that François had stood up and fought with Foucarde, so that Jacques could flee... Of course, François, being alone against five other guys, had finally lost the fight and had been severely beaten... But Jacques had been able to flee unscratched and, in that sense, François had won! So yes, Jacques was important to François, and he was disappointed by the rather cold reception he got from him, when he went to see him that weekend... „Hey! What's wrong with you pal? Why didn't you answer my last letters? Didn't you receive them?" – „...Yeah, I did... sorry if I didn't answer you...", Jacques answered „...You didn't have time?" „No, it's not that..." „Then what?" „(...) I was doing some thinking..." „About what?", François asked... „Well... with you in Paris, studying there... and me here... working on my dad's farm..." „Yeah?" „Well... Can't you see?" „See what?" „I mean... you're studying... and I'm sure you're going to succeed... And I'm happy for you, really... In your last letter, you said you'd like to become a doctor, and that would be nice... but then... reading that got me thinking..." „I don't understand..." „See... I'm sure that before we know it... you'll become a doctor..." „Hey pal... it's not for tomorrow! Do you know how long it's going to take before I become a doctor?" „Whatever... But you see, sooner or later, you'll become a doctor, and I'll still be a farm boy: The same farm boy you see now, who even has problems writing his own name... and tell me, François: Once a doctor, do you think you'll come back to the village, to live the miserable life we live here? I don't think so! You're going to stay in Paris..." „...And so what?" „That's the point! Do you see me living in Paris? I love nature... the woods... I like to go hunting and fishing... In Paris, I would die! So, don't you see... the gap between you and me keeps getting bigger and bigger with every passing day..." „Are you telling me it's over between us? Is that what you're telling me?", François asked his lover, with tears in his eyes... „...I sure wish things would... could be different... But let's face it, François: Our relation is a dead end one!" – „(...) It hurts, hearing you say that..." „I know... And it hurts having to say it, but let's not lie to ourselves... and let's be honest..." „...Is it because you're seeing someone else?" Jacques looked at his friend, and with a very sad smile on his face, he answered: „Are you crazy? Remember: We're in a small village here... who else is gay? Can you tell me?" „No... I can't..." „And it's not tomorrow that I'll find someone like you François: You're just perfect! I wish things could be different... but there's nothing I can do... But I sure wish you the best! I'm happy for you..." „Thanks... and maybe we can stay friends...", François asked... „Sure... But François, please: Go on with your life..." „I'll try... and I sure hope some day, you'll find someone... you're a great guy, you know... And you too, have the right to be happy..." „I suppose so..." Later that day, François went back to Bagatelle, and sat down with Will and Paul... He told them what Jacques had said to him, and that it was over between the two of them... „...I'm very sorry to hear that", Paul said to his young friend... „But you know, François, I think Jacques is right... can you feature him living in Paris?" „I guess not!", François sadly answered... „It's just that life isn't fair"! „...I know... Sometimes, it is not... But look at it the other way: Jacques has set you free! Now, you can look around with new eyes and maybe... you'll see someone you had not noticed before because you were too involved with

Jacques! Someone who's there, waiting for you..." „I sure hope you're right Paul..." „I know I'm right!", Paul answered, with a sincere smile... When Ludwig came back from the greenhouse, Will and Paul told him the whole story... So, he went to see François, and when he found him, he sat down with him and, looking at his best friend, he said: „I heard what happened... and I'm sorry for you François... but I'm sure you'll get over it..." „Yeah, sure...", François answered, with a sad smile...

Was Ludwig really sorry? Well, he felt bad about the fact his best friend was hurting. Sure. But he didn't feel bad about the fact Jacques had broken with François. After all, to Ludwig, Jacques was a distant figure... and he had never given much thought about him... In fact, Ludwig was most satisfied with his „arrangements" with François: He was his wanking partner... They were having fun... so, the hell with the rest. Of course, to Ludwig, those „arrangements" were only temporary... and would last until the day he would meet a nice girl, and would start going out with her... And of course, it never occurred to Ludwig that those „arrangements" could eventually be terminated not by him, but by François, should he meet a nice guy and starts going out with him... No, that thought never occurred to him. Never. Still...

One morning in early September, back in Paris, Paul was alone, having breakfast... when François walked in... „Oh hi, gorgeous!", Paul greeted him, smiling, „Did you sleep well?" „Yeah..." But from the way he had answered, Paul sensed there was something wrong with François. So, he raised his eyes to look his young friend straight in the eyes and said: „Hey pal: Are you okay?" „Sure!... No problem, really..." „Oh come on, François... don't give me that shit! What's wrong?" François sat down, served himself some coffee... then, after a long moment of silence, he started to say: „(...) Well... There's this guy in my class..." „Hu-huh... And?" „Well... he... he's kind of cute...", François said, slowly turning a lovely shade of red... „Oh, is he? And what's his name?" „Philippe..." „Is he from Paris?" „Yes..." „And... you like him?" „... I ... All I said is that I find him cute!" „Of course, of course! (...) Anyway... how is he? How does he look?" François raised his eyes to look at Paul and, with a very big smile on his face, he said: „He's very nice! And very handsome too. He's about seventeen I guess... and he's a bit taller than me... about 1.83 m tall, I would say... He has curly black hair... and lovely blue eyes. Very sexy!" „And have you talked to him?" „Sure... I mean... But of course, I didn't run to him to tell him that I'm gay and that I find him cute!" „... And that you're attracted to him...", Paul added, smiling... „OF COURSE NOT!!!" „... So I take it you haven't jumped on him... not just yet!", Paul said, laughing... „Oh come on, Paul: Don't tease me!" „Okay, okay... But tell me more about him..." „...You should see his hands... They are so beautiful, with long fingers... Everything about him is beautiful! The way he talks... the way he walks... the way he smiles... and, when he looks at me with his beautiful blue eyes, I feel like..." „...Like if you were going to die?" „Yeah!", François answered, laughing... „And yesterday, in class, he accidentally touched my hand, and..." – „...You felt as if an electrical current had passed right through your body?" „Yes!" „And that made you shiver?" „Yeah!", François answered, still laughing... „Well, my friend, I think you have a very serious illness..." „Huh?" „Yup! Very serious case, we got here pal... and it's called 'love'..." „...You think I'm falling in love?" Paul burst out laughing, hearing that question... and he answered: „I'm afraid you have all the symptoms..." „Shit! (...) But I don't even know if he's gay... What if he's not? I can't walk over to him and ask him: „Hey dude: Are you gay?" „Of course you can't..." „So: What the hell am I supposed to do?" „That's not an easy question to answer, you know, and I guess you're going to have to find the answer all by yourself! I can't tell you what to do... all I can do is to give you some hints..." „Like what?" „(...) I don't know... like... At first, I guess you and Philippe could become friends... give yourself time to know him better... and give him time to know you... I know, I know... it's a slow process... but unless one of you decides to bring the „subject", there's no way out: You'll have to take your time... to see where it leads to... and you know, at one point, you could ask him if he has a girlfriend... things like that... And anyway, if he never talks to you about girls, I guess you'll have a good indication..." „Yeah... That would be a good start... I mean..." „Hey pal, as I said, I don't have all the answers for you. You'll have to go with the flow. But just don't try to cross the bridge before you get to the river! Don't scare him away... If he's gay, he's probably as unexperienced as you are, and doesn't know how to act..." „Yeah... I guess you're right..." „In fact, you probably have more experience than he does... with Jacques... you know..." „That's not much! Only once have I fooled around with him... and I got beaten for that! Talk about experience!" – „Yeah! Not much, I guess... Anyway, why don't you invite Philippe over here?" „...It's not my house... I would never do that!" „Don't say that François: You hurt my feelings when you say that, for this is your house, as much as it is mine..." „Sorry Paul... I didn't want to hurt you... But anyway... even if I invite him over here, where would we go? I mean... I would certainly not take him to the drawing-room, you know... it would be like taking him to a „Salon" at Versailles! And I can't take him to my bedroom... I mean... It wouldn't be very „suitable", and how do you think Ludwig would react?" „Guess you're right", Paul answered, laughing... „I never thought about that... I guess we do have a problem here! But anyway, I'll think of something... don't worry!" „Anyway Paul: Thanks for listening to me..." – „Anytime pal! You always know where to find me..." – „Yeah. Thanks!" Indeed, Paul had never thought about the fact that, at seventeen, both Ludwig and François could want to have a place of their own, where they could have fun with their friends... away from the „older" guys... meaning himself, Will, Lutz and Franz! Not that Will and Paul were that much older than Ludwig and François! After all, Will was twenty-two, and Paul had just turned twenty-one! Later, that small „difference" in age wouldn't matter! But for now, it did! And Paul could understand it very well... The „kids" had to be left alone with their friends... So, he started to think about a solution... And of course, as always, it didn't take long for him to find one! One morning, he called madame Louise, his governess, and said to her: „My dear madame Louise... We're going to make a few changes around here, and I need your help..." „Of course monsieur..." „You know... the „petit Salon"... right across the hall?" „Le Salon Bleu, you mean?" „Yes, yes..." „....It's been closed since... well... since your family left for New York..." „I know! Well... we're going to reopen it and transform it... We're going to change all the furniture in there... and put modern furniture instead..." „(...) BUT monsieur Paul... That's a beautiful room... with very beautiful and very expensive furniture in it... What would your mother say?" „My mother? (...) She's in New York and no longer lives here, does she? And we don't use that room, so... But don't worry about the rest of the mansion: I don't intend to touch it!", Paul answered, laughing... „(...) And what do you want me to do monsieur?", madame Louise asked, scandalized... „I want you and your staff to do a good cleaning job over there... Tomorrow, I'll ask a few workers from the company to come over here and I'll ask them to move out all the furniture from that room. I want that room stripped of everything... the carpets...

the drapes... even the chandelier will have to go! Then, I want the room to be cleaned. Can I count on you and your staff to do that?" „Of course monsieur... But..." „No „BUTS"... Paul said... „Just make sure the room is cleaned!" – „Oui monsieur." And of course, the job was done. And of course, madame Louise almost lost consciousness when she saw everything in the room being taken away. And she shed a tear or two, when she saw three men remove the beautiful chandelier... But... After that... she made sure the room was well cleaned! She was mad... she felt sorry... but nevertheless... the room was cleaned! „It's a shame", she said to herself! Two days later, the decorators were at work! „What the hell is going on over there?", Will asked Paul, one morning... „...The other day, I saw the furniture moved out of that room...", Ludwig added... „Ah! That's a surprise!" Paul answered, beaming... „But I forbid all of you to go in there, you hear? Now, swear to me you won't go in there before I tell you to... And you, too, François... Swear to me!" Of course, they all swore... But needless to say, they were all very curious... And a few days later, when all the work was finished... Paul said: „Now my friends... come with me!" Will, Ludwig and François followed him across the great hall... Then, Paul opened the doors to what used to be the „Salon bleu" and, looking at François and Ludwig, he said: „Welcome to your own den!" They all walked inside the room... and couldn't believe their eyes... The room was so... modern... the furniture... the wall-papers... the drapes... even the lighting... „Oh shit!", Ludwig exclaimed... „It's so nice in here..." „Your mother is going to be mad like hell", Will said to his lover... „To hell with her!", Paul answered, laughing... „...It's fantastic...", François said... „And it's for us?" „Yup! For Ludwig and you... and your friends, of course. Now guys, you have a place of your own...and we won't bother you in here...", Paul said, smiling... „Cool!", Ludwig answered, laughing... „...And what's that over there?", François asked... „Ohhhhh... but that's the utmost refinement, my friend!", Paul answered, grinning... „I know what it is..." Ludwig shouted... „It's a turntable..." „Yup!", Paul answered, beaming... „And open the door over there...", Paul said... Ludwig opened a door... and saw a collection of records... lots of records! He started to look at the records, one after the other... and he couldn't believe his eyes... „Hey François", he said to his friend... „Look: Glen Miller „In the mood"... and here... „Pennsylvania 6-5000"... and here, look: Benny Goodman..." „Where the hell did you get those records? We can't find them in any store...", Will asked his lover, stunned... „Ahhhh... never heard about the black market before?", Paul answered, laughing his heart out... „But... That's illegal...", Will answered, shocked... „You don't say! And do you think I care?", Paul answered, laughing... Obviously, Ludwig and François were ecstatic... „Can we try one?", François asked, looking at a record... „Sure... They are all yours!", Paul answered... Ludwig took a record out of its envelope, put it on the turntable and then pushed a button... The record started to turn and then, they all started to listen to Glen Miller and his orchestra, playing „Tuxedo Junction"... „Shit", François said... „I had heard about that song... but I can't believe I can finally hear it..." „All those records... and everything else in here... It must have cost you a fortune", Will said to Paul... „Yeah well... guys... this room is your room now: You can have your friends over here and enjoy yourself!" Paul simply answered... And of course, it didn't take long before François found the courage to invite Philippe over there... Philippe couldn't believe his eyes when he saw the place: He had never seen anything like that before! „...Your dad must be a very rich man...", he said to François... „Are you kidding me?", François answered... „My dad is a very poor farmer living in a small village near Chartres. The mansion here, and everything you see around in here belongs to a very good friend of mine... It's almost as if he has adopted me... And thanks to him, I can go to college... cause otherwise, I would still be working on my dad's farm..." Hearing that, Philippe turned to look at François then slowly said: „(...) You're honest with me, François. I appreciate that..." „I'll always be honest with you Philippe! That's the way I am..." Rather than replying verbally, Philippe just nodded, smiling at his new friend... And of course, it didn't take long before the two friends had fun... listening to the records... talking and laughing... Then, the doors opened, and Ludwig walked in... „Oops! Sorry", he said, when he saw François was not alone... „...No problem, pal... Come on in... and meet my friend Philippe...", François said to Ludwig, with a big smile on his face. Ludwig came in and shook hand with Philippe... After a while, the three teenagers were having fun... just as if they had known each other for years... But all evening long, Ludwig kept watching François and Philippe... And he got suspicious... „Yeah", he thought to himself... „Philippe is a good-looking guy... but I mean... Why is François so excited about him? After all... he's just another guy!" And when Ludwig saw that his best friend's eyes were sparkling, he got even more suspicious... but of course, he didn't say a word. Not one word! Anyway, what was there for him to say? That night and after Philippe had gone home, Ludwig and François slowly made their way to their bedroom, and went to bed... As the lights were turned off and as the two friends were laying down on their beds, Ludwig said to François: „... I guess he's a nice guy..." „Huh?" „... Philippe... I guess he's a nice guy..." „Oh yeah! He is. I'm glad you like him..." „(...). Night François..." „Yeah... night..." Ludwig didn't go to sleep right away... Oh no! He started thinking about François and that guy... Was his best friend falling in love with that Philippe? „And anyway... What the hell do we really know about that guy, huh?", he asked himself... „And he's not so funny! (...) In fact, he's rather dull, when I come to think of it..." That's when Ludwig heard a very suspicious noise, coming from his best friend's bed... Of course, Ludwig kept his eyes closed... but he kept listening... Yup! François was wanking in his bed! Ludwig grinned in the dark and said: „...Taking care of your „needs" pal?" „I thought you were sleeping...", François answered, grinning... „I'm not! Need some help with that?" „...Thanks pal: I can manage..." „You sure?", Ludwig asked... „I wouldn't mind..." „Nah! Don't bother... I'm almost there..." „(..) You're thinking about that guy, aren't you?" „Huh?" „...About Philippe... You're wanking, thinking about him, huh?" „Why do you ask?" „(...) Don't know... Just asking...", Ludwig answered. François burst out laughing and replied: „(...) Just turn to your other side, pal, and let me finish my job in peace, will you?" – „No problem...", Ludwig answered, not too happy... François had never refused his „help" before... Now, Ludwig felt bad about it... Was he jealous of Philippe? Nah! Come on... But when he heard François softly moan... the ache inside him didn't dim... „That's not the right kind of guy for François", Ludwig said to himself... „I must warn him, cause he's going to get hurt! Yeah! I'll talk to him about that and tell him what I really think about his new friend...", he decided. „Demain!" (tomorrow...) Having taken his decision, Ludwig went to sleep, not thinking farther than the tip of his nose... and not thinking about how François would feel, hearing that his new friend was a no good... No, that thought never crossed Ludwig's mind!

That morning, Paul was sitting all alone on the veranda, reading his newspaper and enjoying his coffee... Will had already left for the office and Ludwig for college. Then he heard someone coming from the hall, whistling... „...Ah! Your up!", Paul said to his young friend François, with a big smile on his face... „You seem to be happy this morning... I like that"... „Yup! It's a beautiful morning, isn't it?", François answered, smiling... „And I'm starving..." „Good. I'll call madame Louise..." „Don't bother... I'll go tell her what I want for breakfast... What about fresh coffee? You want some?" – „Why not!", Paul answered, grinning... „I'll be back..." Obviously, François was in a very good mood and Paul was glad to see that, since earlier that same morning, Ludwig had shown such an awful temper... When François came back, Paul looked at him and asked: „Hey... How come you're not in class this morning?" „...No school today: We're free. But I'm supposed to meet Philippe at ten o'clock at the library... since we're working on an assignment together..." „Uh-huh... and I suppose that's not the reason why you're whistling that popular song ... what's the title again ... 'Je t'aimerai toujours'...?" François looked at Paul with a big smile on his face... „...Well..." He said, a little embarrassed... „Oh come on François... you're in love, and you can't hide it...", Paul answered, laughing... „...Maybe..." „Yeah yeah... sure! You make a very bad liar, you know?" „Okay, Yes! I'm really in love with him! Are you happy now?" François answered, laughing too... „Good for you!" „...But I don't know how he feels about me..." „Hey, as I've already told you before... take your time! Paris wasn't built in one day..." „I know... But I think he's happy when we're together... He's always smiling... and he has such a lovely smile... and his lips... Oh God! He's so beautiful, it's a sin!" „...And he has black curly hair... and beautiful blue eyes... and very lovely hands with long fingers... yeah, yeah... you've already told me that..." Paul replied, laughing his heart out... „So, when do you intend to invite him over here, huh? So I can judge by myself how this god looks like..." „But he was here last night... and we had fun listening to the records..." „And you didn't tell me he was here? How naughty of you! (...) Why don't you invite him for supper tonight?" „...I don't think that would be a good idea..." „Why?" „Well... I don't think Ludwig likes him very much..." „Oh? (...) Why do you say that?" „...Cause he told me this morning... He told me Philippe wasn't the right guy for me... He even went as far as to say Philippe is a scum!" „Huh? He told you that? That's not like Ludwig..." „I know... I was stunned..." „What did you answer him?" „Nothing. I was too stunned!" „(...) Maybe he said that because he has learned Marie-Hélène is getting married... and he's not too happy about it...",,,Speaking about a scum! (...) But no, it has nothing to do with her... He doesn't give a damn about her. To him... she was just a good fuck once in a while, that's all", François answered, drinking his coffee... ,,Watch your language, young man!", Paul answered, laughing... ,,Anyway... I don't think it would be a good idea to have Philippe over here for supper, because the way Ludwig talked to me about him this morning, I'm sure that if he comes for supper, Ludwig will treat him like shit... and I don't want to be embarrassed..." ,,(...) I will have to talk to him..." ,,Good luck with that! He wasn't in a very good mood when he left this morning..." ,,Yeah... I've noticed that...", Paul answered... ,,Anyway... don't worry... I'm sure it will not last..." ,,I sure hope you're right..." That day, François met Philippe at the library... and they started working hard on their assignment... As François kept looking at Philippe's hands, Philippe finally noticed and said: ,,What's wrong with my hands?" ,,Oh nothing...", François quickly answered, blushing... ,,...And why are you blushing like that?", Philippe replied, laughing... ,,...Let's drop it, okay?" ,,No, no... I want to know..." ,,You're going to laugh at me if I tell you...", François said... ,,No... I swear I won't..." ,,Well... I think your hands are... beautiful!" ,,You think so? (...) No one ever told me that before..." ,,Well it's true..." ,,...There you go again: You're blushing..." ,,I knew you would be laughing at me..." ,,I'm not laughing at you... I swear... I find it cute, that's all..." ,,(...) Let's go back to work, shall we?", François awkwardly answered... Later, as the two friends were trying to find something in a book, Philippe said: ,,Hey... don't turn the pages so fast... I think we've missed it..." ,,Huh?" ,,...Yes... Here... give me the book..." As Philippe was taking the book away from François, he put his right hand right over his friend's hand... and he left it there much longer than needed... François quivered at the touch, and it didn't go unnoticed by Philippe... François raised his eyes and looked into Philippe's deep blue eyes... ,,There you go again...", Philippe said, laughing..." ,,What?" ,,You're blushing scarlet red again..." ,,Oh... cut it out, will you?" ,,Ah come on François... I'm telling you: It's cute..." ,,...Don't say that..." ,,Why? Because you're a guy?" ,,No... I don't care about that..." ,,Good... Cause neither do I... And I think you're cute when you're blushing like that..." – ,,...If I'm blushing, it's all because of you..." ,,Oh? (...) I make you blush?" ,,I told you, Philippe: Cut it out!" ,,No I

won't! I want to know why I make you blush..." „I won't tell you..."
Philippe burst out laughing, and said: „I've told you: You're so cute when
you look like that..." „I'm not cute..." „Oh yes, you are..." „You're cute,
not me...", François answered, grinning... „You think I'm cute?" „(...)"
„Won't you answer my question?" „No!" „Why?" „I don't want to talk
about it..." „Hey dude, I told you I find you cute... the least you could do
is to answer my question...", Philippe replied, laughing... „You want to
know?" „Yes!" „...Okay then! Yes! I find you're cute... and very good-
looking. Satisfied? Now, let's get back to work...", François answered, still
blushing... Later that morning, and since they had finished working on
their assignment, Philippe looked at François and said: „...What do you
do this afternoon?" „Nothing... Why?" „We could go to parc Monceau ...
have something to eat over there... I have a few francs on me..." „So do
I..." „What do you say?" „Why not! ... let's go then..." At that, the two
friends left the library and started walking towards parc Monceau... Once
they got there, François looked around and, mesmerized by the beauty of
the park he said: „Wow! It's beautiful here... I've never seen anything like
that before..." „You've never been here before?", Philippe asked his
friend.... „No." „I think it's the most beautiful park in Paris... and it's so
romantic...", Philippe answered, looking at François... „And I suppose
you bring all your girlfriends over here, for a romantic walk...", François
answered, grinning... „...I don't have a girlfriend... but I brought you here,
didn't I?" „...A guy like you? No girlfriend? Oh come on, pal..." „What do
you mean... 'a guy like me', huh?" „I mean... you're so good-looking... you
must have lots of girlfriends..." „Really... I don't! What about you?" „Me?
Nah! And anyway, they don't look at me!" „Why do you say that? You're
very attractive...", Philippe answered, looking at François with a nice
smile on his face... „You're telling me that just to make me feel good..."
„No no... I'm sincere..." „Hey: Why don't we sit down over there..."
„Where?", Philippe asked... „Over there...", François answered, showing
to Philippe a very nice and quiet spot... „Good idea..." They walked the
short distance to the spot François had chosen... then François laid down
on his back on the lawn... Philippe laid down right next to him... Philippe
was laying so close to him, François could feel his body heat. Their legs
were slightly touching, and François could clearly hear Philippe's
breathing... As Philippe began to slowly stretch his body, his shirt came
up and revealed his perfectly shaped abs... François didn't want to stare

at his friend's perfectly sculpted body, but he couldn't help himself and on a few occasions, he tried to catch a glimpse or two of his friend's gorgeous body. Philippe was so beautiful! Laying there so close to Philippe was having quite an effect on François... and he felt a stirring in his own pants... And of course, before long, he had a hardon! Not wanting Philippe to notice the outline of his hard dick in his pants, François moved his body and turned to lay down on his stomach. His cock was practically leaping out of his pants, and he could feel himself sweating. His heart was thumping so loudly, he was afraid Philippe could hear it... „...It's really so beautiful over here...", François suddenly said, to break the silence between the two of them... „Yeah! I'm glad you like it... (...) So, were you serious when you said you have no girlfriend?", Philippe asked, grinning... „Yes", François answered, rolling his eyes, grinning... Philippe moved his body to lay on his right side and, looking at François with his irresistible blue eyes, he asked: „Why?" „I think you can figure out why, if you put your mind to it...", François answered... „...There you go again..." – „Huh?" „Blushing..." „Yeah yeah... and you find it cute. You've already told me that...", François answered, laughing... „It's true..." (...) „So you think I can figure out by myself why you don't have a girlfriend, huh?" François shrugged, then nodded... „Yeah!", he finally answered. The next few minutes were spent in silence... and François could sense Philippe was staring at him... „Stop that", he mentally commanded him! „...Don't tell me I'm blushing again: I know!", François suddenly said... „And it's all your fault..." „Oh yeah?" Philippe said, laughing... „My fault, huh?" At that, Philippe moved with blinding speed, forcing François to turn over to his back... then, Philippe tackled him and wrestled him... François was taken by surprise, and couldn't tell quickly enough what Philippe was doing: Before he knew it, Philippe was right on top of him... and François was no longer in a position to put up a fight! They both lay there, laughing... and since Philippe was right on top of him, François wondered if it wasn't his friend's hard dick he was feeling, pressing up against his own crotch... Was Philippe really sporting a hardon? François was fairly certain he could feel it... but wasn't one hundred percent sure... Then... they stopped laughing and just stared at each other for a while, panting... „...So... are you going to tell me now, smartass?", Philippe finally asked... François stared into his friend's beautiful eyes, gave a quick, nervous laugh and answered: „No!" „...Oh you... you don't intend to make it easier for me, do you?", Philippe said, grinning, looking down at François with an absolutely magnetic stare... François didn't answer this time, but a small smile curled his lovely lips... Philippe slowly leaned his head... and François suddenly started to feel his friend's hot breath on his lips. God! He wanted Philippe so much! And his scent smelled so sensuous... Then, François felt Philippe's soft, warm lips brush against his own ever so slightly... He quivered, and all his fears dissipated when Philippe moved in for a longer kiss... François totally surrendered to his gorgeous friend when Philippe's lips caressed his: It was the most sensual and erotic sensation he had ever experienced! And he moaned, when Philippe began grinding his very hard dick over his crotch! Oh yeah, Philippe was hard alright! A wonderful heat enveloped them, as the kiss intensified...Philippe's tongue slowly made its way into his friend's mouth and found his tongue.

Now, François was completely lost in the passion of the kiss, and as their lips locked, he wrapped his arms around his friend's back and pulled Philippe closer to him, to press his body against his own...

Through the thin fabric of Philippe's shirt, François began to massage his strong back muscles, and their kiss intensified some more, their tongues engaged in a sweet struggle... Their kiss lasted for what seemed like hours, and François could feel his precum flowing out of his hard dick like a river inside his pants... When their lips finally parted, Philippe looked down at François and softly said: „...I guess I've got my answer..." „I guess you have, haven't you?", François answered, grinning... „... Do you know what François? I'm in love with you! (...) I've been in love with you since the first day I saw you in class..." „.... And do you know what Philippe: I'm in love with you, too! But before we go too far, I must tell you something important... that may change the way you feel about me..." „How could that be?", Philippe asked, puzzled. François tenderly pushed Philippe off of him, and forced him to lay down on his side, right next to him. Both of them were now laying down on the lawn on their sides, facing each other...

„...I must tell you about something very... personal... and if, after you've heard me out, you decide not to go further with me... I'll understand, I swear to you I will..." For a few seconds, François kept staring at his blue-eyed friend, and it's in those blue eyes that he found the courage so speak up. Then, François told Philippe about Foucarde, and the beating he had gone through... and about the consequences... „...They had to do that, in order to save my life!", François finally explained to his friend... Philippe could see tears in his friend's eyes and after a long moment of silence, he said: „...Whatever they did to you François... you're still alive... and you're here with me today... that's all that counts... and if you think that could change the way I feel about you... you're dead wrong mister! But I sure wish I could put my hands on that Foucarde! Oh shit, he wouldn't like the experience..." François grinned and answered: „Oh... Don't worry about that... He was taken care of..." „Good!(...) Is that all you wanted to tell me?" „Don't you think that's enough?", François answered... „...For you, sure! I understand it's terrible... But as I said, for me, it doesn't change anything.... At that, Philippe tenderly forced François to lay on his back again and, maneuvered so he could lay down right on top of him, as he had been a few minutes ago... Philippe looked straight into his friend's beautiful eyes and said: „Look François... I couldn't care less about what you've just told me... All I know is that I'm madly in love with you. Do you understand what I'm saying to you? I AM IN LOVE WITH YOU!!!" He then leaned onto François, and their lips touched. Philippe gave his friend a very tender kiss, and of course, they both quivered... With his right hand, Philippe began to slowly caress his friend's smooth face... Then, he slowly began kissing him all over his face... sweet kissing his nose, his chin... then his lower lip... „...Oh God, Philippe", François softly said... „I love you so much... I need you... I want you..." Having said that, François raked his fingers through Philippe's black curly hair and he began kissing him passionately. Their tongues intertwined as François wrapped his arms around Philippe in a bear hug, nearly crushing the breath right out of him... Through their pants, their hard oozing dicks were squished between them, and more so when François cupped Philippe's ass cheeks with his hands... They both wiggled their hips, squishing their dicks together more firmly... François sighed when Philippe began swirling his tongue all around his mouth... Obviously, both of them had lost all thought and all feelings of the outside world, and they were completely lost in the passion of their kiss... „...You should go elsewhere to do what you're doing, young men... This is a public park, and in case you haven't noticed yet, children are playing around here...", they heard a man say... Their lips immediately parted and Philippe turned his head to look at the man... „Opus!", Philippe said to a middle-aged man, standing there... „Sorry Sir..." The man smiled back at them and said: „...Next time... why don't you go to the Bois de Boulogne? (...) No one will bother you there..." – „Oh?", Philippe answered to the man... „...It's quiet over there, and the park is so big, I'm sure you'll find a nice place where you can hide and do whatever you want to do without shocking anyone... Believe me... When I was your age, I've been there many times... Just stay clear from the Hippodrome de Longchamp", the man said, laughing... „Thanks Sir... We will remember...", Philippe answered, smiling at the man... „...Sure kids... and have fun over there..." „Thanks again..." The gentleman kindly smiled, then walked away... „...I whish we could go there right now..." Philippe said to François... „You have no idea what I would like to do to you... Where I'd like to kiss you..." „Ohhhhhhh... I think I have an idea...", François answered, laughing... „But I'm afraid we'll have to wait, cause it's already getting late, and I have to go back home..." „Yeah! Me too... Too bad, though..." „Hey! (...) Perhaps, we could have a picnic over there next Saturday... just you and me... you know... the Bois de Boulogne is not very far from where I live on Avenue Foch...", François said, with a sexy grin on his face... „Ohhhhh... That would be great!", Philippe answered, grinning... „...I could ask Paul's chef to prepare a nice lunch for the two of us..." „How lucky you are, to be living there with your friends..." „...I know... Believe me: I know!" „...But I don't think Ludwig likes me very much... When I left last night, I had the clear feeling he was mad at me..." „I don't know what's bugging him right now... and I don't understand why he's acting like that with you... really... That's not like him! He's my best friend, you know... and I love him dearly...", François answered, with a sad look on his face... „Is he gay?" François burst out laughing and answered: „...Oh no! Believe me: He's not! (...) He's not straight as an arrow though... but believe me, he's not gay!" „...What do you mean by „not straight as an arrow?" „We share the same bedroom, you know..." „...And?" „...So, from time to time, we jerk-off together... and I've given him a few blowjobs...", François answered, laughing... „...I can't blame you... He's very good-looking you know..." „Yeah! I've noticed...", François answered, still laughing.... „And at one point, I was even falling for him... That's a long time ago... But then, I realized he wasn't gay, and that he would never fall in love with me. It's true that, at that time, I was infatuated with him... but it's no longer the case! He's still my best friend,

though... and it hurts me to see him act the way he does with you..."
„Perhaps, he's just over-protective... Have you tried to speak to him?"
„...Yes... But to no avail. You should have heard what he told me this morning... Anyway... I talked to Paul this morning, and he said he's going to try to speak to Ludwig..." „That's good...", Philippe answered. „Um..."
„... Give him a chance...", Philippe said to François, giving his friend a sweet kiss on the lips... „Now, let's go... before I rape you and we both get arrested..." „Yeah!", François answered, laughing... The day after, Paul tried to speak to Ludwig... but nothing came out of their discussion! Ludwig had remained stubbornly silent! And Will didn't succeed either...
„...Is he sick?", François asked Will and Paul... „...He says he's not... I don't know what's wrong with him, really...", Will said...

SEVEN

One thing was certain for all though: There was a lot of tension in the air on Avenue Foch... and everybody felt miserable... And of course, François was now avoiding inviting Philippe to Avenue Foch, not wanting to provoke Ludwig... Each night, Ludwig would wait for François to go to bed first, and when he was sure he had fallen asleep... he would silently creep into their bedroom to his own bed, where he would lay down in total silence... Although most of the time, François was not yet sleeping... he wouldn't make a move, and would pretend to be sound asleep... François didn't know what to think, and didn't understand why Ludwig was acting the way he was... All he knew was that he felt really, really miserable... Of course, François told Philippe about how things were on Avenue Foch... „Shit! Things must not be easy for you there...", Philippe said... „Not just for me... but for Will and Paul too...", François sadly answered... When he heard that, Philippe decided he had to take the matter into his own hands... If Ludwig was acting the way he was... Philippe knew it was because of him... And he had to do something about it! He didn't say a word about it to François, but decided he would have a talk with Ludwig... François, Ludwig and Philippe were all going to the same college... but Ludwig wasn't in their class... So, one day, Philippe decided to go to Ludwig's class, and wait for him there... When the door opened and as the students were leaving the class, Philippe spotted Ludwig and walked over to him... „Hi, dude...", he said to Ludwig, with a nice smile on his face... „Hi!", Ludwig coldly answered... „What's up?" „...Not much...", Ludwig replied, not even looking at Philippe, walking his way out of the place... Philippe did pick up his 'go away' vibes, but didn't acknowledge them... „Hey... Um... Are you mad at me or something?", Philippe asked Ludwig... „You pace out in such a hurry..." – „Why do you ask?", Ludwig answered... „...I don't know... It's just that I wonder if you're mad at me because ich habe mich mit François angefreundet!" Hearing what Philippe had just said, Ludwig suddenly stopped walking, turned to look at Philippe... and said: „...You speak German?" „...Not really...", Philippe answered, grinning... „But at least, that stopped you from running from me like you were..." Ludwig didn't know what to say and... started blushing... Philippe burst out laughing, and said: „You're just like François!" „Huh?" „...You're blushing..." Ludwig just shrugged his shoulders... but had to admit Philippe had his undivided attention... „...What do you mean by that?", he asked Philippe... „...You're damn adorable, when you're blushing like that..." „Hey pal... Don't try that with me... It won't work! I'm not gay, you know..." „I know Ludwig... François told me. That's the reason why I want to talk to you... You see... You are his best friend, and I know he loves you dearly..." – „...Not the way you think..." „I know, I know... please Ludwig... can we get the hell out of here, go some place... and have a talk... just you and me? Please? I beg you..." Ludwig looked at his watch... then looked back at Philippe and said: „...Okay... But I don't have too much time..." „No problem, man...", Philippe answered, with a broad smile on his face... „I'll take whatever time you want to give me..." „That's not much!", Ludwig answered, obviously annoyed... „Fine!" They walked out of the school and after a while, Philippe said: „Why don't we sit over there on that bench and have a talk..." – „Fine. But your time is running out...", Ludwig answered. „Thanks!" Philippe answered... Both of them sat on a bench-park... then, Philippe turned to look at Ludwig and said: „Look Ludwig... I know you don't like me. Why? I don't know! As I said, I know François is your best friend... No no... please... let me finish, please..." „(...)" „...And as I said... François told me you're not gay, cause I asked him... I know you've been jerking-off together from time to time, and it's O.K. with me... I have no problem with that... But as you said... You're not in love with him... How could you be? You're not gay. And that's okay too. (...) Ludwig, look... I'm not trying to take your best friend away from you... It's just that... I love him! Not the way you do... I'm really in love with him, and I know he loves me... What's wrong with that?" „...I'm not blind, you know..." – „Can I ask you something, Ludwig?" – „(...)" „I understand that, up until the moment I met François... you had him all to yourself... or almost... I can understand how you feel now... really... You think you're going to lose him as a friend, don't you? But that isn't so, Ludwig! François loves you, just like a brother! You will never lose him! Now, I'm sure that, one day, you're going to fall in love with a nice girl... and you will want to be with her, and that's normal... but what will happen to François when, suddenly, you spend less and less time with him, cause you're in love with that girl? He and I are different, Ludwig... I know. But that doesn't mean we don't have the right to have our own life... to be happy, too. We have that right! Just as much as you do. (...) One day, you'll get married with that nice girl... you'll have children with her... and you won't have much time to spend with François. That's normal. But how do you think he will feel when that happens? If by then he doesn't have a life of his own... he'll feel neglected! And he's going to feel bad!" Ludwig didn't answer. He had never thought about that... „...Look, Ludwig... Instead of losing François as a friend, you could gain another friend! Why don't you look at it that way, huh? We could have lots of fun, the three of us... really..." Ludwig turned to look at Philippe and after a while, he said to him: „...Anything else you wanted to tell me? (...) Cause your time is up, pal..." „No... That's all I wanted to tell you... but Ludwig... I know François feels miserable... and I love him so much that, if it can help... I'll stop seeing him, so you don't feel threatened anymore and stop acting the way you do with him: That way at least, you will stop making him feel miserable..." Again, Ludwig didn't answer. He slowly rose from the park bench... then walked away without saying a single word... „Shit!", Philippe angrily said to himself... „What a fool I am... to think I could manage the situation..." After a few minutes, he slowly rose from the bench and walked away, with tears in his eyes... That night, Ludwig skipped supper and went to bed early... Later, François silently walked into their bedroom and made his way to his bed. He undressed and silently went to bed. „...I'm not sleeping!", Ludwig said to him... „Oh... Sorry... I didn't want to wake you up..." „Didn't you hear me? (...) I wasn't sleeping... I was waiting for you!" „...Oh?... What for?" „...I wanted to talk with you..." „...Well... Here I am...", François answered, a little anxious. He began undressing and waited for Ludwig to speak. „I saw Philippe this afternoon, after school. He was waiting for me..." „Was he?... I wasn't aware that he wanted to..." „I know...", Ludwig said... „Why.. I mean... Did you talk to him?" „Not really... He did the talking, I listened." „Oh?" „...I'm a jerk, huh?"

„What?", François exclaimed... „...At least, I've been acting like one, I guess..."

No you're not a jerk, Ludwig: You're my best friend..." „Not anymore I guess... Now that you have Philippe..." „Hey, pal: Philippe has nothing to do with it... You're my best friend, and that will never change..." „Yeah... sure... You're always with him... I don't see you anymore... and you act as if you were avoiding me...", Ludwig said, with a sad voice... „You know what, Ludwig? It's true... I'm trying to avoid you... Not because I want to, but because you act like you are mad at me... and I don't know why! I've been doing a lot of thinking recently... and really... I don't see what I did wrong to make you mad at me..." „That's why I said I've been acting like a jerk... you did nothing wrong, François... it's just that I feel bad..." – „But why?" „I don't know... I guess... I'm a little jealous of Philippe..." „(...) Now... you've got some explaining to do, pal! I'm totally lost! I mean... I think I'm in love with Philippe... no... let's be honest: I'm madly in love with him. True! That's one thing. But as I said, my love for Philippe has nothing to do with you... why would you be jealous of him?" „Come here, buddy... and sit", Ludwig said to his friend, patting the bed beside of him... François walked over to Ludwig's bed, and sat beside his friend. „Look François... I've been doing a lot of thinking, too... and when I say I'm jealous of Philippe, it's because it's true..." „...I don't understand... Are you telling me you're in love with me?" „...No...", Ludwig answered, grinning... „At least, not the way you love Philippe... But since you started seeing him, I've realized how much you count for me... you're my best friend... and I guess... I don't want to lose you..." „...But..." „Let me finish, okay? (...) Yeah, I've asked myself if I was in love with you... if I was gay... you know... It seems everybody around me is gay, so why not me? And I was all mixed up. You know... my love for you... the way I feel when I'm with you... Hell, I didn't know where I stood anymore. Then, I started asking myself a few questions... like... „Do I want to kiss you?"... „Do I want to really make love with you... not just jack-off"... you know... Questions like that... and the answer is no. That's not what I want... As much as I felt bad before, now I know where I stand... and I know I'm not gay..." „But then, why would you be jealous of Philippe?" „...Until you met Philippe, it was only you and me... We were always together... doing stuff together... having fun... Hey: We even used to jerk-off together... But now, you ignore me. I mean... I feel as if I'm an old rag you've decided to toss away, cause it's no longer useful..." „That's not true!" „...Maybe... But anyway, that's how I feel... (...) I know life has not been easy for you over the last few months... In a different way, things haven't been easy for me neither, you know... I left my family and moved to France... I left all my friends back in Berlin... and now... I don't hear from them anymore... I had to learn how to speak French, and get used to a new country, new customs... Hell! Everything around me is foreign... Then I met you... and we became friends... In a way, you're like a lifebuoy to me... and now, I feel like this lifebuoy is being taken away from me... and that I'm going to drown... and... and..." Ludwig had to stop talking, cause his voice was now quivering and tears were running down his cheeks like a river: He didn't want to make a fool of himself in front of François! François delicately took Ludwig's face between both of his hands... wiped away a few tears from his cheeks, then he softly said to him: „Look at me, Ludwig... Look at me (...) I'm so sorry! The last thing in the world I would do is to hurt you... hurt your feelings... I love you, man! And you're not losing me, pal! I never thought about how hard it could be for you to start a new life here in France... I mean... To me, you have everything! You're gorgeous... have a nice personality... you're funny... Hell! What do I have, compared to you? Not much, I guess..." „That's not true", Ludwig said, sobbing... „Anyway... But now, I understand better how you feel and thanks for being honest with me. But you're wrong, Ludwig: You're not an old rag I'm tossing away... I realize that over the last few weeks, I've spent a lot of time with Philippe... I mean... being in love with him like that is all so new for me... But that doesn't mean you're no longer my best friend! How can I convince you, pal? What can I say to make you feel better?" „Well, I guess I'm going to have to stop acting like a jerk, so you will stop trying to avoid me...", Ludwig said, grinning... „Yeah! That would help! And you know, Ludwig, Philippe likes you... He thinks you're a great guy... Stop thinking my love for him threatens our friendship, cause it's not so..." „...I wasn't sincere when I told you he's not the right guy for you! I was just jealous. He is. And he's madly in love with you..." „You think?" Ludwig burst out laughing and answered: „...You should have been there, when he talked to me this afternoon... I mean... The guy is mad about you! he said you felt miserable, because of the way I was acting, and he thought he was the one who was responsible for that... so he said he was ready to stop seeing you, if it would help making things better between you and me..." „Huh?" „Yeah! (...) How do you think I felt when I heard him saying that? Like a real jerk (...)" Ludwig stopped talking, suddenly at a loss for words. Then he said: „...For what it's worth, I'm sorry, François... for the way I've been acting with you... you have the right to be mad at me!" „I'm not mad at you Ludwig! I swear! I was really hurt, but now that I understand, I feel better about the whole thing... Come on man: Give me a big hug!" The two friends hugged for a while, then François said: „I'm here for you, Ludwig... I'll always be... Just as you've always been there for me when I needed you! And I still do... So... can you bear with me for a while? I know I'm spending a lot of time with Philippe... But from now on, I'll do my best to spend some time with you, too... now that I know you're not mad at me..." „Hey! Don't worry buddy: I'll manage..." „No... We'll manage... The three of us!" „(...) So: Tell me... you and Philippe... have you? I mean... did you?..." François burst out laughing and answered: „Not yet! (...) I mean... We've been fooling around... but except for a few blow-jobs... no... we haven't done anything else ... yet..." „Yet?", Ludwig answered, grinning... „Well... Next Saturday... We're supposed to go for a picnic at the Bois de Boulogne... and... you know... We'll see..." – „Ohhhhhhh... a picnic, huh? At the Bois de Boulogne... You don't say!", Ludwig said, laughing his heart out... „...Don't start teasing me about that you bastard..." „Of course not! You know me better than that!", Ludwig answered, still laughing his heart out... „I would never do a thing like that!" „Yeah! And that's exactly why I'm warning you...", François answered, laughing... „I know you too well..." Now that the two friends had made things clear between the two of them, there was a drastic change of atmosphere on Avenue Foch, and everyone there began breathing easier... „...Ludwig and me... We had a little talk the other night... to sort tings out...", François told Paul and Will one morning... „Oh?", Will said... „Yeah!", François answered, grinning... „We needed to talk... And now, everything is O.K. and things are back to normal between us..." „Thank God!", Paul said... „And... what about Philippe?" „Now that Ludwig understands the difference between our friendship and my love for Philippe...everything is fine... So I guess you'll see more and more of Philippe around here... if you don't mind, that is..." „Hey pal... I told you before: This is your home! Philippe is welcome around here as often as you wish...", Paul answered, with a big smile on his face... „Thanks! (...) Um... next Saturday... I was planning... I mean...

I'd like to have a picnic with Philippe... at the Bois de Boulogne... Do you think I could ask your chef to prepare a lunch for us?" „I'll talk to him... don't worry! You'll have everything you need!", Paul answered, smiling... „Thanks again...", François answered, with a big smile on his face... „(...) A picnic, huh? At the Bois de Boulogne, huh?", Will said... laughing... Seeing François was blushing scarlet red, Paul started to laugh and said to Will: „Oh stop that, will you? Look at him now: He's blushing..." „Oh come on dude", Will answered, looking at François... „You're going to have to get used to it, cause I don't intend to stop teasing you... And I only tease those I love, so..." „You're just like your brother Ludwig...", François said, laughing... „Yeah! It runs in the family..." As he woke up, Saturday morning, François was all excited... and it showed on his face! Ludwig opened his eyes... then looked at his friend... „Picnic day, huh?" „Yesssssss", François answered, with a big smile... „I hope you have fun... both of you... I guess today you don't want me there with you, huh?", Ludwig asked, grinning... „Not really...", François answered, laughing... „I wonder why?" „Oh you... Cut it out..." „Okay okay..." „So... what are you planning on doing today?", François asked his friend... „Don't know yet... Think I'm going to walk over to the Bois de Boulogne and spy on you...", Ludwig answered, laughing... Hearing that, François rose from his bed, jumped on Ludwig's bed and began wrestling with his friend... „Smartass", François said to Ludwig, laughing... They wrestled like that for a while, laughing... François was on top of Ludwig... When they stopped laughing, Ludwig looked up at François and said: „I'm happy for you dude! Really! And I hope today will be the best day of your life..." François stared at Ludwig for a second, and he saw sincerity into his best friend's eyes... He smiled... „Thanks, pal!", he said, before giving Ludwig a noisy peck on his forehead... „Hey! What's that for?", Ludwig asked... „It's because I know you're sincere... And it's important to me!" Ludwig grinned and said: „I am! I wish you the best..."

Later that morning, Philippe came to fetch François... and the two friends left for the Bois de Boulogne... François carrying a big blanket, Philippe carrying a big wicker-basket containing their lunch... enough to feed an army! It was a beautiful warm Saturday morning... and everything was just perfect! Of course, the two friends were happy to be together again. They walked down on Avenue Foch... laughing... having fun... Eventually, they reached the Porte Dauphine, at the end of Avenue

Foch. There, they stopped and looked at each other: The vast park... the Bois de Boulogne was right there in front of them... It was as if both of them understood perfectly well that, once in that park, it would no longer be possible to back off... Although nothing had been said about it, both of them knew perfectly well the reason why they were there... Obviously, both of them were a little nervous... and they both felt a little uneasy... The kind of uneasiness we all feel when facing the unknown... And the unknown was right there... right in front of them... in that park... François wished he could tell Philippe „If you don't want to go... fine... let's forget about it...". But then, he wanted Philippe so much... He was praying his friend wouldn't change his mind... For his part, Philippe had no doubt he wanted to go in the park... find a nice spot... and eventually make love with François. No, he had no second thought about that. Sure, he was nervous... but only because he had no experience with sex! And he knew perfectly well François had some. So the only question on his mind was: „What if I make a fool of myself..." They stayed for a while like that... staring at each other... at the park... not saying a word... Then, François decided to take the lead and, with a smile on his face, he said to Philippe: „You nervous?" „Sort of... you?" „Same for me... It's only normal, I guess..." „Yeah!", Philippe answered, looking down at the ground sheepishly... „You're so cute when you look like that...", François said, laughing... „You're damn adorable (...) and if we don't walk into that park right now... I'm going to jump on you and give you a blow-job right here! I wouldn't mind, you know..." „In that case, I think it's better to walk into the park and find a nice spot over there, cause I intend to enjoy that blow-job of yours...", Philippe answered, laughing... „Let's go..." They entered the Bois de Boulogne park and started walking... but of course, neither of them knew where to go... Now, the Bois de Boulogne in not vast: It's huge! As both of them were soon to discover... "Do you know where to go?", François asked his friend... „No... And you?" „Never been here before...", François answered... They both burst out laughing... „Look over there... There's a signboard...", Philippe said. They walked over to a large signboard detailing and explaining every section of the park... They started to study it... and began listening to the other people around them... Obviously, some of them knew the park well... Some were talking about the Lac Supérieur, others about La Grande Cascade, the Hippodrome de Longchamp or the Jardin d'acclimatation. Then, they heard a guy talking to his friends about a very quiet section where all the lovers in Paris like to go... François looked at the guy and said: „I've heard about that section... I wonder where it is, cause some day, I'd like to bring my girlfriend over there..." The guy turned to look at François, and burst out laughing... „Aren't you a bit young for that?", he asked François... „Hey... I said 'some day'... I didn't say tomorrow...", François answered, grinning... „Right!", the guy answered... still laughing... „Anyway, the section I'm talking about is right over there", the guy said, as he showed François the section on the signboard... „Merci!", François answered, grinning... After the guy had left, Philippe looked at François and, with a twinkle in his eye, he said: „...Your girlfriend, huh?" „Go to hell", François answered, laughing... „At least, we know now where to go..." „...It's not boring, being with you...", Philippe replied, still laughing... „Don't worry: If I have my way, you won't have time to get bored today..." „Ohhhhhhh" „Come on dumbass, let's go", François said... „I'm following you, smartass", Philippe answered, laughing... They walked for quite a while, and followed a few trails... Of course while walking, as if he didn't have control over his eyes, François just couldn't stop looking at his friend's gorgeous body and, when he could, at his crotch... François felt a stirring in his shorts, when he saw a sizeable bulge in Philippe's shorts... And what had to happen did happen: Before long, François was sporting quite a hardon in his shorts... Both friends were wearing shorts and short-sleeve shirts... except that, in his case, François was wearing a pair of shorts made out of a stretchy material... so that was a problem now, since his dick was pitching a tent in his shorts... To hide the obvious... François placed the blanket he was carrying over his crotch... and they continued walking, trying to find the perfect spot... After a while, François suddenly said: „...What about that spot over there: It looks perfect... isolated and quiet..." „Nice!", Philippe answered, grinning... They walked over to the spot they had chosen, and Philippe helped François to unfold the blanket and stretch it over the grass... When Philippe raised his head, he couldn't help but notice the big tent in his friend's shorts and he grinned... „What?", François asked, seeing his friend was grinning... He realized Philippe was staring at his crotch, so he looked down at the tent he was pitching: The blanket wasn't covering it anymore! He looked back up and found Philippe smiling... „Nice", Philippe said, still looking at his friend's crotch... „...Oh you...", François answered... „Don't worry... I don't fare better than you do... look...“ Philippe took his friend's right hand and put it over his crotch... where François could feel his very hard dick... „...It's just that it doesn't show in my shorts as much as it does in yours...“, Philippe said, laughing... „Yeah...“ Then, François grabbed Philippe's cock at its base, through his shorts... and squeezed it a little... „Yeah“, he said... „Nice! (...) But before we go any farther... I suggest we have lunch... I'm starving!“ François said... „...So am I... for you!“, Philippe answered, laughing... „Let's keep that for dessert...“ „Okay“, Philippe reluctantly answered... They sat on the blanket and François opened the picnic basket. He started taking all sorts of things out of it... then found a bottle of wine, two glasses and a corkscrew... He raised his eyes from the basket and, looking at Philippe with a startle look on his face, he said: „...I didn't put that bottle in the basket...“ „Look at it... There's a small note attached to it...“, Philippe said. François looked at the note and read it aloud: „Have fun, my friends. Paul.“, the note said... They both burst out laughing... „...That's Paul alright...“, François said... „And there's something else in the basket...“ François took a small bottle out of the basket... „Baby oil...“, he said, laughing... There was also a small note attached to it that said: „Just in case...“ „What's that for?“, Philippe asked, a bit puzzled... „...If need be... I'll explain to you later... it could become handy...“, François answered, laughing... „Whatever...“, Philippe answered, shrugging his shoulders... So they started eating their lunch, drinking some wine... making small talk and laughing... „It's a beautiful place here, don't you think?“, François asked... „Yeah... so quiet... it's as if we were a thousand kilometers away from Paris...“ „...And it's not like at the Parc Monceau: No one will see us here...“, François added... „Yeah“, Philippe answered, a sexy grin cracking his devilishly handsome face...

Then, Philippe looked down at his friend's crotch. He could clearly see the outline of his dick under the stretched material of his shorts... „Ohhhhh“, he said to François, grinning... „It looks like you're excited down there... I know I am, and I think I know the reason why: I'm hard just looking at you and thinking about touching you... I have been thinking about it all week long...“ Philippe was harder than he had been in a long time. His dick was throbbing so hard... he could barely stop himself from grabbing it and squeeze it... He was so horny... „I was wondering when we'd get around to this...“, François answered in a low voice... „come, and lay down beside me..." Philippe did as asked, and as they were both laying on their sides, facing each other, François delicately took Philippe's face between both of his hands and looked at his friend with an absolutely magnetic stare... „You're so beautiful...", he whispered... They were so near to one another, Philippe could feel his friend's hot breath on his lips... Then François leaned a bit further, bringing their lips together in a sweet, gentle kiss. An electric jolt passed between them as his tongue entered Philippe's mouth... The heat enveloped them as the kiss intensified. Then, François rolled over Philippe, and as soon as François was on top of him, and as their lips were still locked, Philippe wrapped his arms around his friend's back, and began lifting his shirt so he could rub his bare back and pull him closer to him, to press his friend's body against his own... As François began attacking Philippe's right ear with his tongue, Philippe started massaging his friend's strong back muscles... François gave his friend's right ear a good tongue bath, then he began nibbling behind it, and he felt Philippe shiver and gasp as he did so... After a while doing so, François returned to his friend's mouth, and their tongues intertwined as Philippe wrapped his arms around François in a bear hug... They kissed like that for a few minutes, groaning and moaning... Through their shorts, they could feel their hard and oozing dicks hard pressed, one against the other... throbbing... Then François pulled away suddenly and, sitting up on his knees, he said to his friend in a husky, breathless voice: „... I want you so much... You're so beautiful..." Philippe responded by rubbing his friend's inner thighs. Then, grinning seductively, he said: „...I want you, too, François.. problem is... this is my first time and... well... I guess I don't really know what to do... I mean..." „I think I'm a little bit more experienced than you... not that I'm an expert... far from it... but I mean... Let's see... what if I make the first move, and service you the way I want to? What if I excite you... slowly... very slowly... until you get to the point that you can't hold back your orgasm? What if I pleasure you until your dick is ready to explode with pleasure? Would you let me do that to you?" „...Oh shit! Yeah...", Philippe answered in a husky voice... „Yeah... Please... do that and teach me..." François grinned and answered: „...Yeah... That's what I'm going to do to this gorgeous body of yours..." Still sitting up on his knees between Philippe's parted legs, François shucked his shirt then raised himself a bit and pulled his shorts and underwear off... For the first time, Philippe was able to admire his friend's perfectly sculpted body. He looked at his throbbing dick and figured it was at least 23 cm long, and quite thick... „You're beautiful, François... So beautiful my love...", he sincerely said... François looked down at his friend and started to laugh... „What's so funny?", Philippe asked... „...You just called me „my love"..." „Yeah... Cause I love you so much François. In case you haven't noticed, I'm madly in love with you, and I think you're the most beautiful, handsome and gorgeous guy in the world..." „I love you, too, Philippe... so much..." At that, François went back sitting up on his knees between Philippe's strong legs and he started rubbing his friend's inner thighs, grinning. Then he leaned onto his friend's body a bit, and began kissing, licking and nibbling his inner thighs... „Ahhhhh I like that...", Philippe groaned... „You've seen nothing yet", François answered, with a sexy grin on his face... Philippe unbuttoned his shirt, slowly sliding it off... François unzipped his friend's shorts and slid them down from his thighs. Then, he plunged both hands inside Philippe's underwear and seized his hard oozing dick... His hands began working Philippe's dick and balls over, and after a while, he slid his underwear down... „...What a lovely cock...", François whispered... François wrapped his right fist around his friend's 20-cm-cock and began to slowly pump, as his left hand cupped his big low-hanging, hairless balls... „Oh my God... Oh my God...", Philippe shouted out... Philippe's dick was so hot and so hard that it felt like it was going to explode right then and there... That's not what François wanted though... So he let go of Philippe's beautiful dick and backed off... He pulled Philippe's underwear all the way down and off of him... then, he leaned onto his lover... for that was what Philippe was now to him: His lover! As François laid down on top of Philippe, and as they were facing each other now, they began kissing passionately and their hands roamed each other's body... Their hard dicks were squished between them and more so when Philippe cupped his lover's ass cheeks... They both wiggled their hips, squishing their oozing dicks together more firmly... Their bare fronts were rubbing one against the other, smooth as silk... After their lips had parted, François began kissing Philippe's lower lip, then down his chin, down on his Adam's apple... ever so slowly... Then he went down and began rubbing and tweaking his lover's erect nipples... Philippe moaned and said: „...Shit! You're good..." „Told you I would torture you..."

„...Don't stop!" „I don't intend to..." François knew Philippe's hard dick was aching for attention, as was his own... But he was in no hurry... Oh no! He was going to take all his time... François moved his hands down to Philippe's abs and around his sides to his back. Then he sat up and began planting little kisses all over his lover's stomach. He dipped his tongue into his navel and he swirled it around... „Ahhhhh", Philippe groaned... before he raked his fingers through his lover's hair... François began kissing and licking his way down to Philippe's dick... Philippe could feel his lover's breath on his mushroom cap, and he quivered when he felt his lover's hot, wet mouth pounce on his throbbing dick. François licked the slick precum off his lover's dick and loved the taste... Then, he took the rest of the head into his mouth... By now, Philippe was out of his mind... François used his hot, wet tongue to circle Philippe's mushroom cap, and he could feel his lover's dick harden even more... Then, all at once, he swallowed his dick down his tight throat... Philippe gasped, startled by the sudden pleasure. Of course, François had done this before, so he just grinned when he heard his lover gasp... Philippe shivered with pleasure as François gently scraped his teeth along his shaft, then sucked as hard as he could on his head... A few minutes of this was about all Philippe could take... and François sensed that... so he pulled his lover's dick out of his mouth... Needless to say Philippe didn't like it... „...Don't worry, babe... it's not over yet...", François said, grinning... Philippe was learning... After a few seconds, François went back to lick Philippe hard oozing dick, savoring the sweetness of his precum... He gave his dick a good tongue bath, then went to suck first one on his ball, then the other... Philippe squirmed and gasped as François did this, his hands grasping the back of his lover's head... „Ahhhh.... YES, oh....that feels so good", Philippe whispered... „Please, suck my cock... Please, it feels so good! I want to feel my cock in your mouth..." His words excited François further, and made him want to suck his cock without further delay... But then, he grinned... He wanted to take his lover's entire dick in his mouth right now... but also wanted to tease him some more... So he decided to lay his head on his lover's stomach, with his lips less than a few centimeters from the tip of his cock, so that he could feel his breath on his cock's head... Of course, Philippe began moaning loudly and said: „Shit... you're driving me crazy! Pleassssssse... suck my cock!" With that, François slowly licked the head of his lover's oozing dick... Philippe moaned and begged for more... François continued to lick the head of his dick... Finally, he took the head of his lover's cock into his mouth, and suck with his lips and tongue, carefully guarding Philippe's cock from the scrape of his teeth... François could tell he had teased his lover to his breaking point... At this point, François was so into it, feeling so good, he just went for it... He attacked his lover's dick with everything he had in him. He sucked, he licked, he rubbed... „....You don't know how good this feels... I never thought it could feel so damn good...", Philippe said, panting and sweating... All François was doing, was sucking his lover's cock like he would want his to be sucked... Of course, it didn't take long before François could tell his lover was getting ready to have an orgasm... François kept on sucking his lover's cock every direction he could, twisting around so that he could suck on his cock with the top of the cock head on his tongue... He kept going... Philippe began thrusting his crotch into his lover's face and started fucking it... He put his hands around his lover's head and began pumping his cock inside his mouth, and then back out. A few seconds later, Philippe's body went totally rigid, with his back arched so his dick was deep inside his lover's mouth. François heard him let out the loudest and longest moan yet... At the same time, he felt a poke at the back of his throat, and then warm liquid in his mouth... François kept bobbing up and down on Philippe's cock as his lover came, and he swallowed all of his cum as it came out... François wrapped his lips tightly around his lover's dick, then raised his head slowly, keeping every drop of saliva and cum in his mouth... He took all his time, tasting it on his tongue. He loved the taste... „....Ahhhhhh", Philippe shouted out... „I can't believe how..." – „....How good it felt?" „YEAH!", Philippe answered, laughing... „I'm in paradise!" „....I know...", François answered, grinning... „I know how you feel..." François was laying there, with his head on his lover's stomach. He looked at Philippe's cock. It looked as if it was getting soft. But François wasn't ready to stop. Oh no... He wanted more... So he began slowly subbing his lover's cock, and it responded by becoming completely rigid and stiff again... so he started sucking it again... „....Oh no, you don't...", Philippe said, grinning... „It's my turn to torture you..." François stopped sucking his lover's hard dick and burst out laughing... „Oh?... And what do you intend to do?" „Just watch me...", Philippe answered, grinning...

Philippe grabbed François, and forced him to lay down on his back... Kneeling between his lover's legs, Philippe took his lover's hard and oozing dick in his right hand and guided it to his mouth... François felt the best feeling he had had in a long time... It made the hair on the back of his neck stand up... Philippe had opened his mouth and put his lover's entire cock in his mouth. Then, he began massaging it with his tongue... He's a fast learner, François thought to himself, moaning... To François, it felt unreal! He was having sex again... really having sex! He was in heaven! Philippe started sucking his lover's dick and, after a while, François said: „...Let's take the 69 position..." „Huh?", Philippe answered... „What's that?" François grinned, then he moved his body, tugged at his lover's leg until Philippe followed his direction. He guided his legs over his body and, as Philippe's legs went over his lover's body, he felt a warm, wet feeling on his dick... Now, François was on his back with his head in between Philippe's legs... he had opened his mouth and put his lover's entire cock in his hot mouth. He started to suck on it again... Philippe did the same, and took his lover's dick deep in his mouth... Each of them was responding pleasure points by sucking harder... François put his hands on Philippe's ass cheeks and began pulling him into him... as his lover's cock kept going in and out, in and out of his mouth... François forced Philippe to slow his pace... Then, he concentrated only on the head of his lover's cock. He licked and sucked... slowly. Philippe followed the lead... and began slowly massaging his lover's oozing dick with his tongue... „...That's it...", François said, moaning... He went back sucking Philippe's dick again, swirling his tongue around the bottom side of his cock head. That drove Philippe crazy... and he let out a loud moan... Philippe understood the lesson, and did the same to François... Slow at first... then fast... then slow, fast again... Then after a while, François paused and said to Philippe: „...It's perfect my love... But I want more from you... I want you to fuck me! I want to feel your big dick deep inside me..." – „...You sure?" „Oh yeah! I've been dreaming about that for so long... you wouldn't believe me... Come on... lay on your back, and let me do the rest, will you?" „Hell yeah...", Philippe answered, with a sexy grin on his face... He laid down as asked and stared at François. François went to the wicker-basket to retrieve the small bottle of lotion Paul had placed there... Then he put some of the liquid on his finger and slowly penetrated his asshole. He felt no pain and smiled... In fact, it felt damn good. With his finger in his ass, François began probing slowly around and after a few seconds, he added a second finger to the anal action. Now he had two fingers in his ass... sliding them in and out... Finally, a third finger was added and again, there was no pain, only pleasure... All the while, Philippe was laying there... looking at his beautiful lover.. mesmerized by him... François walked back to Philippe and for a few seconds, he just kept staring down at his lover's sexy naked body... his gorgeous dick... Shit, he was horny! Then, François sat on his knees right next to his lover, and reached for Philippe's nice hard dick... and began running his fingers from the base up to the tip, just barely making contact... Philippe sighed and moaned when François used his other hand to give his balls a tender squeeze and a light tug... „Oh shit...", Philippe moaned..."Feels sooooooo good!" After a while, François stopped teasing his lover's balls, took the lotion... and smeared some all over Philippe's already oozing cock... „Oh my God!", Philippe said... „Now I understand why Paul gave us that lotion..." – „Hu-huh", François answered, grinning... Now François was kneeling on the blanket, with Philippe between his legs... Since he was now straddling his lover over his crotch, François reached back and grabbed Philippe's cock. Again, he spread the lubrication around generously, massaging his lover's dick with it... Philippe was now moaning and panting... Again, François smiled at his lover... Now, François wanted Philippe to fuck him... but he wanted to go slow... He wanted to be in control right now, knowing his lover had no experience at all... as much as he wanted his lover's dick in him, François was afraid that if he let Philippe take the lead... his inexperienced lover would probably shove his big dick right in and up to the hilt, not knowing any better... And that would hurt! No... François had to be in control, to teach his lover how it was done... François took his lover's throbbing dick and placed the head of it on his well lubed asshole... He looked at Philippe and whispered to him: „Hold your dick straight up stiff... Philippe grabbed his dick with both hands, as François put each of his hands on each ass cheek and spread them apart... Then, he slowly lowered himself onto his lover's dick... When the dick head breached pass his sphincter muscles, the pain shot through him for a second... François paused, and after a while, the pain started to turn to pleasure... Slowly, he lowered himself a bit more, and his lover's cock started to slide in... It didn't hurt at all... and François was happy to see his love chute was responding nicely... He lowered himself further, and before long, his lover's entire cock was inside his ass... It hurt a little... but François knew that his ass muscles would soon loosen up, and that the pain would pass... While his ass muscles were relaxing, François leaned onto his beautiful lover and began kissing him, lightly at first... then passionately, swirling his tongue all around his lover's mouth... Then, François started to slowly swivel his ass on Philippe's dick... and Philippe uncontrollably let out a long and deep moan, as his dick was massaged by his lover's tight ass muscles... François lifted himself back up as far as he could without letting his lover's cock pop out of his ass... then he let it slide all the way back in again. And as soon as Philippe's dick was as far in his ass as it could go, he started lifting himself and lowering himself, again and again... To both of them, the pleasure was not measurable... and as Philippe's dick sent wave upon wave of pleasure through his body, François cried out in ecstasy... As he felt his dick going in and out, in and out of his lover's love chute, Philippe started moaning louder then he had yet... not believing it could feel so good... „Oh my God, François... How can it feel so good?", he asked his lover, gasping... François grinned... and after a while he said: „...Time to try something else dude!" „Huh?" „...Yeah... It's hard to support my weight, you know... so let's try a new position..." At that point, François lifted himself and his lover's dick slid right out of his ass and popped out of it... François didn't lose time and went on all fours. As soon as he was on knees, he grabbed his tight, compact ass cheeks with his hands and spread them apart. Looking at Phillippe, he said: „Get down on your knees, and fuck me from behind..." Philippe kneeled down and positioned himself behind his lover... François reached in between his own legs and grabbed Philippe's dick. He guided it towards his asshole and once it was in place he spread his ass cheeks some more and said to his lover: „...Now you can take over... but go slowly..." „...Like that?" „Yeahhhhhh, perfect! Now continue to go in until you are all the way in my ass. Don't stop unless I ask you to..." Philippe did as asked... Each cm of his cock brought François more and more pleasure... and he let out a moan when he felt his lover was all the way in his ass... „Now, babe... you can start fucking me... but at first... go slowly okay?" Philippe responded by slowly moving his cock back, then back in... and before long, he was fucking his lover at a slow, but steady pace... „Does that hurt?", he asked... François burst out laughing and answered: „Hell no! It feels soooooo good!" And after a minute or two, he whispered to Philippe: „...Now... you can fuck me as hard as you want..." Philippe quickened the pace and went full steam, slamming his dick into François. His balls were now slapping his lover's ass cheeks, and he seemed to be crazed with passion, breathing loudly, and moaning non-stop! Philippe leaned down onto his lover's back and with his right hand, he reached under his lover to get hold of his hard dick. When he found it, he wrapped his fist around it and began masturbating his lover... „Ahhhhhh, YEAH!", François moaned... feeling his lover's hand all the time riding up and down his oozing prick... Then, François began to contract his ass muscles from the outside in and back, causing Philippe to really feel like his cock was being massaged... „Oh shit!: I don't know how you can do that... but the feeling is incredible...", Philippe whispered... Philippe was really going at it now, his big dick hitting his lover's G-spot with each and every one of his thrust... François looked back as best he could and looked at his lover's beautiful face: His eyes were closed and his mouth opened and closed slowly, as little grunts and moans come from deep in his throat... Then with his hand, Philippe began to bob faster on his lover's dick, pounding it with all he could... Suddenly, he gasped several times, and his muscles tensed... „Ahhhhh! I'm going to cum, François... I can't hold it anymore... I just can't..." As he kept driving his dick in and out of his lover's tight ass, he heard François say: „...Shoot... deep inside me... I want to feel your hot jizz... I'm just about there, too..." A second later, Philippe clenched his jaw, drove his dick as far as he could inside his lover... then... several volleys of his young juice shot out of his dick and into his lover's tight ass... „Oh my God... Oh my God... Ohhhhhhhh", he moaned... „Unnnnnnnh", François moaned loudly, as Philippe was still working his oozing dick with his fist... „Oh Yeah!", Philippe moaned... „Oh yeah", he shouted, as he felt François convulse under his ministrations, and as the after shocks of his orgasm reverberated throughout his body... After their orgasms had subsided, they just stood there for a while, and let roll the tide of emotions which threatened to drown them... When their breathing had returned to normal, Philippe slowly pulled his spent cock out of his lover's asshole... Both lovers felt totally exhausted, and so for a moment, they just laid down on the blanket, side by side... Then, Philippe turned to look at François and, grinning with pride, he said: „You enjoyed that, huh?" „Yeah... It was okay, I guess...", François replied nonchalantly, refusing to feed his lover's ego. „Not bad!" Philippe burst out laughing and replied: „Well, from what I've seen and heard, you were not complaining..." François turned to his side to look at his lover and, laughing his heart out he answered: „You were the best, babe! I swear! You were good! (...) And you: Did you enjoy it?" „Shit François: I never felt so good in my life. Thanks! You're fantastic. Really!" François grinned, hearing that... He felt so happy... The two lovers laid down like that for a while... looking up at the perfect, blue sky... drinking in the calm and quiet all around them... „I think we should get dress, and start walking back home... It's getting late...", François later said to his lover... „I guess you're right...", Philippe answered. „Hey! Why don't you stay for supper with us... I'm sure Paul won't mind..." „You think?" „I know...", François answered, laughing... They walked back up on Avenue Foch and when they got to Paul's mansion, Philippe, a bit apprehensive, asked his lover: „Are you sure Ludwig won't mind if I go in and stay for supper?" – „I'm sure he will be glad to see you! Trust me!" Indeed, Philippe received a hearty welcome from Ludwig who was very happy to see François and Philippe. He was sincere, and it showed... „Thanks buddy, for what you said to me the other day: It opened my eyes...", Ludwig said to Philippe... And of course, Philippe was most welcome to stay for supper... „No problem!", Paul said to François smiling... „And you will be able to introduce Philippe to Lutz and Franz, since they'll be here for supper too..." That night, as they were all sitting at the table in the vast and richly decorated dining-room, Ludwig look at the others and said: „No, no, no, no guys (...) That doesn't work! Look at us here... only guys around the table! I'm going to have to work on it... and next time, I'll do my best so that I can introduce to you my next girlfriend... And of course, she's going to be good-looking, with a good education... well-mannered... and very good at giving me blow-jobs: That's a must!" Of course, they all burst out laughing... Yup! Ludwig was his old self again! „...Oh François?", Paul asked him from across the table... „Did you find a bottle of wine in your picnic basket?" – „...Oh yes! Thanks! We both enjoyed it...", François answered, with a big smile on his face... „Um.." Will said, looking at François... „And did you find something else I had placed in there for you? Huh? Did you find it?", he teasingly asked... „What was it?", Paul asked his lover... „Oh...", Will started to say... „WILL", François shouted... „PLEASE" „Okay okay, I won't tell...", Will answered, laughing his heart out... And of course, once again, he had succeeded teasing François, since his young friend was now blushing... „Oh yes, Will... we did find your little bottle!", Philippe answered, grinning... „Only problem is: We didn't bring it back, since there was nothing left in it when we finished drinking it... So yes... We drank it all... but can't say we really liked the taste though..." Will burst out laughing hearing that... François looked at Will, and with a big smile on his face, he said to him: „Does that answer satisfy your curiosity?" Will looked back at Philippe and said: „I like your sense of humor: Welcome amongst us, pal!" They all burst out laughing... Even Lutz, Franz, Ludwig and Paul... who had no idea about what the hell the others were talking about!

Later that night, François, Philippe and Ludwig went to their own den, where they started to listen to their American records... Will, Paul, Lutz and Franz went to the drawing-room, to have a cognac... That's where Lutz told his three friends: „I've got a letter from my brother Hans..." „Where is he stationed?", Will asked... „Stalingrad", Lutz answered, looking down at the carpet... All the others raised their eyes and started staring at Lutz. They all knew what Stalingrad meant! „He's been badly wounded...", Lutz said, with tears in his eyes...

EIGHT

„Yeah...", Lutz said to his friends... „My brother Hans has been badly wounded at Stalingrad... He's supposed to be air-lifted from there, and sent to a military hospital in Germany..." „Where?", Franz asked... „We don't know yet... I guess we'll have to wait and see. At least, he's still alive...", Lutz answered. „I've heard it's an inferno at Stalingrad...", Will commented. „...It's hell on earth...", Lutz replied to his best friend. At the end of January 1943, Lutz got news that indeed, his brother had been air-lifted from Stalingrad and had been transferred to a military hospital at Oberwesel... „How is he?", Franz asked his lover Lutz... „He's being treated for shrapnel wounds to his legs... He was badly hurt, and he can't walk. But in his letter, he said that later, with therapy, he should be able to walk again..." „...I guess the war is over for him...", Franz said. „Yes: It is!" A week later as they were having supper at Paul's mansion, Lutz said to his friends: „I'll be on leave for a week starting March 2nd... and I'm going to travel to Oberwesel to see Hans..." – „Where the hell is that?", Paul asked. Lutz grinned and answered: „In Germany of course... It's a small village on the Rhine River, south of Koblenz..." „I can't go with him...", Franz said... „My request for a week vacation has been refused by the embassy..." „Hey...", Will said... „I'll be on leave too... Maybe we could go with you..." „Why not...", Paul added... „Cool", Ludwig said, with a smile on his face. Will looked at his young brother and said to him: „No, Ludwig... You can't come. You would have to miss school, and that's out of the question. Sorry, dude!" – „Oh come on bro!", a very disappointed Ludwig said... „Maybe next time...", Will replied... „But not this time..." On March 2nd, 1943, Will, Paul and Lutz boarded a train to Köln. Once there, they had to take another train to Wiesbaden... but there was a six hours waiting period between the two trains... „Hey... Instead of sitting here, waiting... Why don't we go for a walk... have a beer... see the cathedral... They say it's one of the most beautiful in the world...", Will suggested... „Yeah, let's go guys...", Lutz answered, smiling... The three friends walked out of the train station and then... they were shocked! They looked around them, and all they saw was total destruction. As they walked through the great city, they saw for themselves what the British bombs had done to Köln in May 1942. In short, there was nothing left there, standing... Ruins... Nothing but ruins! The center of the city had been completely wiped out. Everything around them had ben destroyed... except... the beautiful cathedral! As they were walking towards the cathedral, they saw it had been damaged... but not badly. „...It's as if the Allied pilots had tried to avoid damaging it...", Lutz commented. „Well, if so... it only shows the RAF is more human than the Luftwaffe... because following Göring's orders, the Luftwaffe totally destroyed Coventry... including the beautiful cathedral the British had over there...", Will stated. „Göring? You mean the big „swine"?", Paul asked, grinning... „Himself!", Will answered, laughing... Of course, what they were suspecting was true: Strict orders had been given to the allied pilots not to bomb the cathedral... and although Cologne endured exactly 262 air raids during the war... at the end of it in May of 1945, the cathedral was still there, standing... and almost unscratched! After their visit to the Cathedral, Lutz said to his friends: „Let's go back to the station... I've seen quite enough..." „Hey... What about our beer?", Will asked, grinning... „Look around, pal: Where do you think we could go to have a beer, huh? There's nothing left around here..." They had to agree... and so they made their way back to the station, amidst the debris of what was once a beautiful city... At the station, the mood was somber... and they remained silent. No one wanted to talk about what they had seen... And anyway, there was nothing to say about it... And they were quite relieved to leave Köln when their train got ready to leave, and when they left the station, Paul said: „I'm breathing easier now..." „Yeah!", Will answered, with a sad look on his face... „Let's get the hell out of here..." Their train made a stop at Bonn, then at Koblenz... and finally they arrived at Oberwesel, and went to the military hospital where Hans was admitted.

Lutz was very happy to see his brother Hans was doing well, and Hans was happy to see them. Of course, Hans knew Will well from childhood, since they had grown on the same street, back in Berlin. And he also knew

Paul: They had met in Berlin back in 1941, just before the start of Hitler's campaign against Russia... „...The therapy is going well", Hans explained... „And in a few months, I should be able to walk again. I guess I'm lucky, compared to my comrades I left behind at Stalingrad. The Sixth Army doesn't exist anymore..." „What?", Will exclaimed, stupefied... „But... that's not possible... I mean... The Sixth Army was so strong..." „Yeah! Exceptionally strong... with 850 000 soldiers...", Hans answered, with a disabused look on his face. „But... What happened? All we heard was that the Wehrmacht had experienced a setback at Stalingrad but...", Lutz started to say before being suddenly interrupted by his brother Hans who said: „A setback? Are you kidding? It's a defeat unmatched in scale to what we have ever seen in history!" „(...)" „But how could that be, Hans?", Paul asked... „You ask me how that happened?", Hans answered, looking around to make sure nobody else but his friends were listening... „I'm going to tell you how it happened!", he said, furious... And after a pause, he began explaining: „You see, last November, the Russians have launched an offensive and have sealed a ring around Stalingrad, where we were. This is how the entire Sixth Army found itself trapped... inside the resulting pocket... we were calling it „Der Kessel". 850 000 of our soldiers were caught in the Kessel... Of course, at that point, it would have been possible for us to break through their lines, but in order to do so, we would have had to evacuate Stalingrad... And Hitler refused!" „Huh?", Will said... „Yeah!", Hans answered... „And do you know why? (...) Because the big swine, Göring, told the Führer the Luftwaffe could supply the Sixth Army with an air bridge! An air bridge! Can you believe that, huh? To feed 850 000 men... and supply such a big army with fuel and ammunition... How ludicrous! But Hitler believed him and re-iterated his orders of „no retreat"... and „no surrender". So we stayed at Stalingrad..." „And?", Lutz ventured to ask his brother... „And what do you think happened, bro?", Hans replied, looking at Lutz... „The air bridge was a total failure... and it didn't take long before we began starving! Before long, we were out of fuel... and our guys began dying like flies... of malnutrition, frostbite and diseases. It's a miracle I was air-lifted from that hell before Von Paulus capitulated to the Russians." „I can't believe what you're telling us...", Paul said... „Yeah, well... it's all too true. And while the big swine was spending some good time on his estate of Karin Hall, drinking French champagne, eating Russian caviar and admiring all the paintings he has stolen from the occupied territories... the Russians were slaughtering us by the thousands..." „Where are those guys now?", Will asked... „We don't know... All we know is that they were taken and sent by the Russians to labor camps...", Hans answered, with tears in his eyes... „I've heard that when Von Paulus surrendered, less than 100 000 of or guys were still alive..." Of course at the time, Hans and his friends had now way of knowing that not until 1955 would the Russians allow the handful of survivors, 6 000, to go back to Germany... 6 000 survivors, out of an army of 850 000 soldiers. „My God! (...) I don't know what to think...", Will commented... „You don't know?", Hans said, looking at Will straight in the eyes... „I'm going to tell you: It's obvious to me Stalingrad was a turning point... It's the beginning of the end for the Reich, I'm telling you guys. The war is lost..." „Oh come on Hans...", Lutz said... „I understand it was bad over there... but I mean... We'll..." Hans turned to look at his brother and said to him: „.....Poor Lutz... You don't know what you're talking about... I'm telling you: At Stalingrad, we have lost the war. We'll never recover from that defeat..."

And Hans was right. The Wehrmacht never recovered from that defeat. And contrary to what the British or the Americans like to think, they didn't win the war in Europe: The Russians did! And that's the reason why Roosevelt and Churchill remained silent at Yalta, when Stalin told them the Soviet Union intended to keep all the territories the Red army would „liberate" up until the end of the war... which meant all of Eastern Europe! Roosevelt and Churchill had no choice but to agree. Of course, Churchill was furious... but Roosevelt had to yield to Stalin, since by then the Red Army was too strong to be defeated and anyway, America had its hands full with the war in the Pacific and wanted to see the war in Europe come to an end... whatever the cost...

„Anyway, Lutz...", Hans concluded... „As soon as I'm better... I'm going back home! By then, I will have been discharged from the Wehrmacht..." „Yeah!", Lutz answered, smiling at his brother... „Good for you..." „Maybe you could come to Paris, and stay with us for a while...", Paul said... „Hey... Why not?", Hans answered, smiling... „Yeah, bro: Life must go on...", Lutz said... „Right! And I'm still alive...", Hans replied. „Right!", Lutz answered.

On their way back to Paris, Will, Lutz and Paul kept thinking about what Hans had said about the war... As their train was leaving Köln, Lutz looked at his best friend and asked him: „Will... Do you really think the war is lost?" Through the window, Will looked at all the ruins all around them... then answered: „.... It's only a question of time, you know. But yes, Lutz... I really think Hans is right. The war is lost, thanks to Hitler!" – „I wish I could strangle him!", Lutz answered... „You're not the only one...", Will replied, with a sad look on his face. „...And if you need my help, dismembering the big swine... you can count on me guys...", Paul said, laughing... „Ohhhh... I would love to do just that...", Lutz answered... Eventually, they reached Paris... and started to breathe again... „Thank God, we're back!", Paul said... „Yeah!", Will and Lutz answered, with a big smile on their face... Periodically Will, Ludwig and Lutz would make calls to Berlin, to talk to their families over there, thanks to Paul's direct phone line to the capital... „I hope I won't lose that line...", Paul said to them one night... „Why would you?", Will asked... Paul grinned and said: „...I don't know. You know my business partners in Berlin? Well... they have decided to buy me back..." – „Huh?", Will said... „But why?" „Well... over the past few months, some business opportunities have arisen... to invest into some industries in Germany and Poland... and I've refused..." – „But why?" „(...) In each case, I've studied the documents... the balance-sheets... and in each case, it didn't make sense: No salaries were paid to the workers... Of course, I asked my business partners questions about that... and all they told me was that the workers were „for free"... and that I shouldn't ask too many questions about that! That didn't make sense! So I vetoed the investments... and I guess they got tired of me..." „And?", Will asked... „Well... In our partnership contract, it is clearly stipulated that if you want to get rid of a partner, you have to offer him to sell to him your shares... at a fixed price... and if he decides not to buy your shares, he has no choice but to sell his own shares to you, at the same price. It's called a 'shot gun clause'... Anyway, they offered to sell me their shares... knowing I wouldn't buy them... and so, I had no choice but to sell them mine. And that's what happened: They bought me out!" „How did they pay you? With Reichsmarks?", Will asked his lover Paul... „Yeah! They paid me in Reichsmarks... deposited on my bank account in Switzerland... and the same day, I used all that money to purchase gold! I didn't want to get stuck with Reichsmarks... and I tell you, Will... I made a hefty profit", Paul answered, laughing his heart out... „...So... You no longer have any investment in Germany?", Will asked... „Oh, I still have some...

but not much! That's why I say I wouldn't be surprised if they decide to cut my direct phone line to Berlin..." Fortunately... that never happened!

Then one night in September of 1943, François asked Paul: "Um... can Philippe stay over here for the night? It's late... and the Métro (subway) has stopped working..." – „Huh?", Paul said, looking at his young friend... „Well... With Ludwig, we were having fun in our den, listening to our records... and we didn't keep track of the time... Now... it's getting late, and if Philippe doesn't stay here for the night, we have a big problem!", François explained to Paul... „Well... we do have a problem here, don't we?", Paul said... „Where do you want him to sleep? All the other bedrooms have been closed for... what? Three years? He can't sleep in one of them..." „Hey", Ludwig said... „No problem... He'll sleep with us in our bedroom... All we have to do is to push our two beds together... that way, we'll have enough space in there for the three of us... what do you think Paul?" „....Well... If it's okay with you, Ludwig... then I guess...", Paul answered... „No problem!", Ludwig answered, laughing... „Okay then...", Paul finally said... before saying to François: „Hey you... Come here... Yeah, you! Do I smell beer? Have the three of you been drinking?" „...Um...", François answered, a bit embarrassed... „Oh come on, Paul...", Ludwig said, coming to his best friend's rescue... „It's Friday night... we only had a few beers, that's all..." Paul looked at them for a minute, then said: „....A few beers huh?... Sure! You smell like you drank plenty... Don't let Will see you like that...you hear? I can't believe I'm covering for you guys! Now, go to bed..." „Yessss!", Ludwig and François answered, knowing perfectly well Paul wouldn't say a word to Will about that: Will felt responsible for his younger brother and was...well... rather stiff about alcohol... Paul was more... liberal! „... I can't resist you guys!", Paul finally said to Ludwig and François, laughing... as the two young friends were running to their den to fetch Philippe... who was... well... a bit buzzed out! The three friends went upstairs to François and Ludwig's bedroom and then pushed their two beds together... „...That's perfect!", Ludwig said, looking down at the result... They all went to bed and finally turned the lights off! Of course... they didn't go to sleep right away... and started talking and making jokes... But eventually, they did go to sleep.

And later during the night, François... who was sleeping between Ludwig and Philippe... woke up... then listened in the dark for a while... and finally turned to Ludwig and whispered to him: „... Are you doing what I think you're doing?" Ludwig smiled in the dark and answered: „...Can't help it... Sorry, pal!" „You make me horny!", François answered... „Me too...", they heard Philippe say, from his side of their makeshift bed... Both Ludwig and François turned to look at Philippe, laughing their heart out... „You were not sleeping?", they both asked their friend... „... What do you think? (...) And with that hardon I have...", Philippe answered, grinning... „... You have a hardon, too?", François asked his lover... „Yeah!", Philippe answered... „And I'm oozing so much, you wouldn't believe it..." „... So am I...", François answered, grinning... „What the hell are we going to do about that, guys?", Ludwig asked his two friends... „...We're going to take care of our needs... won't we?", François answered, laughing... „Hey guys... Don't worry because I'm here in bed with you two... I don't care, you know...", Ludwig said... „So if you want to fuck... feel free to do so..." „Oh come on Ludwig!", François exclaimed... „No no... I swear... I don't care... Besides, I'd like to watch, if you see what I mean... Oh, come on guys... let's do it!", Ludwig finally said... „Hey, pals...", Philippe said... „There's something I've been wanting to do for a long time..." „What's that?", François asked his lover... „Well..." Philippe started to say... „Since you've lost most of your hair „down there"... I mean... Yeah... So what?", François said... „Well... I want to shave... to look like you... I find it very sexy...", Philippe answered, turning on his side in the bed to look at François... „What?", François exclaimed... „You find it sexy?" „Yeah!", Philippe admitted... „Don't you, Ludwig?" „Um... I don't know... Yes, I guess... After all, Will, Paul and Franz are all shaved „down there"... and I must say... well... they look good...", Ludwig answered... „Oh come on, guys...", François said... „No, I swear I like it François...", Philippe said, looking at his lover in the dark... „So let's move on to the shower..." – „Are you kidding?", François answered... „No!... I've been thinking about that for a while...I'm telling you...", Philippe replied, grinning... „...Let's go guys...", Ludwig said, laughing... „Yeah!", Philippe answered. So they all walked over to the bathroom where Ludwig turned the lights on... „Do you think the three of us will fit in there?", he asked his two friends, looking at the shower... „No problem!", Philippe answered, laughing... „It's quite big!" They all entered the shower and indeed, it was large enough to accommodate the three of them... „Who's first?", Ludwig asked, laughing... „Me...", François answered... „It won't take long... But first, let's take a shower..."

Before long, the three of them were standing under streaming water... As François began to soap and wash Philippe's back, Philippe took a soap and began rubbing his hands all over Ludwig's rippling stomach working up a lather with Ludwig's eyes closed against the water, his huge cock hanging over his sack and water and soap dripping from his foreskin... He looked incredible... Philippe pushed backwards with his body, forcing François against the cold tiles, his butt against his François' crotch. Then, Philippe began making grinding movements, and his lover's cock responded quickly by growing hard and poking at him, as he rubbed himself against François. Philippe was still rubbing his hands over Ludwig's chest and all over his hard stomach... his fingers finding their way through his blond pubic hair. Finally, Philippe felt Ludwig's big dick in his hand. He was still soft. He bent down and gave Ludwig's dick a kiss... Then, he took it in his mouth... Ludwig's soft cock filled his mouth and he started to play around with it with his tongue... Of course, it didn't take long before Ludwig started getting hard and soon enough, Philippe felt him coming to life inside his warm mouth... As Philippe kept making grinding movements with his butt against his lover's crotch, he heard François moan softly... Ludwig pulled away from the streaming water and looked down at Philippe who was sucking on his hard cock: God, the guy was talented! Ludwig was groaning and moaning so much by now, François knew his best friend was about to cum. He leaned forward to Philippe and whispered in his ear: „Don't make him cum... not yet... We've just started..." „Un-huh", Philippe answered, letting go of Ludwig's throbbing dick... „Hey! What the hell are you doing...", Ludwig said... „I was almost there..." „Yeah... That's the problem with you straight guys: You just don't know how to make it last for a while...", Philippe answered, grinning... „Fuck!", Ludwig answered... „Yeah... I hope you will fuck me... with that nice, big dick of yours...", Philippe answered, laughing... „Don't count on that!", Ludwig answered, laughing... „That would be queer..." „No it wouldn't", François said... „And anyway... who cares? As long as it's fun..." „Yeah well...", Ludwig started to say... then closed his mouth, not saying anything else... since he didn't really know what else to say... „Hey! Don't forget we have a shaving job to do guys...", Philippe said, grinning... „Yeah!", François answered. Philippe turned around to face his lover and stared at his face, with water trickling down its beautiful contours. He leaned in to him and their hard cocks collided.

He wanted him so bad. He kissed him, his hands finding their way to his lover's hard dick, stroking it a few times. François moaned into his lover's mouth then, as their lips parted, François said: „Let's do me first...“ François laid down on the shower floor, and Ludwig shut the water off. He then turned to Philippe and said: „I'll get what we need...“ Ludwig got off the shower and a few minutes later, he was back with a pair of scissors, shaving cream and a razor... François did nothing but stretch out on his back on the floor: Philippe did the rest, as Ludwig was watching, giving his hard, aching dick a few, firm squeezes... Philippe went to work with the scissors, reducing his lover's bush to coarse stubble and Ludwig watched breathlessly when Philippe lathered his lover's manhood and began shaving him clean. François grinned at Philippe as he rubbed his hand over the newly shaven pubes above his cock: It felt wonderful! „Now... it's Ludwig's turn!“, François said, raising from the floor so Ludwig could lay down there... „...Um...“, Ludwig said... „I'm not really sure guys... I mean... I love my pubes...“, he said, looking down at his blond pubic bush... „Oh come on Ludwig... What the hell! It's only hair... it will grow back...“, Philippe said to his friend, laughing, playing with the pair of scissors like some demented barber... „Okay okay...“, Ludwig finally said, laughing... „But be careful down there... and don't cut my dick! That's my pride and joy, you know...“ „Don't worry dude: I'm in control!“, Philippe answered, laughing... So Ludwig laid down on his back on the floor, stretching out his body... „Now... be careful!“, he warned Philippe again... „I said not to worry, pal!“, Philippe answered, grinning... Ludwig nevertheless felt a sick wave of apprehension... Then, Philippe grabbed his friend's dick and started to play with it... and of course, Ludwig felt his cock swelling... François knew his best friend was apprehensive, so he decided to do something to divert his attention. He moved over to Ludwig's face, put his legs on both side... then lowered himself down over his friend's face... so that Ludwig now had a perfect view of François' asshole... „What the hell do you think you're doing?“, Ludwig said to François... „If you think I'm going to lick your hole, you're dead wrong!“ „...Well... You can't lick my balls, can you?“, François answered... Hearing that made Ludwig feel bad: François knew how to make him feel cheap! Ludwig looked up at his friend's hole... it was rosy pink and hairless... and so fresh and clean... „Oh... What the hell!“, Ludwig said... „Just lower yourself a bit more, will you... bastard...“

François grinned and did as asked... Ludwig pushed his face into his best friend's ass crack... François had a big round muscular ass and Philippe could hear Ludwig's tongue and lips attacking his asshole. What a sight! François moaned, feeling Ludwig's hot tongue all over his hole... And it felt so good! Ludwig would never admit it... but licking his best friend's asshole was making him very horny, and Philippe could see his big dick was leaking like crazy... Philippe began to focus on his work... but was distracted by François, who was moaning... Philipe looked up at his lover, who was facing him. François was straddling Ludwig's face, and Philippe could see Ludwig's tongue going in and out of his lover's asshole. He grinned... and couldn't believe his eyes: Ludwig was really eating his lover's ass! And of course, Philippe got a massive boner: He was getting off on this just as much as François was... Then, Philippe took the pair of scissors and started snipping round Ludwig's tangled pubes... reducing his blond bush to coarse stubble... He then lathered Ludwig's dick and balls with soap and started to shave him... Since Ludwig's big dick was getting in his way, Philippe grabbed it, pulling it this way and that, shaving round the root of it and up the sides... Ludwig kept bucking under Philippe's hand, trying to get off in his fist... „Keep still", Philippe said to him... „Or I'll cut you..." Ludwig grunted... but stopped bucking... „That's better, dude...", Philippe said, grinning... Then, he started handling Ludwig's balls, squeezing them... stretching them... soaping them and scraping off the hair... Ludwig was moaning so loud, François could feel his tongue vibrate, buried deep inside his asshole... „God, Ludwig... You're good!", François moaned to his friend... „You don't know how good that feels..." Finally, Philippe threw down the razor and began to admire his handiwork... „Yup, dude... you look good... You look very good...", Philippe said to Ludwig... „And your dick looks even bigger..." Ludwig removed his tongue from François' hole... and when François raised himself up from his face, Ludwig looked down at his hairless dick: The cool air on his bare skin made him horny... Now, his dick and balls were as smooth as silk, as smooth as on the day he was born. Indeed, his huge cock looked even bigger... and was dripping sticky precum all over his shaved skin... „Nice job...", he said to Philippe, grinning... „I like it... thanks dude! (...) Now my friend... it's your turn!" – „Oh yes...", François said to Philippe, laughing... „And I'm the barber!" Philippe smiled as he took Ludwig's place on the shower floor... „...Take your time... and don't cut me!", Philippe said to his lover... "Don't worry babe... I love your dick too much, I'll handle it with very good care..." François looked at his lover's large, black pubic bush... then raised his head to look at Ludwig, standing there... with his hairless dick in his hand... "...Don't just stay there like that... you're not a dummy, are you?", François said to Ludwig... "Have your asshole eaten by Philippe..." "Yeah!", Philippe said... "Come sit over my face dude... and let me please you..." "Are you kidding?", Ludwig answered... "No guy will ever touch my hole... ever..." "Oh stop that...", François answered... "I've put two or three fingers up in your ass in the past... and you didn't complain at the time, if I remember correctly..." "...Well... That was different...", Ludwig answered, going red in the face... Then, after a pause he said: "If I do it... Please, don't ever tell anyone I did it... no matter what okay?" Both François and Philippe nodded... "You promise?" "Yeah, yeah...", they both answered, grinning... So Ludwig walked over to Philippe's face, placed his parted legs on both sides of his head... then lowered himself, so his asshole was directly hovering over his friend's mouth... As he was facing François, Ludwig said to him: "I can't believe..." "Shut up, and do it...", François answered, laughing... "...A bit lower...", Philippe said to Ludwig... "That's it, pal..." With his warm, slippery tongue Philippe began to play all around Ludwig's beautiful rosebud... and it didn't take long before Ludwig started to moan and groan... Then, Philippe drove his tongue deep inside Ludwig's fuck hole... Ludwig shuddered... gasping and moaning... "Fuck my hole with your hot tongue...", Ludwig shouted... begging to be royally tongue-fucked... "You like the feeling, huh?", François asked his best friend, grinning... "Hell! It feels sooooo good... I never thought...", Ludwig answered... "Yeah! I know!", François answered, laughing...

Then François took the scissors and began to cut the hair away from his lover's dick and balls... and then, he started so shave them... François was so gentle, Philippe lost himself in the movement and before long, his big, black bush was history! Tilting his head slightly to one side, François gazed at his lover's hairless crotch and said: "God! Philippe... You're so beautiful..." When Ludwig finally raised his body from his face, Philippe raised his head to look down at his hairless dick and said: "Hum... You've done an excellent job... I like the way my dick looks... Not as big as yours, Ludwig... but not bad, huh?" The three of them laughed... staring at each other... „Yeah...", François said... „Ludwig has the biggest dick... but doesn't know how to use it..." „The hell with you...", Ludwig answered, laughing... „You made me eat your ass... and then, I was forced to have my asshole eaten by Philippe... but that's how far I'm going to go with you, guys..." „Oh... You were forced to eat my ass, huh?", François answered, laughing... You're bigger and stronger than me... so how did I do that, huh?" „...Well... I don't know...", Ludwig answered, grinning... „But you did it..." „Yeah! Sure! And you loved it!", François replied... „...You swore you two will never tell anyone...", Ludwig said, looking at his two friends... „Yes... We did!", Philippe answered... „And we'll keep our mouth shut... don't worry Ludwig..." Ludwig grinned and replied: „Good!"

„Look, Ludwig... Don't worry! What's going on here tonight between the three of us will remain between the three of us... I swear to you!", François said, looking Ludwig straight in the eyes... „Beside Ludwig... let's be honest: You've always wanted to satisfy your curiosity... So tonight... it's you're only chance to do so! Later, you'll find yourself a nice girl to go out with... and you'll probably marry her... and make love to her... and if you don't satisfy your curiosity tonight, you'll always ask yourself if you haven't missed something... isn't that true?" „...You're the devil, you know that?", Ludwig answered, laughing... „It's for your own good I say that...", François answered, with a sincere look on his face... „I know you, Ludwig... and I know you won't rest until your curiosity is fully satisfied..." „...Come on dudes... Let's take a shower... look at all the hair on us and all over the floor...", Philippe said... They all looked down at the floor... where their pubes were all mingled... and they began laughing... Philippe turned the water on, and hot water began streaming on them... They washed their strong, smooth bodies... and then, after they had all cleaned, they walked out of the shower to dry up... Then François looked at Ludwig and Philippe and, with a very sexy grin on his face, he said to them: „...Let's go back to bed... Tonight is THE NIGHT"... „Yeah!", Philippe answered, grinning at his lover... „What do you mean by THE NIGHT?, Ludwig asked, a bit puzzled... „...Let's go to bed... You'll see what I mean soon enough...", François answered, with the same sexy grin on his face... „You won't make me do things I don't want to do, huh?", Ludwig apprehensively asked... „Hey, pal... You know me better than that..." „...Yeah... and that's why I'm asking you... You're the devil you know... and I wonder if I wouldn't follow you to hell!", Ludwig answered, grinning... François turned to look at Ludwig straight in the eyes... and after a moment of silence, he answered: „(...) Not to hell, Ludwig, to heaven!" At that, François looked at Philippe and winked at him... „...Yeah", Philippe answered... „Let's go to bed... I'm so tired..." „Oh yeah?", Ludwig answered... „And if so... what's that, that I feel hard pressed against my thigh, huh?" – „...You mean... my hard, oozing dick?" „Hu-huh...", Ludwig answered... Philippe looked down at Ludwig's hard, hairless dick... and grabbed it, giving it a few squeezes. Then, looking back at Ludwig, he replied: „...Speaking about a hard dick, huh? Guess we're going to have to take good care of it before we go to sleep, won't we?" „...You're as bad as François...", Ludwig answered, laughing... „Worse!", Philippe answered, giving Ludwig and François a sexy grin... „Much worse!" „Ohhhhh", François answered... „It's going to be a long, hot night..." „Oh shit!", Ludwig answered... „Yeah!", François replied, as the three friends were walking back to their makeshift bed... „A very long... and very steamy night, count on me, straight boy!", François answered, looking at Ludwig, grinning... „Oh my God!", was all Ludwig could answer... „Look pal...", François said to Ludwig, looking his best friend straight in the eyes again... „If that's not what you want, no problem... and we'll just go to sleep. I don't want you to wake up tomorrow morning, hating us... If we do it with you, it's because you want to. Tomorrow, I don't want you to feel bad about it... do you understand what I mean... You've got to be sure what we're about to do is what you want! Cause if not, you better say so right now. And we won't be mad at you, far from it!" Ludwig looked at François... and after a few seconds he said: „...As long as you two don't ever tell anyone... no matter what!" „We swear...", François and Philippe answered... „...But Ludwig...", François added... „If we do it... We do it all the way... I don't want to hear you say „It's queer.." or „That's gay...", you understand?" „Okay", Ludwig answered... „Except for one thing: No kissing! You two can kiss all you want, but leave me out of it, okay? For the rest... no problem... as long as you swear..." „...We did Ludwig... No one will ever know about what we're going to do tonight... We swear to you...", Philippe said. „Yeah!", François added... „(...) Then... Let's do it guys", Ludwig answered, grinning, becoming hornier and hornier... „Yeah!... Let's do it!"

Ludwig led the way to their bedroom, followed by his two friends... François couldn't help but to glance at Ludwig's beautiful ass cheeks right in front of him: He reached his hand out and squeezed, and heard Ludwig chuckle as he did it... Once in the bedroom and as Ludwig was about to lay down on the bed, Philippe stopped him and said: „...No.. Don't lay down... just stand here, beside the bed..." And as Ludwig stood there, Philippe knelt in front of him and immediately went to work on his friend's big, hard dick... taking it down his throat like he'd been doing this all of his life. François stood beside Ludwig and started licking his large, pink nipples, while slowly stroking his own big, oozing cock... Philippe opened his throat some more and Ludwig groaned with his entire hot dick inside his young friend's mouth and throat. Ludwig began to hump Philippe's beautiful face, and his eyes rolled into the back of his head as he felt his knob enter and exit his tight throat... As Ludwig was slamming his big dick in and out of Philippe's mouth, François turned his body and began sliding his hot palms down Ludwig's smooth muscular backside until his hands touched his hot ass cheeks... Ludwig turned his head back as far as he could to look at François and, gasping, he said to him: „...Are you going to..." „Fuck you in the ass? (...) Ohhhhh yeah! But first, I'm going to make sure you're ready for it..." Then François knelt behind Ludwig, put his hands on his tight, compact ass cheeks and spread them open, exposing his friend's beautiful rosebud... Then, with his hot tongue, he started to lick all around it... „Oh shit... That feels good...", Ludwig exclaimed moaning and groaning, wiggling his ass with his hard, oozing dick lodged deeply inside Philippe's tight throat... When Ludwig felt his friend's tongue enter his asshole, he began to moan louder and when Philippe looked up at his face, he saw the looks of pleasurable bliss on it... By now, Ludwig's breathing was heavy and Philippe sensed it wouldn't take long before he started cumming... so he let go of Ludwig's cock and began to give his balls a good tongue bath... then kissed and nibbled on his inner thighs... while François on his knees behind him was giving Ludwig a tongue bath of his own... With Ludwig panting and sweating, François grabbed the bottle of lotion he had brought with him from the bathroom and smeared some all over his right hand and fingers. Using his well lubed middle finger, he began to play all around Ludwig's moist hole and Ludwig moaned lightly when he felt the tip of his friend's finger enter his sweet hole... It felt so good... and before long, he began wiggling his ass and grunted as his friend's finger slid deep inside his hole. Philippe went back sucking Ludwig's knob while fumbling his nuts in their sack... Using his middle finger, François began wiggling around inside Ludwig's bum and the young, blond stud gasped when François located his tender prostate... Then, François pushed in a second finger and Ludwig sighed when François began twisting his two fingers around... „Oh my God!... You're good, guys... You're good!", Ludwig moaned, looking down at Philippe working hard on his dick with his hot, velvety mouth... After a while, François inserted a third finger inside Ludwig's hole... Then, Philippe removed his mouth from Ludwig's hard, throbbing dick, raised to his feet, looked at his blond friend and said to him: „Oh no, dude... You're not cumming yet... cause I want you to fuck me with that big dick of yours..." Ludwig grinned and answered: „At your command... sorry if I can't stand at attention though... but you see... I have a few fingers up my ass..." Philippe laughed then turned around, thrusting his hot looking ass out behind him... „...Here", He said to Ludwig, tossing him the lotion... „Smear some all over your cock... then all over my asshole, and lube it well..." Of course, Ludwig did as asked and seconds later, as Philippe was spreading his legs offering him his ass, Ludwig began lubing it... When he was sure his asshole was pretty well lubed-up, Philippe said to Ludwig: „I'm ready dude... take your time... go slowly with that big cock, will you?" Philippe grabbed his ass cheeks making sure they were completely separated, telling Ludwig to put his dick head right over his rosebud... „...That's it dude... Now, push slowly..." Both Ludwig and Philippe grunted when the head of Ludwig's cock penetrated his friend's ass... Philippe's ass lips squeezed his cock so Ludwig, not knowing what to do, asked his friend: „Do you want me to take it out?" „Nooooo", Philippe answered, grinning... „It's just that your dick is so big... it hurts a little... just give me some time to get adjusted, okay?" „...You tell me when you're ready, huh?" „Yeah...", Philippe answered, trying to relax... „...Okay now... you can push... slowly...", he said a bit later... Ludwig started to thrust his hips forward and his big, oozing dick sunk in another few centimeters into his friend's tight hole... „Ohhhhhh... That's tight... Oh God!", Ludwig moaned... „Does it hurt?" „...No... Go for it pal... all the way in...", Philippe moaned. „You sure?" „Yeah!" Ludwig pushed harder and before long, his big 25-cm-dick was buried deep inside his curly, black haired friend's ass, up to the hilt...

„...Stay still for a while, okay?", Philippe said to his blond friend... „...(...) Okay now, that's perfect, Ludwig: Fuck me now...", Philippe finally said... Gingerly Ludwig began to work his hips back and forth, with François' fingers still buried deep inside his own hole... When Philipe started to moan, Ludwig asked him: „Can I fuck you a little faster dude?" „...As fast as you want, pal...", Philippe answered gasping with lust. As he began to fuck Philippe harder and faster Ludwig exclaimed: „Ahhhhh... your ass is so tight... so hot... it's much better than Marie-Hélène's pussy, I swear..." – „...Glad you like it...", Philippe answered, moaning... „Yeah...", Ludwig replied, grinning. Then he turned his head to look at François behind him and said to his best friend: „...You still want to fuck me, huh?" „Yeah!... I'm going to fuck your cute, bubble butt while you fuck Philippe... you'll see buddy... you'll love the experience. Stay still for a few seconds... and don't cum... can you do that?" „Hey... I'm doing my best here..." „Yeah... well, stop fucking... don't cum just yet!" – „Okay okay...", Ludwig answered, grunting... „Just trust me pal... You'll love it...", François said... Reluctantly, Ludwig stopped fucking Philippe and said: „...I'm almost there... Don't wiggle your ass Philippe, don't squeeze your ass muscles dude, cause you're going to make me cum..." A few seconds later, he said: „Okay now... it's safe..." „...See... it's not so hard to gain control over your dick, dickhead!" François said to Ludwig, laughing... „Now what?", Ludwig asked, a bit apprehensive... with his dick deep inside Philippe's love chute... „Ahhh... Don't worry, pal... Now at first, it's going to hurt for a few seconds... but that won't last, I swear to you... then, you're going to love it. Just do what I tell you to do, okay?", François answered... „...Yeah...", Ludwig answered, turning his head to look at François... „I trust you... I don't know why, but I do..." At that, François removed his fingers from Ludwig's asshole... took the lotion and smeared a generous amount on them, then re-entered his friend's ass, spreading the lotion all around and deep inside... Ludwig moaned, and began wiggling his ass with his best friend's fingers deep inside him... Then, François smeared another generous amount of lotion all over his dick... „Now, spread open your ass cheeks for me, will you?", François asked Ludwig... „I can't believe I'm doing this...", Ludwig answered... „Shut up and do as I say..." „Okay okay..." With his left hand, François located Ludwig's asshole. With his right hand, he guided his hard dick right over it... „Ready?"... „I guess..." François began to slowly push... Ludwig grunted... As he felt the head of his cock was starting to penetrate Ludwig's rosebud, François said to him: „It will be better if you try crapping... but of course, don't really shit..." „Huh?" „...You'll see... just do as I say..." Ludwig grunted, looking as if he were about to take a huge dump. François trusted his hips forward and soon enough, his dick head breached past Ludwig's sphincter muscles... „Oh shit... it hurts... it hurts...", Ludwig cried out... „Well, pal... you're no longer a virgin...", François answered, chuckling... „Yeah well... it hurts like hell!", Ludwig replied.... „It won't last... Take it like a man, Ludwig... come on..." „Easy for you to say..." „I've been there before... I tell you... it won't last..." And indeed, a few minutes later, it didn't feel so bad anymore... „...Much better now...", Ludwig suddenly said, with his stiffy oozing like never before deeply within Philippe's bum... „Now don't move... I'm going to take my dick out of your hole, put some more lotion on it.... and I'm going to put it back, okay?" „Okay..." After François had smeared some more lotion on his hard dick he said: „...Now, back it goes..." He re-entered Ludwig's tight asshole, and Ludwig moaned... „Not bad, huh?", François asked him... „...It starts feeling good...", Ludwig answered, grinning... „Okay... I'm going to push my dick all the way inside... slowly... okay?" „Go ahead, pal..." Again, Ludwig grunted as he felt François slowly push his hard prick all the way inside his hole... „How does it feel?", François asked... „Like I was going to explode!", Ludwig answered... „We'll give your ass muscles time to adjust... it won't take long..." With his arms, François grabbed Ludwig from behind, holding him tightly against him. Ludwig leaned back against him, feeling his best friend's hard cock deep inside him... François kissed Ludwig's neck and Ludwig's whole body went weak. Then François whispered in his hear: „You're so tight... it feels so good to be inside you..." Ludwig moaned. He was not feeling the pain anymore... While he was kissing Ludwig's neck, François began to run his strong hands across his friend's chest and rippled stomach... Ludwig's dick was a raging hardon and as he trusted his hips forward, he went deeper inside Philippe's ass... which made Philippe moan... Ludwig lifted his arms and reached back and began stroking François hair... „Ohhhhh.... you were right, pal... it does feel good...", he said to François...

François began to slowly pump his dick in and out of Ludwig's asshole, his hard dick filling his friend perfectly... and he knew he was hitting that incredibly tender spot near the top end of his friend's back passage as he was thrusting in to the hilt... then out again... As Ludwig began to trust his big dick deep inside Philippe's hole, François decided to stay still... and let Ludwig do the job... When Ludwig felt ready to really ride Philippe... he pulled his dick almost all the way out of his friend's chute, thus forcing François deeper inside him. Then Ludwig re-entered Philippe's arse, forcing François' dick to slide almost all the way out of his own chute... In.. and out... in and out... Yeah! Ludwig had found his rhythm... His face was a picture as he took all Philippe had to give, sodomizing him forcefully, repeatedly and roughly... withdrawing and re-entering his friend's arse, fucking him as deeply as he could, and receiving the same treatment from François... François started nibbling on Ludwig's ear... and he heard his friend moan softly... Then, Ludwig leaned forward onto Philippe's back, forcing his friend to go on all fours... He wrapped his arms around his friend's waist and went to find his dick. When he found it, he started wanking it... hard and fast... François was forced to lean onto Ludwig's back... and then, his hands went in search for his blond friend's nipples... It didn't take long for his fingertips to find them, and he began pinching them, wiggling his hips... Ludwig moaned and groaned, tossing his head back arching his back, driving his cock deeper inside Philippe's hot fuck hole. François stretched Ludwig's nipples twisting, tugging, and pinching them hard hearing Ludwig's cries and whimpers... François grinned and began kissing Ludwig between his shoulder blades... While Ludwig was fisting Philippe's hard, oozing dick, François pulled his hips back, and Ludwig did the same. Then, François rammed Ludwig's hot fucking buns so hard that Ludwig's cock slammed into Philippe's tight hot ass. The three of them shuddered gasping and moaning as one loud cry! „Ohhhhh fuck me, François...", Ludwig shouted, begging to be royally fucked. With his forearms wrapped around Ludwig's hard washboard abs, François began to swing his hips back and forth... fucking his tight asshole with Ludwig in return plowing his fuck pole into Philippe... Ludwig gripped Philippe's broad shoulders while kissing his nape when Philippe raised his torso. Philippe shivered, begging to be fucked harder and harder... Ludwig in turn asking François to do the same thing to his hungry to be fucked tight butt... Ludwig and François were working up quite a sweat fucking butt. When François ground his groin into his best friend's ass, Ludwig would ground his groin into Philippe's hot hot bum! „Will you guys fucking cum!", Philippe shouted, panting... „I can't take it anymore... I'm about to bust both my nuts up front here...", he cried out... Ludwig's cock was by now throbbing and near to bursting... „I'm almost there, man...", he answered, panting... „I'm so close, I'm so close...", François shouted, gasping, not caring it would only be precum he would shoot... „Cum Ludwig... cum deep inside me...", Philippe commanded... Ludwig only managed to thrust two or three more times before spurting a wad of teenage spunk deep into Philippe's arse... „Ahhhhhh...", he shouted out, as the feeling of orgasm clearly went through him several times... With Ludwig's body pressed hard on top of him, his cock pounding his arse... and as he felt the pressure building from his balls, Philippe shouted: „I'm cumming... Oh shit! Keep wanking my dick Ludwig... I'm cumming..." At that, he began emptying his load... and his body shook with the feeling of complete release and utter pleasure at the act... Although out of breath, Ludwig nevertheless kept wicking him... while his dick was still deep inside him... And he pushed it even deeper... Philippe could feel Ludwig squeezing his throbbing cock, and he shot another load of his hot young jizz... Then, as François began to climax deep inside Ludwig's tight ass, he became louder and louder... and he shouted out when his precum burst deep inside his best friend's love chute... „Ahhhhh shit guys...", he shouted, as he felt Ludwig's ass muscles squeezing his cock... „Shit! It feels so good..." Both Ludwig and Philippe grinned hearing that, too happy to see François had reached an orgasm... As their orgasms slowly ebbed, Ludwig grinned broadly... „Thanks guys... I owe you one...", he said to his two friends.

As the three of them were now laying on the bed, François turned to Ludwig and, with a grin on his face, he asked him: „So... tell me Ludwig... did you like it?" „....Hell... I never thought it would be so good guys, really..." „So... are you gay now?", Philippe asked him, laughing... „Sorry guys... as much as I loved it... I still like women... but I loved to be fucked by you François, and of course... I loved fucking you Philippe... but... something was missing, if you see what I mean...", Ludwig answered, laughing... „Hey dude: You're straight... that's not our fault!", François answered, laughing... „Yeah...", Ludwig replied, grinning... „It's not my fault either: I love big tits..." „Hey... that's your problem, not ours!", Philippe answered, laughing... „Anyway... before you get a girlfriend with big tits to fuck with, I hope I'll have a chance to be fucked by your big dick...", François said, chuckling... „...Sure! Anything to please you, pal!", Ludwig answered, still laughing... „But not tonight... give me a break, will you? I'm exhausted..." „So am I...", Philippe added... „Okay okay...", François answered, giggling... „But you owe me one, dude!" „...And don't hurry to get yourself a girlfriend... I loved being screwed by your stiff prick... and next time, I want to taste your cum...", Philippe said... „Ohhhhhhh...", Ludwig exclaimed... „Lots of fun in store for us, huh guys?" – „Count on us...", François and Philippe answered with one voice.

During the fall of 1943, Philippe was invited on a few occasions at Bagatelle, Paul's estate outside Paris, to spend weekends over there with his friends and of course... they had lots of fun! One night, as the three friends were alone at La Vacherie, the private and very secluded pavilion located on the estate, Ludwig said to his two friends: „Do you know what I'd like to do?" (...) Just watch you two fuck... you could give me a show, what do you say guys?" – „...Oh? And what would you be doing?", François asked, grinning... „Just sit there and watch... and wank of course...", Ludwig answered with a sexy grin on his face... „What a pervert you make!", François answered, laughing... „But I like the idea... What do you think Philippe?" – „Let's give him a show!", Philippe answered, grinning... „Okay... Let's go to our bedroom..." Once there, Ludwig undressed as fast as he could and sat on the bed, with his back leaning against the bed head board... Philippe began to undress... but François stopped him and said: „I have a better idea... Let's undress each other... slowly... Let's give that pervert over there a good show!" And of course, Philippe agreed! François walked closer to his lover and began kissing him full on the mouth. His kiss was soft and tender... and Philippe relaxed, enjoying his taste... „...That's so sexy", they heard Ludwig say from where he was sitting, with his fist wrapped around his big, hard dick... slowing stroking himself... Not only was he enjoying the show his two friends were doing for him, but he was also enjoying every sensation running through his body while sitting on the bed with his legs outstretched, wanking... His cock was clearly hungry for attention, and he was taking care of it! After their lips had parted, Philippe said to François: „Lift your arms..." François did so and Philippe pushed his shirt upwards, his hands running over his lover's body as he did so... he then lifted the shirt over his head... Then Philippe went down on his knees before his lover and began caressing his hard dick under the thin fabric of his pants. François moaned... Slowly, Philippe loosened his lover's belt, making sure that in the process he was touching his hard cock through his pants... Then he undid the button of his pants and unzipped him slowly. He slipped his hands inside his lover's pants, again just pressing against his hard dick and then pulled the pants down. François was now only wearing his white shorts. His dick was so hot and so hard that it felt like it might explode. And the head was oozing lots of precum... François gripped the sides of Philippe's shoulders, stepping out of his pants. Then he kicked them aside. Philippe pressed his lips onto his lover's hard, throbbing dick, and François cried out in sheer ecstasy when he felt the tip of Philippe's tongue trace the underside of his hard cock shaft through his shorts... Not too far from where they were standing, Philippe and François heard Ludwig moan... They grinned. Then, François gasped when Philippe's fingers began tugging his shorts. He held his breath. Philippe slowly lowered his shorts down to his ankles. François raised his right foot then his left as Philippe removed his shorts, tossing them aside. „...What a show, guys... You're surpassing the Lido in Paris. I swear!", they heard Ludwig say... „...Oh? You've been there?", François asked him... „Nah... just heard about it... But I'm sure the show over there is not half as good as the one you're doing now...", Ludwig answered, grinning...At that, Philippe tilted his head upward and his lips touched his lover's hard, oozing dick.... „Oh Philippe... ohhhhh...", François whimpered moaning feeling Philippe's hot tongue licking his hard shaft... Then Philippe slowly rose, licking his way up on his lover's stomach... First, he pressed his lips into his lover's navel, then kissed and licked his way up to his right nipple... François began panting and gasping feeling the tip of Philippe's hot tongue licking his erect nipple. His beautiful fingers ran through Philippe's curly, black hair as Philippe switched nipples to torture and suck his left nipple... „...I love watching you...", Ludwig said in a husky voice, slowly masturbating... „Keep going guys... slowly..." Philippe grinned... then wrapped his right fist around his lover's thick 20-cm-dick and began to slowly pump it... His lips left his lover's left nipple and made their way to his mouth... Now that he was completely standing up, Philippe let go of his lover's dick and wrapped his arms around his lover's back, so he could rub his bare back and pull him closer to him, to press his body against his own... Then, Philippe moved in for a deep kiss. His tongue slowly made its way into his lover's mouth and found his tongue and their kiss intensified like a battle... François wrapped his arms around Philippe's back and slowly began to lift his shirt... Philippe stopped kissing François and smiled at him. Then he slowly began to unbutton his shirt... slowly sliding it off behind him... „Yeah... that's the way to do it...", Ludwig moaned in the distance... François began massaging his beautiful lover's pecs, squeezing his hard nipples. Philippe responded immediately to this, rolling his eyes back in his head and moaning. François gave his lover a sexy grind and continued stimulating his nipples, driving Philippe wild... Then, François moved his hands down to his lover's abs... and after a few seconds, he began planting sweet little kisses all over his smooth stomach. He planted his tongue into his navel and he swirled it around... Philippe groaned under Ludwig's watchful eyes... With his hands, François wandered to his lover's belt buckle and undid it, then slowly removed the belt and threw it across the room. He moved to Philippe's fly and unbuttoned and unzipped it, then slowly slid his pants down over his thighs. He then plunged both hands inside his underwear and seized his cock... As François was working his hands over his lover's hard, oozing dick and balls, Philippe slid his pants and underwear down to his ankles. He backed off for a second so he could kick them off... François knelt in front of Philippe and his wet mouth pounced on his lover's throbbing dick. He slowly licked the slick precum off the head, then took the rest of the head into his velvety mouth... His tongue circled round and round, and Philippe felt his dick harden even more when François swallowed it all down his tight throat... „Ohhhhh...", Philippe whimpered moaning... Then François raised to his feet and pressed his hard nude body into Philippe's, wrapping his arms around him... their hard, oozing dicks squished between them... Both of them moaned and groaned, French-kissing again... François wrapped his right hand around his lover's hard cock shaft. Then he squeezed his oozing knob and Philippe gasped... „Okay guys...", Ludwig said... „You've fooled around long enough... Now I want to watch you two fuck..." François looked at Philippe and grinned...

Philippe hopped on the bed and knelt between Ludwig's parted legs. Ludwig was still sitting on the bed with his back resting against the bed head board, so Philippe was now facing him in a short distance. Philippe went on all fours between Ludwig's legs, and he leaned onto his friend's crotch, where he began kissing his big, smooth balls. Ludwig groaned when Philippe started sucking his nut sac... François knelt right behind Philippe and he said to his lover: „Spread your legs a bit, babe..." Philippe, still on all fours, spread his legs and the next thing he felt was François kissing the area between his balls and his hole... Then François began to suck his balls, one by one... After a while, he moved to his lover's rosy, hairless hole and with his hot tongue, he began licking all around it... „Ummmmmmm", Philippe moaned with Ludwig's hard cock in his mouth, sucking it good... up and down... up and down... „Ahhhh Yes... Ohhhhh... that feels so good...", Ludwig whispered... Philippe grinned and continued to go up and down, from the base of Ludwig's cock to the tip... Then Philippe slowed his pace, concentrating only on the head of Ludwig's dick. He licked, he sucked, slowly... He began swirling his tongue around the bottom side of his cock head. He was driving Ludwig crazy... and so he kept going... slow at first... then fast... slow again... As François was still working his asshole with his hot tongue, Philippe used his right hand to reach behind him to grab his lover's cock and placed the length of it between his ass cheeks. He pressed his lover's hard, oozing dick against his well lubed asshole and rubbed his lover's cock head around it. François loved it. Then Philippe slowly pushed his ass back and his lover's cock started to slide in... Philippe uncontrollably let out a loud, long, and deep moan as his lover's dick began to sent wave upon wave of pleasure through his body as it slowly slid into his ass... Now that he was all the way in, François began moving backward and forwards... slowly at first... then going harder and faster as his breathing also increased... „Wait wait wait...", Ludwig said... „I want to watch you fuck him from under..." As Philippe was on all fours, Ludwig turned in the bed on his back then slid between Philippe's arms down to his crotch. Looking up, Ludwig now had a perfect view of Philippe's balls hanging right over his mouth... and of François' big dick pushed deep into his lover's tight ass... For his part, Philippe had Ludwig's hard, throbbing dick right in front of him... so he leaned onto it and took it in his hot mouth... „Oh shit...", Ludwig shouted... „Okay François... start fucking...", he said to his best friend... As François began to fuck Philippe's ass slow and steady, Ludwig reached up and took Philippe's smooth balls into his mouth, giving them a very pleasurable tongue bath. Of course, while doing so... Ludwig kept looking up... watching François fuck Philippe's ass... Philippe was giving a lot of attention to the job he was doing on Ludwig's hairless dick while he was getting a good fuck from François... While sucking on Philippe's balls, Ludwig couldn't stop watching François' big dick going in and out, in and out of Philippe's tight ass... And he loved the show! Philippe was moaning softly... loving the feeling of being fucked while Ludwig was giving his balls the best tongue bath he'd ever had. When Philippe felt he couldn't hold it any longer, he let go of Ludwig's dick and moaned: „...Ohhh... I'm going to cum dudes... Ahhhhh... I'm going to cum..." Ludwig let go of Philippe's balls and took his hard, throbbing dick into his mouth... Philippe let his orgasm engulf his body as he shot his load down Ludwig's hot mouth... Ludwig dutifully swallowed everything, watching François' dick sliding in and out of Philippe's asshole. François was giving it to him good now, fucking his lover much faster and harder... his cock racing in and out of his tight arse... and then he came, going into overdrive, slamming his hips into Philippe's ass... The sight of this made Ludwig hornier than ever: There's nothing better than watching another guy reach orgasm... and soon, his own dick got very rigid deep inside Philippe's mouth and soon, Philippe could tell his blond friend was about to shoot... As Ludwig climaxed he became louder and louder and shouted out when his young cum burst inside his friend's mouth... Philippe sealed his lips around Ludwig's dick and Ludwig groaned. Philippe gulped every time Ludwig shot another wad... Ludwig's cock was pulsating... Tenderly, Philippe began sucking Ludwig's knob hearing him sighing before his lips tightened around his hard cock rod again, moving his head back and forth... And only after he had swallowed Ludwig's final trapped wad did Philippe pull his head off Ludwig's cock... Ludwig's teen jizz tasted so good... and Philippe was hungry for it... Ludwig was gasping... and François was groaning, slowly moving his hips back and forth... feeling his last rope of clear liquid oozing out of his prick deep inside his lover's hot ass... Then... François pulled out of his lover and collapsed onto the bed... Ludwig moved out from under François, then turned and laid on his back right beside his best friend. As for Phillippe, he collapsed onto François and as their breathing was returning to normal, they began kissing... „Shit guys... That was HOT!", Ludwig then said... „What a show... Thanks dudes..." – „This has been one hell of a fuck...", Philippe answered, chuckling... „Yeah!", François answered, laughing... „One hell of a fuck... And do you know what, Philippe? I think I'm starting to have a little crush on you...", he added, laughing his heart out... „...Only a little crush, huh?", Philippe answered, looking at his lover with a sexy grin on his face... „Okay okay... a big, big crush...", François answered, still laughing... „That's better!", Philippe answered... „...Time to go to sleep, dudes, before you make me feel horny again...", Ludwig said... „Ohhhhh... is that so?", François answered to his best friend... „Well dude... the night is not over yet..." And indeed, the night wasn't over! It had just begun! And much later, when they finally went to sleep... they all slept the sleep of the totally satisfied!

NINE

The fall of 1943 was beautiful, as much as the summer of that year had been... To Paul, life was perfect... and all you could hear on Avenue Foch were laughs... and of course, a few moans now and then. One evening, Paul was in the drawing-room reading a book when he heard Will play a beautiful song on the piano. „...What's that song?" he asked, looking at his lover... „You like it?" „...Yeah!" „It's called „Lili Marleen...". it's a big hit, you know. It's been translated in English, French... Russian... everywhere, they sing that song...", Will explained. „...But it's a German song, isn't it?" „Yeah! But it speaks about love... and love, like music, knows no boundaries... look at the lyrics here..." Paul took the partition and began reading the lyrics... „Vor der Kaserne, vor dem grossen Tor, stand eine Laterne. Und steht sie noch davor, so woll'n wir da uns wiederseh'n. Bei der Laterne woll'n wir steh'n. Wie einst Lili Marleen... Wie einst Lili Marleen..." And the song went on... speaking about the love of a simple soldier for his girlfriend he couldn't be with, because of the war... „Yes... It's beautiful", Paul said, giving the partition back to Will... „I hope this madness will stop one day... When I think of all the guys our age that are dying as we speak... fighting a war no one except Hitler wanted. Each one of them has a face... a life... They are like you and me... All they ever wanted was to live happy, to love and be loved! I wish we could run away from it all...", Paul said. „Well... We can't!", Will answered with a sad look on his face... „And remember: I'm a soldier... I couldn't run away like that..." Paul raised his eyes to look at Will. He hated to be reminded Will was a soldier... „At least, you're not at the front, fighting and killing people...", he answered. „...Let's hope it doesn't come to that...", Will slowly answered. „Don't tell me you would fight for Hitler!", Paul shouted... „For Hitler? Never! But to defend my country...

my family... Yes! I would fight for them, Paul." "I don't want to speak about that...", Paul finally answered, panicking at the thought of seeing Will leaving for the front... "Hey! Don't get panicky, my love! It's not as if the Reich was threaten... And the war could end sooner then we think...", Will answered, trying to reassure his lover. From that moment, Paul never stopped thinking about the fact that, one day, Will could very well be sent to the front should more soldiers be needed over there... He had to think about something to make sure Will would never have to leave him... He knew Will loved his country, his family... He could understand why his lover would sacrifice his life to defend the ones he loved. But Paul could never let him go! Never! No. "Will's name will never be added to the endless list of dead soldiers, killed for nothing", Paul said to himself. "No way! No fucking way!" Problem was: Paul had no idea... no plan... So he kept thinking about it, and decided he would have to talk to Franz about that, since he knew his friend would never let Lutz go either! "Two heads are better than one", he said to himself. A few days later, Paul talked to Franz about his worries, and his friend grinned before saying: "....I'm glad to see I'm not the only one worried about that... I just can't stop thinking about that..." – "Well, let's worry together. Perhaps, if we work together on this, we will find a way out...", Paul answered. "Yeah!", Franz answered. A week later, on November 25, 1943, madame Louise (Paul's governess) entered the drawing-room to tell him: "Monsieur Paul... you have a call in your study..." "Who's calling?" "...A man named Herr Koch... He's German, with a very strong accent..." "Herr Koch? Are you sure?", Paul asked, in a worried voice... "Oui monsieur..." Paul knew perfectly well who Oberstleutnant Heinz Koch was: He was Will's superior officer... Paul had not seen him since 1940, when he had been arrested because he didn't have his I.D. papers on him... Why was Herr Koch calling him? Had something happened to Will? Or to Lutz? Paul ran to his study and took the phone... "Oui... Paul de Brion speaking!" "Monsieur de Brion? This is Oberstleutnant Koch speaking... do you remember me?" "Of course Sir... Has something happened to Will... or to Lutz? How come you have my phone number?" – "(...) Look monsieur de Brion... I know you and Will are... very good friends, shall I say... and you know I've always loved Will as my own son..." – "(...) Yes Sir, I know..." "Don't worry... nothing happened to Will... nor to Lutz. They are fine. They don't know I'm calling you though... I must see you... as soon as possible. It's urgent." „Tomorrow..." „No. Today! It's very urgent!" „Very well Sir." And they agreed to meet later that same day at Paul's office on the Champs Elysées... „How are you Sir", Paul asked the German officer, as he was introduced into his office... „Fine Fine...", Oberstleutnant Koch answered, smiling at Paul... „You haven't changed much monsieur de Brion, since the last time I saw you... You have matured... but still looking as handsome as you did three years ago..." „Thank you Sir... Please, do sit down..." Paul was very anxious to learn why Her Koch wanted to see him so urgently... and it showed on his face. „(...) If I wanted to see you monsieur de Brion... It's because... I know you and Will are very... close to one another... What you two do together is none of my business... and don't worry, that's not the reason why I am here today... no. And I also know Lutz is a very good friend of yours... I understand you speak German, monsieur de Brion... would you mind if I'd switch to German?" „Not at all", Paul answered, giving the German officer a friendly smile... „Thank you. (...) I've received a telegram from Berlin this morning... „Yes...", Paul answered, with a worried frown... „(...) Perhaps you haven't heard yet... But during the night of the 22nd to the 23rd, Berlin was the main target of a massive air raid..." – „Huh?" „Yes... Saturday night... The RAF began bombing Berlin... and according to the secret reports we've received... there is not much left of Berlin to see..." „I'm sorry to hear that...", Paul answered, trying to guess why Oberstleutnant Koch was telling him that... Then Herr Koch raised his eyes to look at Paul straight in his eyes. After a long moment of silence he said: „You see monsieur de Brion... during the last bombing... much of Berlin was under clouds, so the RAF pilot's didn't know what they were bombing... and... most of the damage was to the residential areas... West of the Centre..." Paul raised his eyes to look at Herr Koch: Now, his face was as white as the wall behind him... „I think you've been to Berlin on a few occasions... so, I guess you know the city well...", Herr Koch added... „...Yes, I do...", Paul slowly answered. „...As I said, the other night, most of the damage was to Tiergarten... Schöneberg... Spandau and... Charlottenburg..." „Charlottenburg? But... that's where... where Will's family lives, as well as Lutz's!", Paul shouted... „Yes!", Herr Koch answered, with a very sad look on his face. „Charlottenburg was severely hit..." Paul suddenly raised from his chair and walked around his desk to Herr Koch... „...You don't mean...", he started to say, as he was now beginning to see why Herr

149

Koch wanted to see him... „Yes, I'm afraid...", Herr Koch answered, with tears in his eyes... „Are they..." „Please monsieur de Brion... please, sit down, will you?" Paul walked back to his chair and sat... „...Thousands of deaths... thousands are homeless... Because of the dry weather conditions, firestorms ignited... And to make things worst, the sirens didn't go on in time to warn them. They didn't suffer, monsieur de Brion. They were all sleeping. They never realized what was happening to them. They all died instantaneously..." „.... Will's parents? (...) and Lutz's?" „All of them... There's nothing left standing on their street..." – „But..." „(...) When the giant demolition bombs felt, they blew away blocks of houses, making rubble of the entire district, blasting bodies out into the streets... According to our reports... in the ruins, on the streets, in the branches of trees where bombs had blown them... lay the dead. Some with their eyes wide open, staring..." Paul was silently crying... listening to Herr Koch... „The telegram I received this morning from Berlin was to tell me I had to announce Will and Lutz... their parents have been killed during the bombing... but I didn't have the courage to do so...", Herr Koch said, with his eyes full of tears... „I just didn't have the courage...", he added, covering his face with his hands... Paul turned his head to look at a large window, and through that window he could see people walking up and down the Champs Elysées... They were smiling... Some were laughing... For a while, he looked at them through the window... Then, right before his eyes... he saw Will's mother... his father, his sister Karen... Then he saw Lutz's parents... They were all smiling at him... He could see them talk... their lips were moving... but he couldn't hear them... Then he started to cry like a baby... After a few minutes crying... Paul raised his eyes and looked at Herr Koch... Herr Koch took an envelope from his pocket and gave it to Paul, saying: „Here... I've obtained a leave for Will and Lutz... They must go to Berlin, to identify the bodies... or at least, what remains of them... Can I count on you?", Herr Koch asked, with tears running down his cheeks... „I've personally asked the authorities in Berlin not to dispose of the remains before Will and Lutz get there... and they reluctantly agreed... You know, there are so many dead... They hurry to bury them as soon as possible into mass graves... to make sure diseases are not spreading. You'll find them at the morgue..." Paul raised to his feet and walked over to Herr Koch... then sat onto a chair next to the German officer. He took the envelope and looked at the German officer straight in the eyes and said: „Thank you for all you did Sir... and count on me: I'm going to take them to Berlin...(...) And what about your own family, Herr Koch?" „Oh, my family is not in Berlin. We're from a small village in Bavaria..." – „Good for you", Paul answered, before asking: „And what about you?" – „What do you mean?", the officer asked... Paul looked at Herr Koch, and then said: „Herr Koch... I have no doubt you are a very intelligent man... and you're a good man... (...) You know as well as I do that sooner or later, the Reich will lose the war. It's only a question of time. You know... with Will and Lutz... we went to see Lutz's brother at the Oberwesel military hospital... He was wounded at Stalingrad... We know what happened over there..." „(...) Oh..." „...I... wouldn't like to see you -and I don't intent to see Will nor Lutz- sent to the Russian front! Do you understand?" „(...) I'm too old for that...", Herr Koch answered.... „I'm happy to hear that... But look at me Sir: Will and Lutz are much younger than you are, and I'll do all I can to make sure they are not sent over there... do you understand me?" „(...)" „...If I need your help, Sir... Will you help me? Can I count on you Sir?" „What are you asking me to do?", the officer asked... „For the moment... nothing! But if I need your help in the future... will you be there for us?", Paul asked, looking at the German officer straight in the eyes... „(...) Yes... I'll be there for you, count on me monsieur de Brion". „Thank you Sir. Now tonight, I'm going to talk to Will, Lutz and Ludwig... and we'll go to Berlin as soon as possible..." – „Thank you monsieur de Brion. I knew I was right to ask for your help, even if you're French..." Paul looked at Herr Koch and answered: „French... German... I don't give a damn about that... I love them, and that's all that counts to me..." – „(...) I knew". „Yes", Paul answered, with a sincere smile on his face... After Herr Koch had left, Paul gave Will a call and told him: „Hey... Would you ask Lutz and Franz to come tonight... We could have supper all together..." – „Sure...", Will answered... That night... they all had supper... and after the supper, they went to the drawing-room to have coffee... „You too Ludwig... come with us", Paul told Ludwig, seeing his young friend was walking to his den... „I have something to say..." They all sat down, and coffee was served... Then... Paul rose to his feet and, with tears in his eyes, he looked at his lover and at his other friends... „I have something to tell you (...) Oh God, help me!", he said... Then... he told them everything... „(...) That's not true!", Ludwig cried out... „That's not true. That's a lie..." Paul simply sat down and looked at Will, his eyes full of tears... „I wish it wasn't true... I swear to God, I wish it wasn't true", Paul finally said. Will took his brother into his arms... Lutz simply sat there... shocked! „Say something Lutz...", Franz said, looking at his lover... Lutz slowly turned his head to look at Franz. He opened his mouth... but no sound came out of it. Franz took Lutz into his arms and began kissing his hair... Lutz just didn't move. He had no tear in his eyes... nothing. He was just sitting there... staring... Then, after a while he rose to his feet and shouted: „I Want to kill him! I'm going to kill him with my own hands!" „Huh?", Franz asked... „(...) Hitler! I'm going to kill him... that bastard!" „Now guys... please... sit back, will you... I've got something else to say...", Paul said. They all went back to sit and looked at Paul. „(...) This is the worst day in my life... and it's yours too... It took all the courage I have to tell you that... I... But I know one thing...", he said, looking at Will... „You still have Ludwig and me...". Then, looking at Lutz he added: „And you Lutz, you still have Franz as well as your brother Hans... So, we'll built on that guys... count on me. We may be bleeding tonight... but we are still alive, and we are together." Will was holding his young brother Ludwig tight against him, kissing him all over his hair... „(...) I have something here for you Will...", Paul said... „A letter your mother gave to me more than a year ago, making me swear I would give it to you, should something bad happen to your parents..." Will took the envelope, opened it, and began reading aloud his mother's letter: „My dear son... If you're reading this letter, it's because something happened to your father and to me... I gave it to Paul, knowing he loves you as much as we do! We have trusted you and Paul with Ludwig's life. Now, your sacred duty is to take good care of him. We know that, with Paul's help, you will... Your sacred duty is not to fight for Hitler... Please! Your sacred duty is to the ones you love! We love you Wilhelm... Please, please... take good care of you, of Paul and of your baby brother... And Ludwig: Swear you will obey Will and Paul. They are your parents now! (...) We love you both, Will and Ludwig... We will always love you. Be happy sons... and go on with your life. Make us proud of you! p.s. Paul... we love you, and count on you!" After Will had read the letter, they all started crying like babies... Will was holding Ludwig, his strong arms wrapped around his younger brother... Will looked up at Paul and said: „Come here you... We're family..." Paul walked over to Will and Ludwig and the three of them hugged in a tight embrace... Paul raised his head to look at Lutz and Franz and said: „Come here you too... We're all family here..." Later that night, Paul looked at them and said: „I called Kurt... and he's ready to ay the four of us to Berlin tomorrow..." „(...) No", Will said... „Ludwig is staying here... it's too dangerous..." Ludwig looked at Will... „Look Will", Ludwig said to his brother... „I'm not a baby anymore... I want to go. I need to be there. Besides, if we die going there... We'll all die together..." „(...) He's right, Will", Paul said, looking at his lover... Will looked at his young brother and, after a while he said: „(...) Okay. You're coming bro..." „Thanks Will", Ludwig answered, giving his brother a peck on his forehead... „I love you..." – „I love you too bro...", Will answered, caressing his brother's hair... „I love you so much..." – „I know...", Ludwig answered... Then François walked into the drawing-room, smiling, coming back from the library where he had spent his evening. Looking at his friends, he realized something wrong was going on. As he sat, Paul told him everything. François was speechless. Later that night, Paul took François to his study and told him: „Look François... As you know, you can't come to Berlin with us. Only three people can travel along with me... And I won't hide from you that our trip will be a dangerous one, since every day and every night the Allies keep bombing Germany..." „I want to go with you...", François said, looking at Paul with tears in his eyes... Paul smiled at him and said: „I know you would like to come... but you can't" „But you're all I have... if you die..." „No François... You understand why you can't come, don't you? You must live your own life François... You're going to be eighteen soon... and You're doing well in College. You must go on with your dream of becoming a doctor, if that's what you want to become... Now, you've always be very mature for your age... so look at me... and listen to me well..." François raised his eyes to look at Paul... „All was so sudden", Paul started to explain... „I didn't have time to make a lot of planning... so... first, take this..." – „What's that?" „That document makes you the official tenant of a flat... not too far from here... So if something bad happens to us, you'll have a nice place to stay..." Then Paul knelt in front of François and said to his young friend: „Now François... look at me... good... You see François, I love you as if you were my own brother... here...", Paul said, giving François two envelopes. A very thick one... and a very thin one. „In the thin envelope, you'll find my last will... don't open it unless you hear I have died, you understand?" – „Yes", François

answered, his eyes full of tears... „Now open the second envelope..."
When François opened the thick envelope, he saw it was full with Swiss
Francs... „You have a small fortune in there...", Paul started to say... „And
I give it to you. Whatever happens to us, it's yours to keep François. Don't
you deposit that money into the bank. Don't change that money into
French Francs, you understand?" „Yes", François answered, sobbing...
„You have enough in there to make it through University... and well
beyond that..." „...That's not what I want Paul... I don't want money... I
want to be with you..." „Hey! I swear... We don't intend to die... Relax pal!
It's just in case... And as soon as we're back, I'm going to tell you what to
do with that money. Don't worry, okay? We'll be back!" „You swear?",
François asked, his eyes still full of tears... „(...) I can't François", Paul
answered, giving his young friend a peck on the tip of his nose... „But I
swear we'll do our best to stay alive and to be back as soon as possible..."

TEN

At four o'clock the day after, Paul, Will, Lutz and Franz met their friend and pilot Kurt at the Bourget Airport... Kurt looked at his friends and said: „Paul told me about your families... I'm so sorry guys... You don't know how much I'm sorry... (...) Ready to go?" „Yes", they all answered. So they left Paris... and as soon as they saw they had crossed over the Rhine river, they got nervous, as they realized Kurt was screening the skies to make sure no enemy planes were flying above them... „(...) Don't worry guys...", Kurt finally said to his worried friends... „Usually, they come at night..." As they were nearing Berlin, Paul looked out and said to his friends: „Look at the beautiful sunset..." Kurt looked back at Paul and said: „You're looking at the East, Paul..." „So what?", Paul answered... „Have you ever seen the sun set over there? (...) You're not looking at the sunset Paul... You're looking at Berlin burning...", Kurt replied. And through the portholes, they all looked at the sky... so beautiful... so yellow and red... A city was dying down there... right before their eyes... „That can't be", Ludwig said... „Oh yes pal...", Kurt replied... „That's our city burning..." Then, Kurt started to listen very carefully into his headphones... The others in the plane heard him exclaim: „What?" Of course, they couldn't hear what Kurt was hearing in his headphones... what the guy at Tempelhof Airport was telling him... „(...) No", they heard Kurt answer into his microphone... „No... I can't go there... I'm coming from Paris, and my tanks are almost empty (...) Yeah (...) Okay... just send a car over there, to pick us up, will you? (...) Yeah. Thanks", they heard Kurt say to the guy at Tempelhof... „What's going on...", Will asked Kurt... „Can't land at Tempelhof... Too much smoke over there, cause of all the fires in Berlin..." – „But... where the hell are you going to take us?", Will asked, worried... „Well...", Kurt answered, grinning... „The Führer might be crazy... but he knew what he was doing when he ordered highways to be built all over Germany... We will use a highway near Berlin to land our plane... At Tempelhof they said there is no smoke over that highway...“ „(...) Are you crazy or what?“, Paul shouted... „A highway? What's that?“ „(...) You'll see soon enough...“, Kurt answered, laughing... And indeed a few minutes later, they were landing on a beautiful highway... At the time, only Germany had highways... Only in the late 50' would highways start to be built in America and elsewhere in the world... After Kurt had landed his plane with it's passengers, they all got off the plane and looked around... „...Look at the barn over there...“, Kurt said... „I'll drive the plane right over there...“ „Why?“, Lutz asked... „You want to ay back to Paris, don't you?“, Kurt asked... „Oh... sure...“, Lutz answered, not knowing what else to say... „Well... we need a plane in good condition to go back... If the RAF pilots see our plane, they will destroy it...“ So Kurt slowly drove the plane to the barn they had stopped, then they all helped him to roll it inside the barn. After that, Kurt closed the big doors and went to talk to the farmer. A bit later, he was back and said to his friends: „No problem... It's okay. We can leave the plane there...“ Soon after, they saw an army car arrive... The driver stopped his car and looked at Kurt, saying: „Leutnant Weiner?“ „Yes“, Kurt answered, grinning... „Ah...“, the driver answered, smiling at the pilot... „I was ordered to pick you up here... I hope you made a nice trip...“ – „Could have been worst...“, Kurt answered... „(...) So... you're going to Berlin, huh?“, the driver asked... „Yes... to the Adlon Hotel...Can you drive us there?“, Paul answered... „Huh?“, the driver answered, looking at Paul... „Where?“ „(...) The Adlon Hotel...“ „Well you have a problem Sir... The Adlon doesn't exist anymore! Completely destroyed...“ „Huh?“, Paul answered... „Yes Sir... There's not much left standing over there... Hope you have another place to stay, cause the Adlon... well...“ „No problem pals“, Kurt said... „You'll all stay at our home... My parents are not rich or anything... and the house is not very big... but at least, you'll have a place to stay. And I know our house has not been damaged...“ They all agreed, and thanked Kurt for his kindness... „It's only natural guys... you would do the same for me...“, Kurt answered... „Let's go...“, the car driver said... So they all went to Berlin... and soon, as they got near the city, they realized the air was thick with smoke over there... „Do you have handkerchiefs with you?“, the driver asked them... „Wrap them around your head to cover your nose and mouth...", he explained to his passengers... „That will help. (...) Where do you live, Leutnant Weiner?" Kurt explained to the driver where his home was located... and the driver answered: „Okay... But I'm afraid we'll have to drive through the center of the city to go there... all the other avenues and streets are blocked by debris..." As they were driving through Berlin, all they could see was destruction. A few buildings were still burning... „No more water to put out the fires... the water mains are busted", the driver explained... „So they just let them burn..." They finally made it to a large Avenue they all recognized... or at least... tried to recognize: Unter den Linden... Not much was left standing on what used to be the Champs Elysées of Berlin... „...I can't believe my eyes...", Ludwig said, stunned, as they were driving near the Brandenburg Tor (Brandenburg Gate...), or what was left of it... „What about the New Chancellery?", Will asked, secretly hoping it had been reduced to rubbles... „Unscratched...", their driver answered... „But don't worry guys... the Allies will be back...", he said, grinning... knowing from what his passengers had already said that they were not Nazis... As they reached Kurt's home, Kurt said: „Welcome to my parent's house..." Their driver left them there, and they all went inside where they were introduced to Kurt's parents: „...We are truly sorry to hear about your parents...", Kurt's father said... „It's terrible... but you are most welcome to stay here with us... for as long as you need to... or for as long as this house is standing, I should say..." The day after, Kurt borrowed his father's car and drove his friends to the morgue... „Ah yes...", the man at the morgue said to them... „We were expecting you...(...) Herr Lutz Reinberger?", the man asked... „Yes, that's me...", Lutz answered... „You're first... Please Sir, follow me..." Lutz followed the man to another room, and about twenty minutes later, he came back... looking sick and crying... Franz went to him and took him into his arms... „Herr von Rundstedt?", the man asked. Will and Ludwig rose to their feet and both of them answered „Yes" „you're next..." „No Will... Don't go there...", Lutz shouted to his best friend... „Don't go... it's a nightmare over there..." Paul rose to his feet, looked at Will and Ludwig and said to them: „Let me go, please. I knew them well, and I'll be able to identify them... Don't worry. I don't want you two to see them like that..." „...But we have to...", Will started to say... „No ... you don't. I'm here. I'll go.", Paul answered...

„Let him go...", Lutz said to Will and Ludwig... „I wish I had not gone there... I'm telling you, don't go!" Will looked at Ludwig and asked his brother: „...What do you think bro?" After a moment of silence, Ludwig answered to his brother with tears in his eyes: „Let Paul go...". „Okay", Will answered, looking at Paul... „Will you do that for us?" Paul looked back at Will and Ludwig and with a very sad smile on his face and answered: „I will...". Then, looking at the man in charge of the morgue, Paul said: „I'm ready Sir..." Indeed, Paul was able to identify Will and Ludwig's parents and their young sister Karen... Their bodies were atrociously mutilated, and some parts were missing... „...That's all they found...", the man in charge of the morgue said to Paul... „I'm sorry..." – „Thanks", Paul answered with tears in his eyes, feeling sick... „Do you have a lavatory around here?" – „Yes... to your right...", the man from the morgue answered... „Just give me a few minutes, will you?" „Sure" Paul went to the lavatory to throw up... After a few minutes... he came out of the lavatory, looked at the man still standing there, waiting for him... and said: „Thank you Sir... I needed that..." „I understand...", the man answered. „Let's go back to the others, shall we?", Paul said... They walked back to the room where his friends were waiting... Paul then looked at Will and Ludwig and said: „(...) It's them. I have no doubt whatsoever. It's them... All three of them..." „(...) Thanks Paul, for what you just did...", Will answered, crying... „Ummm...", the man in charge of the morgue said... „May I ask you what you intend to do with their remains? It's impossible to find a coffin nowadays in Berlin, you know..." Paul walked over to the man and took him apart, and the two of them started talking. Paul gave the man a very generous tip and, looking down at all the Reichsmarks Paul was giving him, the man finally said: „...It will be done tonight Sir... and you can come by tomorrow morning. The funeral urns will be ready..." – „Thank you Sir", Paul answered... As they were all leaving the morgue, Paul explained to his friends the remains would be cremated during the night... and that the urns would be ready for pick up the day after... „That's the only solution...", Paul stated... „Yes", they all answered... After that, they all went back to Kurt's house. Of course, no one of them was hungry... and all of them went to sleep on empty stomachs... It took them a long time... but finally, they all fell asleep... Then, the sirens went on... „What's that", Paul asked, his heart pounding... „Quick", they heard Kurt's father shout... „No time to get dress... we have to run to the shelter as fast as we can..." All they had time to grab was their coats and their shoes... „Come... quick...", Kurt's father said... „Follow us..." They all ran outside of the house... then down the street to a bomb shelter... As they were running down the stairs, Paul almost fell... but Ludwig took hold of his friend's arm and helped him... „(...) Thanks dude!", Paul said to Ludwig, with a grin on his face... „Sure...", Ludwig answered, grinning... „What are friends for, huh?" „Yeah..." They all went deep under the ground and walked into the bomb shelter, where they all sat down on the floor. It didn't take long before the shelter got crowded... They all sat one next to the other. Then, they heard Kurt's mother say: „Our Father, Who art in Heaven, Hollowed be Thy Name (...)" Then, they heard voices all around them, saying: „(...) Thy kingdom come, Thy will be done..." Paul looked at Will... took his lover's hand into his and softly said: „(...) On earth as it is in heaven..." And they all started to recite the prayer which Jesus Christ had thought to His disciples... After the last „Amen" had been said... a total silence fell ... They were all waiting... and waiting... Then... They heard the first bombs fall... The pounding went on... and on... and on... and dust started to fall onto them from the ceiling... „Do you think it will hold?", Will asked Paul, looking up at the ceiling... „It will... I'm sure it will! I didn't come all the way to Berlin to die in this bomb shelter! No way!" Paul answered, smiling at his lover... Then, the bomb shelters lost power and all the lights went off... Seconds later, they saw people all around them light up candles... some even had with them old oil lamps... Obliviously for most of them, it wasn't their first time in there, and they were getting used to it... As the kept hearing the deafening sound of bombs falling above them, Paul turned to Kurt's father and asked him: „... Do you think the bombs are falling right above us?" Kurt's father grinned and answered: „...No... From the sound we hear... I'd say they are falling West of here... If they start falling right above us, you'll see and hear the difference... that's if we are still here to hear them fall..." Paul grinned and answered: „Don't worry Sir... I'm sure we'll be okay! We're going to make it through..." „I sure hope you're right son...", Kurt's father replied... „I sure hope you're right..." Fortunately for them, the air raid on Berlin in the night of the 24th to the 25th of November 1943 was a small one... and after what seemed to be an eternity... silence came back... along with the electricity... Then they heard the sirens again... telling them the raid was over... „That's it for the night, folks! Welcome to Berlin...", Kurt's father said... "Let's go upstairs, to see if we still have a house, shall we?" With the rest of the crowd, they slowly made their way out of the bomb shelter. When they finally reached the street level, they went out and looked around them... The air was hard to breathe... with all the smoke... Instinctively, they all put handkerchiefs over their nose and mouth... "You're getting use to it, huh?", Kurt's father asked them... "Shit!", Ludwig answered... "Yeah...", Lutz and Franz said... "Let's go, shall we?", Kurt's father said... "Let's go see if our house is still there..." They started walking, holding to their handkerchiefs... As they were walking, they all looked at the buildings burning not too far from where they were... Even with their handkerchiefs, it was hard to breathe... "Put it back over your nose...", Paul said to Will, seeing his lover was suffocating... "Yeah...", Will answered, coughing. "... Never come to Berlin without a handkerchief...", they heard Kurt's father say... "It's rather handy around here nowadays..." They all laughed... As they were walking towards Kurt's house, Kurt turned to his Mum and Dad and said: "...I hope it's still there..." With all that smoke around them, they couldn't tell... "Do you see it?", Kurt's Mum asked him... "I can't Mum... the smoke is too thick to see...", Kurt answered. But they all knew perfectly well that if the smoke was so thick all around them... it was because buildings and houses were burning not too far... "Do you see it now?", Kurt's Mum thanked her son for the second time... "Not yet Mum... not yet..." As they were all walking back towards Kurt's house in Berlin, all they could see around them was destruction, and buildings burning. The smoke from the fires was thick and they were all wearing their handkerchiefs over their nose and mouth... They were walking in the middle of the avenue, to stay away as far as possible from the burning structures and from time to time, they would pass right next to people standing there... looking at a building burning... not moving... just sobbing, looking at their home being destroyed by the fire. Eventually they turned on a street and, in the distance, they saw Kurt's house... It was still there... unscratched. "Thank God!", Kurt's mother said, looking at their house... "It's still there..." They all went inside the house and tried to get some rest. Although they were all exhausted, no one was able to fall asleep... as their nervous tension was just too high. So they started to drink coffee... or chicory rather... since coffee was a long gone product from the shelfs in Germany. When the sun rose, hidden by the smoke from the burning fires, Paul looked at Kurt and in a very low voice he whispered to him: „Do you have a shovel here?" „...Yes... Why?" „We've got a job to do... at the cemetery..." Later that morning, they all went to the morgue to get the funeral urns. Then, they went to the cemetery where Will and Lutz families had plots... Due to the events, a formal funeral was out of the question. So they walked over to the von Rundstedt's plot, where Lutz dug a hole large and deep enough to contain Will's parents as well as his sister's urns... A prayer was said... and then, they moved on to the Weiner's plot, where Lutz's parents were put to rest. Another prayer was said and after that, they remained silent, looking at the graves... tears running down their cheeks... After a while... Paul softly said to his friends: „Now... let's go my friends. Let's go... let them rest in peace." They all went back to Kurt's house, packed their belongings... and as they were about to leave, Kurt's father said to them: „I'll drive you to your plane... no problem!" „Are you sure dad?", Kurt asked his father... „Don't worry son... I'll be fine!" Kurt kissed his mother good-bye and then his father drove them through Berlin -or what was left of the once beautiful city- then to their plane. Once there, as they were about to board the plane, Paul took Kurt's father apart and said to him: „Sir... That's all I have left...", giving the man a bundle of Reichsmarks... „Promise me you and your wife will leave Berlin as soon as possible... Please Sir?" Kurt's father looked down at all the Reichsmarks Paul was giving him... then smiled at the young Frenchman... „(...) Why are you doing this?", the man asked... „Because you're a good man Sir... and because your son Kurt is my friend. That's why! I want to make sure you and your wife don't get killed in that damn city... The RAF will be back and perhaps next time, you won't be as lucky as we were last night..." The man looked at Paul and answered: „You're a good man too Paul... God bless you!" – „Are you going to leave Berlin?" „(...) Yes, we will... I swear to you we will!" – „Good!", Paul answered, smiling at Kurt's father. And as he had said, that very same day, Kurt's parents left Berlin for good. And thank God they did, for a few weeks later their house was indeed totally destroyed during a bombing... Once they had all boarded the plane, Kurt looked back at Paul and said to him: „(...) I know what you did Paul... I owe you..." „No my friend, you owe me nothing! ... Thanks to you, we all made it to Berlin, to pay our last respects to Will and Lutz's families. Without your help, it would never have been possible. Now, take us back to Paris, will you? And preferably... in one piece!", Paul answered, smiling at his friend... Kurt laughed and answered: „My friends... here we go! Hold on to hour hats!" And a few hours later, they safely landed at the Bourget Airport... „Thank God, we're back", Paul said, looking at the terminal... „Yeah!", they all answered in one voice. A page of their life had been turned... and from now on, things would never be the same anymore. But they didn't know it yet.

ELEVEN

A few days later, as Paul was walking into the drawing-room on Avenue Foch, he noticed the lid over the grand piano had been shut down... He asked madame Louise, his governess, about it and she simply answered: „Monsieur Will asked me to do it. He said he won't play anymore..." „(...) I see", Paul answered with a sad look on his face... „And I understand..." „I hope you do, because I don't... I loved to hear him play... he plays so beautifully...", madame Louise answered. „Yes", Paul replied... „I know. But that's his decision, and we're going to respect it, won't we?" „Oui monsieur...", madame Louise answered, with a sad look on her face. Then, and before they even noticed it... 1944 was there! „Happy new year!", Paul said to his lover, kissing him... „Happy new year to you too...", Will answered... „The new year can't be worst than the last, huh?" – „No", Paul answered „I don't think so..." Thank God they didn't have a crystal ball to look into the future... One night of April 1944, as they were all having supper at Paul's mansion, Lutz said: „(...) My brother Hans is going to be released from the hospital. Franz and I have been talking about that... and we've decided Hans will come to Paris, to live with us. He can't go back to Berlin, since there's nothing left for him over there..." „Good!", Paul said... „He'll be safe here, with us..." „I hope you're right...", Lutz answered. „You don't seem to be sure about that...", Paul answered, looking at his friend... „(...) Look Paul... The way things are going, I don't know... How long do you think we'll be here in France, huh? On all fronts, the Reich is..." „Yes, I know", Paul said... „And if you want to know, I think it's only a matter of months before Hitler is defeated. Now guys, it's time to talk!" „(...) What do you mean?", Will asked his lover. „Look... I mean... It's obvious Germany has lost the war. At least, that's what I think... and I sure don't intend to stay still and see you guys sent to the front. No way!", Paul answered. „(...) Are you asking us... to desert... and to go to the enemy?", Lutz angerly asked... „No guys... That's not what I'm asking you to do. But I'm asking you to save your skin, that's what I'm asking you..." – „What do you mean?", Will asked, looking at Paul straight in the eyes... Paul took all his time. He looked at Will... then at Lutz... and he finally said: „Hitler will bring down Germany with him... He doesn't care... And you all know it. Germany -or what's left of it- can't be saved. You know that too. Do you want to die, fighting for him? There's nothing left to fight for... As hard to say to you as it is, Germany is vanquished! (...) Now, what do you intend to do? And if I have to shoot you myself in a leg or in a foot to save you from being sent to the front... I will... I swear I will..." Franz looked at Lutz and said to his lover: „No way I'm going to let you go to the front! You have no one left in Germany to fight for! Thanks to Hitler, they are all dead! I won't stay here and see you go... and get killed for nothing. And if I have to, I'll do the same as Paul said: I'll shoot you in a foot, to make sure they can't send you to the front. I swear I will!" „(...) Calm down guys...", Lutz answered... „I mean, it's not as if we had to leave tomorrow for the Russian front, huh?" „(...) No", Paul calmly answered... „But it could come to that..." – „Yes...", Will answered, looking at Lutz... „It could come to that..." They all remained silent for a while. Then, Will asked Paul: „So...What do you want us to do, huh?" „I don't know yet... I don't know. We'll have to think about that..." Early in May of 1944 Hans, Lutz's brother, was discharged from the military hospital and came to Paris, to live with his brother and Franz... One night, as they were all having supper at Paul's mansion, Hans unrolled a large map of Europe he had brought with him. „Let's study the situation guys, shall we?", he said to his friends... So they all looked at the large map as Hans began to explain to them: „To the East, the Russians are on the offensive again. They have already taken Kiev, and are pushing towards the Dniestr River... here... To the South, in Italy... the Allies are pushing towards Rome, and I have no doubt the city will soon fall into their hands. Now, we know the Allies are massing troops all over England so.. we can expect them to soon try to land somewhere... here... in France!" „Where?", Paul asked Hans, raising his head from the map to look at him... „Don't know", Hans answered. „Can't the Wehrmacht stop them from landing?", Franz asked... Hans looked at his brother's lover and answered: „I doubt it. You see, over the last few months, whole regiments have been moved out of France and sent to the Russian front, thus weakening our defenses here, in France. So I guess unless the Kriegsmarine can sink the landing ships as soon as they leave England, I don't see how we could stop the invasion..." „...I'm sure their landing ships will be well protected... A few might be sank, but the rest will reach France...", Lutz commented... „Right!", his brother Hans answered. „That's what I think too..." „...Do you think Paris could be threaten?", Paul asked, with a worried look on his face... „Look Paul", Hans started to say, turning to friend... „If the Allies land in France, they will want to take Paris, that's for sure! That would be the grand prize... the city of light... That would be a very big lost for Hitler..." „In that case... we must prepare ourselves... make plans...", Paul answered. „Yes", Hans whispered... A few days later, Franz called Paul. „Hey... remember what we talked about the other night...with Hans?" „Yes...", Paul answered. „Well... I've been doing some thinking, and I think I have a plan..." „Huh?", Paul answered, all excited... „Yup!" „Well... don't keep me waiting... What is it?" „.... Can't tell you at the moment. I'm at the embassy (...) Anyway, you know that next week it's going to be my birthday... or have you forgotten?", Franz asked, laughing... „...Of course not...", Paul answered, laughing too... „Well... my friends here at work are throwing a small party for me... and you, Will, Lutz, Ludwig and Hans will receive an invitation..." „Oh?" „Yeah. And I've ask our official photographer to be present... to take pictures of all of us as a group... but also of our friends separately..." „Huh? (...) But why?" „Ahhh... That's my secret... and it's part of my plan...", Franz answered, still laughing... A few days later, Paul, Will, Lutz, Ludwig and Hans all went to the Swiss embassy to attend Franz's birthday party and, indeed, they were all photographed... „...Why the hell can't I smile?", Lutz asked the photographer, when is turn came to be separately photographed... „...Oh come on Lutz!", Paul said... „Have you ever seen pictures of your Mum and dad?" „Yeah sure!" „Well... Were they smiling on those pictures, huh?" „....No. But why can't we smile?" „I don't know Lutz", Franz answered... „But that's how it's done. So shut up, and don't smile, please?" „Okay okay... but only because you ask...", Lutz answered, not happy at all... So all the pictures were taken, and obviously, Franz was very happy! A few days later, Franz called Paul: „I've got to see you...", he said. „Sure... Why don't you and Lutz come for supper tonight?" „No no... just you and me! (...) I could be at your office on the Champs Elysées at ten, tomorrow morning...", Franz said. „Sure... But you've got me worried..." „No need! You'll be pleased..." „Okay then... At ten tomorrow morning..." „Fine!" And indeed at ten the morning after, Franz was sitting right in front of Paul in his office... „So I'll be pleased, huh?", Paul asked Franz, grinning... „Yup!", Franz answered, with a big smile on his face... Then Franz took something from a large envelope and gave it to Paul... „What are those?", Paul asked... „Look at them...", Franz answered, beaming... Paul took the first passport, opened it... looked at the picture in it... then, he went through the second... the third... then the fourth... „I don't understand... Swiss passports? For Lutz, Will, Ludwig and Hans? (...) Why? (...) They are fakes, aren't they?", Paul asked, stunned... „Oh no... they are not! Those are real and valid Swiss passports! Our friends are now Swiss citizens..." – „But... those are not their names...", Paul said, looking at the names in the passports... „Of course not!" Paul took one passport and again opened it... He saw Will's picture in it, but the name under it said „Wilhelm Schmidt", from Kloten, Switzerland. Then he opened another one... with Ludwig's picture in it... „Ludwig Keitel", from Einsiedeln, Switzerland... „All those guys really do exist. Each one of them has the right age... and they are all... farmers!" „Farmers?", Paul asked, looking at his friend... „Yup!", Franz answered, laughing his heart out... „But why? I don't understand..." „Look Paul... I've borrowed their identities... Those guys are farmers, they don't travel, and they've never asked for a passport! Probably never will either. And certainly not before this damn war is over! Where would they want to go?" „...So that's why you wanted those pictures taken at the embassy the other night!" „Yup! (...) So now, with those passports, not only can they come to Switzerland... but they can go to Spain, Portugal... even England, where they would never get arrested, just because they are Germans... So if we ever have to flee someday, it will be easy to cross the borders..." „Right!", Paul answered, laughing... „Great idea... But for the moment, let's keep that a secret between you and me, shall we?" „Of course...", Franz answered, grinning... Paul looked back at the Swiss passports right before his eyes and then said: „You're brilliant, Franz!" „Thanks!", a beaming Franz answered. And that brilliant idea didn't come too soon for on June 6th, 1944... the Allied did land in Normandy, and began pushing East and South...

TWELVE

At the end of July, Paul called Oberstleutnant Koch, Will and Lutz's superior officer... „I need to see you Herr Koch... it's urgent!", Paul said to the German officer... And they met... „...Do you remember, last November, when you said we could count on your help?", Paul asked the officer... „Yes" „Are you still ready to help us?" „Yes... But how can I help?", the officer asked. „The Allies are closing fast... and I've heard the Résistance in Paris is very active..." „...Yes... They are shooting at our guys from every corners. We've already lost a few of our guys..." – „That's what I've heard...", Paul answered, looking at the officer. „And I want you to report that Will and Lutz have been shot, but that their bodies haven't been found..." – „What?", the German officer exclaimed... „Yes Sir... That's what we need you to do, in order to save their lives. And as soon as it's done, let me know: I'll make sure Will and Lutz really disappear from Paris, never to be seen in the city again... No one will find them!" There was a long moment of silence, as Herr Koch was obviously thinking about what Paul was asking him to do... „(...) You're asking me to falsify a report! (...) And do you realize that as soon as such a report is filed with the authorities, both of them will be officially dead... both of them will cease to exist..." „Precisely! That's what we need...", Paul answered, grinning... „Can you do that?" The German officer looked at Paul straight in the eyes... then said: „I could be shot should my superiors ever find out about that false report... (...) But I said to you I would help you, and I'm a man of honor! I think I can manage something... But don't do anything before I give you a call. And don't tell Will and Lutz! I want them to act as normally as possible right until the last moment. And as soon as I call you, do what you have to do to make sure they really disappear from view! No one must find them... cause otherwise, we will all be shot!"

„Thanks Sir! And don't worry about that: Not only will they disappear from Paris, but each one of them will have a new identity! And shall you ever need my help, remember: I'll be there for you, just a phone call away...", Paul answered. „Thanks monsieur de Brion. I shall remember that..." Two days later, Paul got a call from Oberstleutnant Koch: „Tomorrow morning, they will be officially dead!" the officer laconically said. „Thanks!", was all Paul answered. That night, Lutz, Franz and Hans came for supper and after the meal, Paul told his friends: „Will and Lutz... tomorrow morning, the two of you will be officially dead!" „Huh?", Will and Lutz exclaimed... Paul burst out laughing... then explained everything to them... „First thing tomorrow morning, we're all moving to Bagatelle...", Paul stated. Then, looking at Lutz and Hans he said: „Tonight, you're not going back to your eat on rue Lapérouse: It's too dangerous. You'll spend the night here, so we can leave very early tomorrow morning. And Franz... I suggest you go back there, and pack their belongings..." „Yes", Franz answered... „I'll be back later..." „Oh and Franz?", Paul said... „Yes..." „Don't bother packing their uniforms... just get rid of them, and make sure no one finds them..." „Yeah!", Franz answered, laughing... „I can't believe we're doing this...", Will said, looking at Lutz... „Want to go fight for Hitler on the Russian front, huh?", Lutz answered, looking at his best friend straight in the eyes... „No", Will answered, looking down at his two feet... „Not really..." „And don't forget Will... we have Oberstleutnant Koch's blessing... and he's our superior officer!", Lutz added... Will raised his head to look at Lutz and after a few seconds he answered: „That's true... He's a good man. I sure hope he's going to be okay! „Oh don't worry about him...", Paul said... „I've already contacted our friend from the Résistance and I've explained every to him. And before the end of the week, Herr Koch will be kidnaped... Our friend swore to me they will take good care of him... and when the time comes, they will make sure he can go back to Bavaria..." „Are you kidding?", Will exclaimed! „No...", Paul answered, laughing... „I told Herr Koch I would be there for him... and I will! Of course, he doesn't know about our plan... but as soon as the guys from the Résistance put their hands on him our friend will explain everything to him..." „You're the devil!", Lutz said, laughing... „Oh and that's not all", Paul said to his friends as he gave them their new passports: „Thanks to Franz... you are all Swiss citizens now... Always carry them with you, so should you get arrested, you'll be able to prove you're from Switzerland, not Germany…" „Right", they all answered, each one of them looking at his new passport! And of course, they were all laughing… „Franz is brilliant!", Lutz said, laughing, looking at his passport… „Yeah! That's what I told him", Paul answered, laughing… „Now guys, we have work to do: Let's start packing… I brought a big truck from the head office. It's parked in the underground garage… and you'll find empty boxes in it… use them to pack all you want to bring with you at Bagatelle…", Paul said. Later that night, Franz came back from rue de la Pérouse and said to Lutz: „I've packed all my things… and all of Hans' belongings… and a few of yours…" – „What did you do with the rest?", Lutz asked, a bit puzzled… „I've spread your cloths evenly between the two bedrooms… Remember: Will and you are supposed to share that eat, and Hans and me are not even suppose to live there. So if tomorrow the military policemen go there… they will be convinced you two left for work as usual, not knowing what was going to happen to you later…", Franz answered, grinning… „Good idea…", Paul answered…. „And what did you do with their uniforms?" „I burned them in the fireplace… and I didn't leave the Wat before they were totally destroyed by the fire. I've even removed the zippers and all the buttons from the ashes…" „Gook thinking!", Lutz answered, laughing… „Hey you!", Franz said to Lutz… „Dead guys are not suppose to be laughing…" „Oops!", Lutz answered… „But I'm not dead yet… according to my schedule here, I still have a few hours to live…", he added still laughing… „Darn!", Franz answered, laughing too… „So I guess I'll have to wait before I can put my hands on your car…" – „Hey, that's true… What about our cars?", Will and Lutz asked Paul… Paul looked at them and said: „I'll have them seized!" „What?", Lutz exclaimed… „Yes! You're dead! And remember: You and Will never paid to me the sale price! So, I have the right to claim back the two cars. Then, I'll sell one to Franz, so he can go to work at the embassy, and come to bagatelle every weekend…" „Yeah… but where will Franz live from now on?", a worried Lutz asked Paul… „Oh no problem!", Paul answered, with a big smile on his face… „You see… last November before we left for Berlin, I had taken one of our Wats off the market, so François could move in it, should something bad happen to us. And that Wat is still empty. So now Franz: It's yours!" „Where is it located?", Franz asked… „Not too far from here… on rue Galilée… on the corner of rue Vernet…" – „Perfect!", Franz answered… „Here is the key…", Paul said.

„Fine... So tomorrow morning, as you all leave for Bagatelle, I'll move my things over there..." Franz said, smiling at Lutz... „Will you come to Bagatelle next weekend?", Lutz asked his lover, not too happy to see that they would be separated during the week... „Count on me!", Franz answered, giving his lover a sweet kiss... Very early the morning after, Paul, Will, Ludwig, Hans and François were leaving Paris... and Franz was taking possession of his new Wat on rue Galilée. In August, the situation in Paris became very unstable as the Allies were closing on the city and the danger of an uprising became evident. Most of the personnel at the Swiss embassy were invited to leave Paris... and Franz gave the ambassador his phone number at Bagatelle, where he told him he could be reached. He then left Paris and went to Bagatelle, where he told his friends about the latest news... „There's an uprising in Paris... and I saw German POW's being led through the streets. Some were treated roughly... others were killed... According to the rumor Général Leclerc, with his Forces and armored vehicles are heading for Paris.(...) When I left, the Métro (subway), the Gendarmerie and the Police were on strike... and orders have been given so there is going to be a general strike starting from tomorrow...", Franz explained. „Won't General von Choltitz fight to keep the city?", Ludwig asked Franz... „It doesn't look like he intends to...", Franz answered. However Von Choltitz did some hard fighting that cost Leclerc's 2nd Division 35 thanks and many vehicles... But in the end, he knew there was not much he could do to stop the French Résistance and Leclerc's Free French Forces... And contrary to the legend, Hitler never ordered Von Choltitz to burn Paris to the ground. It's true that bombs were placed under bridges all across the city, to slow down Leclerc's troops... but they were never detonated. And so, on August 25, Von Choltitz, the military governor of Paris, capitulated... On the same day, Général de Gaulle, leader of the Free French Forces moved back into the War Ministry on the rue Saint-Dominique, then made a rousing speech to the population from the Hôtel de Ville. This was followed on August 26 by a Victory parade down the Champs-Elysées, with German snipers still active. On the 29th, joyous crowds greeted the American Forces... and on that day, another Victory parade down the Champs-Elysées took place. By that time, the city of light had been secured, and the Germans had stopped fighting in the capital... Paris was free again!

THIRTEEN

The news of the Liberation was greeted with a kind of uneasiness at Bagatelle... Of course, all were very happy to hear Von Choltitz had capitulated... but Will and Lutz felt sorry for their comrades that had been killed... and for all the others that had evacuated Paris only to be sent to the Russian front... „For them, the war is not over yet...", Hans commented... „And I'm afraid they are about to learn what hell is all about..." „What's going to happen now?", Lutz asked his brother... „The Allies will keep pushing towards Germany I guess..." „...Unless Hitler capitulates...", Ludwig said... „Are you crazy? Hitler will never capitulate. Never! He will bring Germany down with him... that's what he's going to do!", Hans angerly answered... At the end of September, Franz returned to Paris, as he had been called to resume his work at the Swiss embassy... and Ludwig and François went with him, to live with him on the rue Galilée, since they had to go back to College... That's about the time Paul got a letter from his father, telling him his family was coming back to Paris... „Thank God we no longer live on Avenue Foch...", Paul said to Will... „Can you imagine us living there, with my mother? It would have been hell!" A few weeks later, Paul had a call at Bagatelle from his father: His family was back! The day after, Paul drove to Paris and met his father at the Head office for the first time in four years... Both of them were very happy to be reunited... and of course, many tears were shed... „When I last saw you... you were a teenager Paul. Now, you're a grown man, and a very handsome one", Paul's Dad said to him... „And all those years, you did a fine job here... and I know it wasn't always easy for you. I can't thank you enough, son... I'm so proud of you!" „Thanks Dad. I'm so happy to see you again. (...) And how is mum?" „(...) Oh... she's fine, I guess... But you won't be surprised to hear that she doesn't want to see you...", his Dad sadly answered... With a sad look on his face, Paul replied: „Oh... I'm not really surprised Dad... But I'm sorry she feels that way about me and Will..." „And I must tell you that she has given strict orders to your sister and your brother not to ever contact you...", his Dad added... Paul looked at his father with tears in his eyes and said: „I should have known... But how is Catherine? And how is Pierre? Have they changed?" „Oh... They have grown, you know... Your sister Catherine is now eighteen... and your brother Pierre got sixteen last month... and he's a fine young man. He looks a lot like you... tall, blond curly hair and he has your sparkling green eyes... And of course, now that we're back, he talks a lot about you... and wants to see you." „I wish I could see him...", Paul sadly said... „Life isn't easy for him you know... Your mother said he's gay! Just like you! And she said it's all my fault..." „Your fault? But why?", Paul asked, stunned to hear his mother was blaming his father... „She says it runs in my family... That it couldn't come from her side, since no one was gay in her family..." „That's bull shit! Like if some of them would have admitted they were gay, even if they were. (...) But I don't understand why she says Pierre is gay? Is that what he said?" „No... didn't have to. Two or three months before we left New York city, she caught him with one of his friends and... Well, they were..." „Oh, I see...", Paul answered, grinning... „Yes. And since then, it's been a living hell for your brother... She said that, with some help from the Church, she's going to change your brother, and make sure he doesn't sin anymore..." „You're kidding me, are you? If he's gay... she can't change him... that's stupid!" „I'm watching her closely. For now, she's only talking... but should she start acting, I'm going to have to reason her...", his Dad said... „You can count on me Dad, should you need my help..." „So... I understand you and Will are now living at Bagatelle... I intend to visit you over there. I want you to introduce me to Will", his Dad said, smiling at his son... „And you're most welcome to visit us Dad. Will is dying to meet you, and so are all the others..." „The others?" So Paul explained to his Dad who Lutz, Hans, Ludwig and François were... „I'm happy to see you have such good friends Paul..." „So.. Why don't you come to see us next Sunday?", Paul asked his Dad... „I guess that could be arranged... yes. But I will come alone..." „I understand...", Paul answered, with a sad grin on his face... „Now, I hope you will keep working here, at the Head office..." „(...) No Dad... I took care of the business while you were gone, but now that you're back, I intend to do something else with my life..." „Oh... And what do you have in mind?" „We haven't really decided yet... But you remember Will and I bought a sugarcane plantation in Martinique three or four years ago... and... we're thinking about moving there... you know... we're kind of fed up with Europe!" – „You would leave France?" „Why not? And you know, it's not as if Martinique was a foreign land... it's part of France..." – „Nevertheless... it's a shock to hear you say you want to leave. I just found you back, and you're already talking about leaving..." „Don't worry dad", Paul answered, grinning... „We're not leaving tomorrow..." „Thank God! (...) Anyway, we'll have time to talk about that, won't we? And expect me to be at Bagatelle next Sunday..." „We'll be expecting you for dinner Dad...", Paul answered, with a big smile on his face. And indeed on Sunday, Paul's father drove to Bagatelle... and as he was parking his car in front of the Château... he heard some one shout from the trunk: „Open the trunk..." Paul's father remained still... just to make sure he really had heard a voice... „Please Dad... open the trunk...", he clearly heard... He walked over to the trunk and opened it... „Thanks Dad!", his son Pierre said, beaming... „It's not too comfortable in there, you know..." „What are you doing in there?", his Dad asked, dumbfounded... „What does it look like I'm doing here, dad? I knew you were coming to see Paul today... and so... here I am!", Pierre answered, laughing... „Your mother will kill us..." „I don't give a damn about her Dad... It's my life we're talking about, and I won't let her decide what's good for me!" – „...We'll talk about that later son. But now that you are here... well... there's not much I can do... or that I want to do to prevent you from seeing your brother..." Pierre smiled at his Dad, and the two of them were walking towards the Château... „Paul won't believe it...", his Dad said... „Well, here I am!", Pierre answered, as Paul was about to answer the door... „And I intend to stay here with Paul... I don't intend to go back to Paris, Dad..." Pierre stated. „Huh?", his father said, as the big door was opening before them... When Paul opened the door, he saw his Dad standing there... „Hi Dad...", he said, smiling... Then he realized someone else was standing there too, right next to his Dad... Paul looked at the young man, and it didn't take long for him to realized who he was: „....Pierre? Is that you bro?" „Yup! That's me bro...", his brother Pierre answered, laughing his heart out... Paul walked over to his brother, took him into his arms, and with tears in his eyes he said: „I

173

can't believe it's you... you're so tall... you're..." „Yeah!" Pierre answered, laughing... „but if you keep hugging me so tightly, you'll pull the last breath away from my poor lungs..." „Oops...", Paul said, laughing... „Sorry! But I'm so happy to see you... but... How come..." „It's not my fault", Paul's Dad said, rolling his eyes... „He heard me say to your Mum I was coming to Bagatelle to see you... and he just hid himself inside the car trunk. That's where he made the trip... hidden in the trunk!" Paul burst out laughing, hearing that... then he said: „Well... come on in, please. We have so much to talk about. Let's join the others..." As they walked into a beautiful salon, Paul introduced his Dad and his brother to Will... then to the others... „I've heard so much about you Will... I'm glad we finally meet...", Paul's Dad said, smiling. „So am I, Sir...", Will replied, smiling too. „....And there's no point trying to deny the fact that you two are brothers...", Lutz said to Paul and Pierre... „You two are so much alike..." „Yes guys... That's my baby brother alright...", Paul proudly answered... „The last time I saw him, he was just a kid..." – „Well, he's not a kid anymore", Lutz said, laughing... „Just look at him..." „I guess he has grown a bit since 1940...", Paul said, laughing too... „Rather, I should say he has grown a lot..." After dinner, they began talking about all the events of the last four years... There was so much to talk about... But sooner or later, Pierre knew he had to talk to his Dad and his brother about his plans... and he decided the sooner the better. „Look Dad... I don't want to go back to Paris. It's a nightmare for me with Mum... She's going to drive me crazy... Since we came back, she's been on my back non-stop... she even forbid me to try to locate the friends I had before we fled Paris..." „But why?", Paul asked... „She said she doesn't want me to „contaminate" them..." „You're kidding?", Paul asked, not believing his ears... „No... I swear... that's what she said... Anyway, I've tried to locate them, but they all fled when we did, and I don't know where they are now, so..." „But what have you been doing since you came back to Paris?", Will asked... „Not much... Since we left four years ago, so many things have changed in Paris, and besides, all my friends are back in New York... not here... so the other night, I wanted to go out, to see a film... but Mum refused. She said it's too dangerous. So I had to stay home and read a book to Mum and Catherine, while they were busy, knitting..." They all burst out laughing, hearing that... „Poor Pierre...", Ludwig finally said... „Don't laugh... it's not funny!", Pierre answered, with a sad look on his face.

„...Perhaps I could spend more time at home with you...", his father said. „Even if you do Dad, it won't help: She's after me, and you know that as well as I do!", Pierre answered... „So that's why I say I want to stay here with Paul... if Paul agrees, of course... I can't go back Dad. I can't. And if you force me to go back, you'll have to chain me to her beloved grand piano, for if you don't, I will run away as soon as I can..." His father looked at Paul, not knowing what to say... „Look Dad.. If Pierre wants to stay here with us, I have no problem with that... He's most welcome to stay. After all, Bagatelle is already a refugium peccatorum..." „A what?", Ludwig asked... „...A refuge of sinners...", Paul answered, grinning... „...What am I going to tell your mother?", their Dad asked... „The truth! That's all! And don't worry so much Dad... She'll be glad to get rid of me... the „sinner"...", Pierre answered... „I guess there's no point forcing you to come back to Paris..." „No Dad... cause as I said... I would run away! I just can't stand her anymore!" „(...) Fine! You stay here for now. I'll be back next weekend, so we can talk about your future. About what you intend to do with your life... Think about that, will you? I understand you don't want your Mum to decide for you... and that's normal... But you have some thinking to do, if you don't want others to make decisions for you." „I will... but one thing is certain: I'm not going back home with her..." Their Dad went back to Paris... and of course... madame de Brion was very mad. At first. Then, she said to her husband: „Two sinners together... They make a fine pair! (...) Let him live with Paul, if that's what he wants. He's hopeless. At least, we won't see this good-for-nothing welter in his sins..." „How can you say that?", he asked his wife... „...Don't look at me with that sly look on your face. You know as well as I do that your youngest son is no better than your oldest..." „...That's your point of view, not mine. They are my sons, and I love them, whatever their sexual preferences..." „...And I suppose you agree to that?" „That's not what I said. I don't have to agree to anything. But I don't judge them, that's what I mean!" „...Do as you wish... I don't care... as long as I don't see them!" „You won't!" The next weekend, monsieur de Brion went to Bagatelle... and told his sons about their mother's reaction... „I knew she was going to say that...", Pierre said... „And I don't care!" „(...) You'll have to go to college...", his father later said... „(...) It's too late for this year..." „Maybe... but next year...", his Dad replied... „Yes Dad... next year!", Pierre answered. That year, each weekend, Ludwig and François would bring

175

back from college their books... and teach to Pierre all they had learned the previous week... and with Paul's help, Pierre was learning... Paul and his brother also had time to have a serious talk about their... sexual preferences... „...She caught you in the act, huh?", Paul asked his brother one day... „Look... my friend was only giving me a blow-job... not much, huh? But anyway Paul, I've known that I'm gay for at least three years now, and I have no problem with that whatsoever...", Pierre answered, grinning... „I see... But you've never been going out with girls, so..." – „Have you?", Pierre asked his big brother... „(...) No, but..." „Again Paul, I know who I am, as much as you know who you are..." – „Okay... It's your life after all... I just wanted to make sure..." – „Yeah yeah...", Pierre answered, laughing... „Don't worry for me bro..."

FOURTEEN

As April of 1945 came, they were all happy to be able to spend sometimes outside the Château... The winter had been rather rough on them, and they were all a bit restive. They all wanted to do something with their life... Fortunately, during the winter, they had been able to do some work in the greenhouse... but now that the snow had melt, they began thinking about going to La Vacherie, the small, secluded pavilion located on the estate, near the lake... „At least if we go there, it will be a change... I'm sick and tired staying here, doing nothing...", Paul said to his friends... And of course, they all agreed... So as soon as the temperature was warm enough, they all went to La Vacherie, to spend some time over there... And when Hans, Lutz's brother, saw Paul, Will and Lutz walking around naked... he asked them: „What the hell is going on here, huh?" Lutz burst out laughing... and answered: „Oh... It has always been like that around here... but if you want to keep your shorts on, no problem bro. You do what you want. It's up to you... But for us, when we're here... we wear nothing... it gives us a sense of freedom, that's all!" Minutes later, Pierre was walking around... stark naked! It took Hans more time to get accustomed to the idea of walking around in the nude... but before the end of that day, he was as naked as all the others... „Come on bro... We won't rape you, you know... We all know you're straight, so... feel comfortable...", Lutz said to his brother, smiling... Two days later, as they were having coffee in the salon, back at the Château, Hans walked in and said to his friends: „I've been listening to the BBC last night... If what they say is true, the Allies have crossed over the Rhine River and are not too far from Leipzig... and as for the Russians, they're heading for Berlin and should soon be there..." „You're kidding...", Lutz exclaimed. „No... it's only a matter of days before the war in Europe is over...", Hans answered... „What about Hitler?" „They say he's still in Berlin... and he said he will defend the capital, until the Allies and the Russians are defeated...", Hans answered, with a grin on his face... „What a lunatic...", Will answered... On April 30, 1945, as they were all listening to Radio Berlin, they heard the speaker announce the Führer had died... while defending Berlin... „...Sure!", Lutz said... „Can you imagine him, with a gun... fighting to defend Berlin?" − „I wonder what really happened to him...", Will said... They didn't know it yet, but the truth was that, as Soviet forces had entered Berlin itself and were battling their way to the center of the city where the Chancellery was located... Hitler has shot himself in the head, deeply buried inside his bunker... When the Soviet troops took the Chancellery that night, Hitler's body had already been reduced to ashes... burned according to his orders by SS guards... As they were listening to Radio Berlin, they heard the speaker say that Admiral Dönitz was now Germany head of state... and that he had vowed to continue fighting... „With what? For what?", Ludwig asked... „They're going to make me vomit...", Lutz answered... „Anyway... whatever Dönitz says... the war is over. And thank God, we lost it!", Will said... „...How can you say that Will...", Lutz asked his best friend. „If we had won... can you imagine how it would have been like, with Hitler at the helm? Can you?", Will answered, looking at Lutz... „(...) It's just that I feel sorry Germany had to be destroyed, in order to get rid of him..." − „I know how you feel Lutz... all the Führer left behind him are ruins...", Hans sadly said... Finally, on May 8, 1945... they heard Germany had capitulated... „Thank God! It's over!", Will shouted out when he heard the news... „Yeah...", Paul answered, with a big smile on his face... „And we are still alive!" „Now what?", Lutz asked his friends... „I mean... what are we going to do, now that the war is over?" − „Oh... I did a lot of thinking about that guys... and I think I have an idea...", Paul answered, grinning... „Oh yeah?", Lutz answered, looking at Paul... „What is it?" „Look guys...", Paul started to say... „You already know that three years ago, Will and I bought a sugarcane plantation in Martinique... so I suggest we all move over there and start a business... We could create a new company... we would all be shareholders, and would sell shares to our employees, so they have a stake in the business... That way, we would make sure they are as eager as we are the plantation does prosper. What do you think?" „(..) You mean... We would leave Europe?", Lutz and

Hans asked... „...Do you really want to go back to Berlin... with the Soviets over there? Is that what you want?", Will asked his two friends... „(...) Not really...", Lutz and Hans answered. And so, they all started to discuss Paul's idea... „But what about Franz? I'm not going if he's not coming with us...", Lutz later said... „...I've already talked to him about my idea... and he's willing to give up his job, and come with us... don't worry Lutz...", Paul answered, grinning... „And what about me?", François nervously asked... „I mean... Philippe is here, in Paris... I don't want to lose him..." „No, you won't François. You're going to stay in Paris, and you're going to keep the fat on the rue Galilée... so you can continue going to college...", Paul said, smiling... „...But I want to be with you guys..." „Look François, you remember how you and I have invested the money I gave you last November?" „Yes..." „So, you will have no financial problem... and my Dad has already agreed to look after you... and maybe, later... if you and Philippe want to come to Martinique... well... you'll be welcome to join us over there..." Obviously, Paul had thought about everything. He answered every question... and in the end, he said: „Look... it's up to you guys. We stay in Europe and we continue to rot in France, like we all did last winter... or we move on with our lives, and we start building a new future for ourselves. We're family, so we all go... or no one goes! And if we decide to go... I'm not saying life will be perfect over there. We'll have to work hard, and I don't know how long it's going to take before we see the results of our hard work. I say we give ourselves a year and a half... and if by then we don't like it... if one of us is homesick... we'll all come back. After all, Europe will still be there. But I say let's give it a try..." After a long... a very long moment of silence... they all agreed to go. They had all come to realize there were not too many alternatives... Europe was in ruins. The future looked bleak... The Soviets were all over Eastern Europe... and already, there were tensions between them and the Allies... Would there be another war? Communism was on the rise, not only in France... but also in Italy, in Greece and in many other countries... No... They didn't want to go through another war! No thanks! And they were all fed up with ideologies... „Yeah...", Will said... „Let's give it a try! I say we go... We are young... and there is nothing left here for us in Europe!" – „Yes", they all said... „...And I'm going too...", Pierre said, looking at Paul... „Yes Pierre. You're coming with us, if that's what you want. I've already spoken to Dad about that... and he said it's okay. He

understands..." „Cool", Pierre answered, with a big smile on his face...
„So guys... We are all going then?", Paul asked his friends... „Yes", they
all answered. „We should drink to that", Paul answered... So champagne
was served... and they all drank to their new life...

FIFTEEN

Four weeks later, they all boarded an American liner bound for New York city... „New York city? Why?", Will asked Paul... „That's the only way... and as soon as we reach New York city, we'll take a train down to Miami... There, we will take another ship to Martinique...", Paul explained to his friends... „...Quite a long trip, huh?", Will answered... „Hey... it's that... or we all stay here. And besides, we're in no hurry, are we?", Paul replied, grinning... „I guess not...", Lutz answered... Before leaving France, Paul gave orders so that everything at Bagatelle... all the furniture... his grandmother's grand piano... even the chandeliers and all sconces... be packed, put into containers and sent to Martinique on a merchant ship... along with two cars he had bought, knowing it would be hard to find cars in Martinique by the time they got there... It took them five weeks to reach Martinique... But when they reached Fort-de-France, Paul looked at his friends and said: „Welcome to the New World my friends... a new life is waiting for us here..." Although Paul was laughing, he was as scared as the others! He didn't know what to expect and didn't know much about their new „Homeland"... But then, he looked up over the old Fort Saint-Louis and saw the French flag flying over it... and he smiled to himself. Yes... they were home! He didn't know why, but he felt like crying. He knew perfectly well all the others were counting on him... as if he was some kind of wizard. But Paul knew perfectly well he was not a wizard, and he felt very much responsible for the five others he had convinced to embark on this new journey... and he felt all the pressure on his shoulders. „Shit", he said to himself... „I'm only twenty-four years old! Why do I have to go through all this?". Then, he looked at Will, his beautiful lover... and again, it's in his beautiful blue eyes that he found the courage to fight for his friends... As they were going ashore, a tall man walked to them, smiling. The man looked at them and said: „...Which one of you is monsieur de Brion?" „I am monsieur de Brion...", Paul answered... „Oh... nice to meet you monsieur... and welcome to Fort-de-France. I'm Gérard Langevin... I'm the real-estate agent you bought your plantation from..." „Oh yes monsieur Langevin... I remember you now...", Paul answered, smiling at the man... „Your father wrote to me, to tell me you were coming... and he asked me to greet you. You must all be tired from your long trip, and eager to reach your new home..." the man said... „Yes", Paul answered. „Well... meet Émile... He knows where your plantation is located, and he will drive you there..." „It's a pleasure to meet you monsieur Émile...", Paul said to the tall, smiling Martinican... „Yes...", monsieur Émile answered... „Welcome to Martinique... Now, we'll have to put your luggage in my truck over there...", the man said, pointing to his truck, that looked more like a very old bus than a truck... Ludwig looked at it, then at Franz and... rolling his eyes he said, dubitatively: „Yeah! Welcome to Martinique!" Franz grinned... then answered: „Well... I prefer to be here than in Berlin!" „Shut up, you two...", Hans said... „When in Rome, we do like the Romans... and that truck is not so bad..." – „Shit!", Ludwig answered, a bit dispirited... A few Martinicans help them to put their luggage onboard the big truck. Paul paid them, then he said to his friends: „Let's go pals... Let's go home!" So they left Fort-de-France and their driver drove them to their sugarcane plantation... „Is it far from here?", Paul asked the driver... „Not really... It's in the Southern part of the island... and the island is not so big you know. The only problem is that the roads to the South are not too good... But soon, they will be repaired, don't worry...", the driver answered, smiling... After more than an hour driving on bad roads, the driver finally said: „We're almost there..." Ten minutes later the driver announced: „That's the entrance to your plantation, Sir..." Entering through the plantation's main wrought-iron gate, they all looked in the distance to an impressive, whitewashed mansion on a grassy hilltop... „That used to be the „Maison de maître" (Master's house) the driver said... „That's before the plantation was abandoned years ago..." „Yes", Paul answered, giving the driver a friendly smile... They slowly drove towards the mansion but at one point, the driver stopped the truck, since from that point the private road leading to the mansion was no longer practicable... „I guess you'll all have to walk the rest of the distance...", the driver told them...

„No problem!", Paul answered... „We'll have that road repaired in no time..." – „...Not only the road, Sir...", the driver answered, looking at the mansion... Paul looked up at the big mansion, with its impressive eight-columned two story portico and prominent pedimented gable stretching across the entire front of the building, trimmed by tooth-like dentil molding along the base and the sloping sides... Once near the mansion, he gave a look to the towering, footed columns with ornate Corinthian column capitals that proved the dignity of the original owner... However, from such a short distance, it wasn't hard to see the mansion had been abandoned for may years and needed many repairs. Paul turned to look at Will and all he saw into his lover's beautiful eyes was despair... He gave him a tender smile and said: „Come on... let's go inside..." They silently walked to the mansion's 60-foot-wide stone steps and once on the colonnaded front porch Paul turned to look at the Sea as the plantation was delimited on one side by the beautiful, turquoise Caribbean Sea. He stared at the Sea for a while... then said: „Look at that view guys: It's fantastic, don't you think?" They all turned to look at the Sea, and for the first time in a while, Paul saw them smile... After a while, they walked inside the mansion and entered the sixteen-foot ceiling front hall, with its signature „floating" staircase -a fabulous stairway that winds up either side of the foyer with no visible means of support- „It's beautiful...", Paul said... „Yes Sir... It used to be...", the driver said... „Lots of work to be done though, to restore the place to its original grandeur... and I guess it's going to take a lot of money to do that. Many people would just tear down the mansion and built something more modern..." „Never!", Paul answered, shocked by that idea... He looked at the tall double-hung windows extending from near the ceiling to the floor, making it possible to walk from the house to the porch beyond. He slowly walked towards one of the tall windows, opened it and walked out. Back on the colonnaded front porch, Paul again looked at the Sea. „We're going to restore this place!", he said to himself. „Yes sir!" Will joined him on the porch. He was silent. Paul looked at him and said: „What do you think?" „Do you really want to know?" – „Yes..." „... Have you seen „Gone With the Wind?" – „The film? Sure...", Paul answered... „Well... the place looks a lot like „Tara" in the film... but after it had gone through the Civil War! All that is missing is the Spanish moss... And it wouldn't surprise me to suddenly see a starving Scarlet O'Hara walk through those broken French doors..." Paul turned to Will and, with tears in his eyes, he answered: „That's not exactly what I was expecting you to say..." Will saw so much sadness into his lover's beautiful green eyes, he felt bad for what he had just said. He took Paul into his strong arms, gave him a tender kiss and said: „I'm sorry Paul. Shit! I'm so sorry... Look: There's a lot of work to do to restore this place... but we'll do it! Look at me Paul... We'll do it, you hear? And we will succeed!" „I can't do it alone..." „Hey! I'm here. And so are the others. Now, put a smile on your face, will you?" Paul smiled at Will. His courage was coming back to him. They all needed him. They all counted on him. And Paul knew that. „Yes...", he finally said... „We will succeed!" When they heard some one else walk on the porch, they turned and saw their driver walking towards them... „...Of course Sir, the Maison de maître doesn't look too good now... and as I said, it needs a lot of repairs... but I've worked here in the past, and I know it's strongly built. It's well adapted to the climatic conditions around here... I know it's been built more than a hundred years ago, and since then, it withstood all the natural disasters that occurred on the island..." „(...)" „So..." the driver continued to say... „This is your Habitation Sir..." Paul didn't know yet that in the French West Indies, the term „Habitation" meant the whole estate... including the sugarcane fields, the main house, the out buildings as well as what used to be the slave cabins, set up along a part of the property known as „rues cases-nègres". As such, the „Habitation"... or Plantation... consisted of all the planter's -or master's- possessions... „So you've worked here before?", Paul asked the driver... „Yes Sir..." „What about the other buildings on the estate?" „...Well I would say they also need repairs, Sir... The distillery hasn't actually been in operation since... 1936, I'd say..." „So you know the place well...", Will asked. „Oh yes, Sir", the driver answered, beaming... „Do you have a job at the moment?", Paul asked the man... „...Not really, Sir. Not much work around here, you know..." „...And do you know some of the workers that used to work here?" The driver smiled to Paul and answered: „Of course, Sir... I know them well... they're my friends..." „...Well... if you and your friends are looking for jobs... good jobs... well paid jobs... be here the day after tomorrow...", Paul said to the driver. „We'll be here, Master..." the man answered, smiling... „...Never call me „master" again, you hear? If you and your friends agree to work with us on this plantation, we'll be business partners... and from now on, you call me Paul, okay?" „Yes

Master... I mean... Yes, Sir.. Paul..." Since Paul had already transferred all the money he had in France into a bank account at Fort-de-France... money was no object. Of course, he had not transferred the money he had in Switzerland nor the money he had in the United-States... No. He knew better than that! And his father was taking care of his investments...

SIXTEEN

So two days later, true to his word, the driver came back to the plantation... along with many of his friends. Paul explained to them what he had in mind... and that all employees would have a stake into their business, since they would be shareholders... Of course, Paul had a lot of explaining to do, for this was a foreign concept to the Martinicans.... „We'll share the profits with you?", one of the Martinicans asked... „...Yes! If we make profits, that is!", Paul answered, laughing... „Oh we will...", all the Martinicans answered, smiling... And before long, he plantation was back into business... and the old „Master's house" was repaired... „Magnificent", Will said to Paul, looking at the house once it had been repaired... „You did it!" – „Yeah!", Paul answered..."We all did it!", he added, rather proud of what they all had accomplished... Eventually, the big containers from France were delivered, along with the two cars Paul had bought in France... The furniture, the grand piano... the chandeliers... everything was fitting perfectly well in the big mansion, now restored to its original and formal grandeur. And of course, the road leading to the mansion was also repaired... „...The place looks stunning", Hans said one morning, looking at the mansion... „Quite different from what we saw the first day we got here, huh?" „Yes... We all did a great job guys", Paul answered looking at his friends. Of course, servants were hired to take care of the mansion... and provide for their needs, including a good cook, to feed them well... Yes, life was getting better and better with each passing day! A few weeks later Ludwig, looking at workers digging deep into the ground... asked Paul: „...What the hell are they doing over there?" „...They are going to build a swimming pool over there...", Paul answered, laughing... „Are you crazy or what? The Sea is right there..." Ludwig answered, stunned... „...And do you think Franz will want to swim in the Sea? I don't think so pal... He almost drowned at La Vacherie a few years ago..." „Oh!", Ludwig said, grinning... „I do remember that day..." „Yes and so do I... just as if it was yesterday...", Paul said... „So, that why I've decided to have a swimming pool built here..." „Good idea!", Ludwig answered, laughing... „And I can't wait to tell Franz... and maybe you and I can make a few swimming laps in there, you know... I miss our training... and I don't like to train into the Sea..." „Count on me pal!", Paul answered... A few days later as they were all having coffee on the colonnaded front porch, Paul look at his friends and said: „I suggest we name the plantation „Bagatelle"... That name would serve as a reminder of all the good times and all the fun we had in France, at Bagatelle. What do you think guys?" And of course, they all agreed... And before they knew it... their first crop was ready... and before long, rum was flowing again from their new, spotless equipment Paul had bought from Cuba... „Back into business...", Paul said one day, laughing, as all of their production was shipped over to France, where his father was in charge of the marketing over there... And it was a huge success! And of course, all the profits were shared amongst all the shareholders... „Next year, we'll do even better!" one of the Martinicans said to Paul... „You'll see... Bagatelle will become the most profitable plantation of all the French West Indies...", the tall man added, with a big smile on his face... „...You all did a great job", Paul told the workers and business partners... „I'm so proud of you... and it's all thanks to you!" „...If you were not here, Sir... We would all be jobless...", a Martinican said... „...You see", Paul answered... „L'union fait la force!" (united, we stand). „He was right Paul: It's all thanks to you if we made it", Will said to Paul one evening, as the two of them were sitting on cane chairs on the colonnaded front porch, looking at the calm, beautiful, turquoise Caribbean Sea... „...As I've said before Will... I would never have done it without you Will and the others. You're the one who gave me the courage to go on, day after day. Did I tell you that I'm madly in love with you?" „... Are you?", Will asked, grinning... looking at his beautiful lover... „I've been in love with you since the very first day I saw you... back in 1940... and I've never stopped loving you since. That's six year ago Will... Can you believe it? At the time, I was eighteen, going on nineteen... Now, I'm twenty- five... an old guy!" „...Are you kidding? You're just twenty-five Paul... and you've never looked better... Oh come on, stop that, will you. I'm twenty-six, and I sure don't feel like I'm an old guy...", Will answered, laughing... "And I'm so much in love with you...", he finally whispered to Paul, taking his lover's hand into his... Paul turned his head to look at his beautiful lover... "...We've been through so much since we first met..." "...And I'm here with you today... and so are Lutz and Franz, Hans, Ludwig and Pierre... and it's all thanks to you! And if Lutz and me haven't been sent to the Russian front... again... it's thanks to you!" Paul just smiled back at Will. Then he turned to look back at the Sea... and at the sky. Even though it was after supper, it was still fairly sunny, with just a few clouds around... For a while they remained silent, sitting side by side, holding hands and staring at the Sea... Then dark clouds showed up from what seems out of nowhere and minutes later, it was pouring rain. Since they were sitting on the porch, they were well protected from the rain, so they just stayed were they were... watching... "...It's the rainy season... heavy down pours... it won't last...", Paul softly said... And indeed before long, the rain had stopped and the clouds were gone... "...Can you smell it?", Paul asked Will... "What?", Will answered... "Nature! It smells so good here, after the rain..." – "Yeah", Will answered, smiling... "Look at the sunset... It's so beautiful. We're privileged to be here you know, you and me... We could be dead. And if not, we could be blind, not being able to watch that beautiful sunset..." Paul said... "So true...", Will softly answered... "...Why don't we go for a walk on the beach?", Paul asked Will, grinning... "Yeah", Will answered, smiling at his lover... "It's our own beach after all, isn't it?" "Sure is... and I've asked one of our employees to clean it... Just give me a minute, I'll get two towels... just in case..." "...In case of what?", Will asked, giving his lover a very sexy grin... "Oh... Just in case, you know...", Paul answered, laughing...

SEVENTEEN

A few minutes later Paul was back, holding a blanket in one hand, and a basket with his other hand... „What do you have in there?", Will asked Paul, looking at the basket... „Ohhhhhhh... that's a surprise!", Paul answered, laughing... „Let me give you a hand... I'll carry the blanket...", Will replied, smiling at his lover... So, hand in hand, they slowly walked their way to the beach... only wearing shorts. The warm breeze felt so good on their bare chests and legs... „...The breeze is so warm tonight...", Will said... „Yeah. How would it feel if those same breezes were caressing our entire bodies, huh?", Paul asked... „Let's get naked... no one can see us from the mansion..." „Right!", Will answered, laughing... Two seconds later, the two lovers were on the beach, stark naked... „Where should we lay our blanket?", Will asked, rubbing the back of his neck... „Right there...", Paul answered, grinning. They set down their blanket, and Will sat on the middle of it, with Paul sitting between his firm legs, with his back against Will's bare muscle bound chest... For a while, they just sat there, gazing at the beautiful Sea... Then Paul turned to look at Will and said: „We're celebrating tonight..." „Celebrating what?", Will asked... „Our love... and our new life!", Paul answered, grinning... He reached for the basket he had brought from the mansion, took a bottle and two beautiful crystal glasses out of it and said: „...champagne, my love..." Paul unscrewed the bottle and the cork popped out of the bottle... Then he filled the long flûtes and, giving a flûte to Will he said: „Here's to our love and our new life!" „To our love and to our new life!", Will answered, smiling... They took a sip... and went back gazing at the beautiful Caribbean Sea right at their feet... „Are you happy?", Paul suddenly asked Will, turning his head to look at his lover... Doing so, Paul saw tears going down Will's cheeks... „Hey... What's wrong?" „...I'm so happy

Paul... I wish my Mum and Dad could see us. I wish they could be here with us... you know... I wish they had not died they way they did... I wish..." „Stop that Will!", Paul said... „We can't change the past, can we? And I'm sure they are with us tonight, looking upon us... and they are smiling at us... They loved us so much. And they loved Ludwig so much... I'm sure they are happy for us, and very proud of us..." „...You think so?" „I know", Paul softly answered... „And I know that I love you Will... and people may judge us because we're in love, and I don't care! Nothing is more beautiful than love in this world. And if they choose to make war, if they choose to shoot at one another on battlefields... that's their choice! I've chosen to love you and be with you instead, and that was the best decision I've ever made in my life..." „...I love you so much Paul... so much...", Will softly answered... Paul looked up over Will's shoulders and looked at the moon rising to the East, right above the Mansion... He turned his head to look back at the Sea and gazed at it, as the moon was reflecting off the calm water... lightning up the beach in hues of gray and white... Everything around them was so calm... so beautiful... As he was still sitting between Will's firm legs, with his back against his lover's bare chest, Paul turned a bit and said: „...Kiss me Will, Please? Just kiss me!" Will wrapped his strong arms around Paul, resting his chin on his lover's shoulder... turning his head kissing the side of his ear and nibbling on Paul's neck... „...I love you so much Paul..." Paul turned his head to look at Will, and their lips met, as the warm tropical breeze was now blowing... Will leaned towards Paul and started kissing him full on the mouth. His kiss was soft and tender... just like the sunset on his skin earlier... Paul was growing hard and was aware that his cock was bobbing against his own stomach... While he was kissing his lover, Will's strong hands ran across Paul's chest and stomach, pulling him closer to him. Paul felt Will's cock stirring against his back as his lover was getting hard... His own dick was a raging hardon. He lifted his arms and reached back and began stroking Will's blond hair... „Ohhhhhhh....", Paul moaned... Will's left hand covered Paul's right pec, tenderly pinching his nipple... Paul moaned again... Then, Will's right hand went down... to find Paul's very hard dick... He then wrapped his right fist around his lover's hard, oozing dick, slowly masturbating him... Will continued kissing Paul... then went down to kiss his lover's neck and nape, tickling them with the tip of his tongue... „...You're driving me crazy...", Paul said, begging Will for a kiss, twisting his head... Will leaned over, placing his hot lips on Paul's lips. He wiggled his tongue, tickling Paul's upper lip before he captured his lover's tongue, sucking it into his mouth... Will leaned back with Paul leaning down farther on him. Will's fist was still wrapped around Paul's hard, oozing dick... masturbating his lover faster and faster... Paul was moaning and groaning, his heels dug into the sand, raising his hips a bit higher... „Ahhhhh", Paul moaned... „You're going to make me cum!" „Yeah...", Will answered... „Shoot..." „Oh shit... Here I cum...", Paul shouted, panting, before firing four ropes of cum landing all over his chest and abs, with Will still squeezing his hard cock. Paul uncontrollably let out a loud, long, and deep moan... As his body was going limp within Will's embrace, Paul turned his head to look back at his lover and said: „That was soooooo good Will..." „...I guess so, huh?", Will answered, lightly laughing... Paul could feel Will's throbbing dick hard pressed against his back. He had to take care of it... He slowly rose to his feet, turned to look down at Will, still sitting on the blanket, wondering what Paul was going to do next... Paul sat on his knees between Will's strong parted legs and reached for his big, beautiful dick... and ran his fingers from the base up to the tip, just barely making contact. A smile crossed his face when he heard Will moan... Paul then leaned, opened his mouth and put his lover's entire cook in his mouth and began massaging his hard shaft with his tongue... That made the hair on the back of Will's neck stand up, every muscle in his body to tighten up... and he threw his head back, moaning... It felt so damn good! Will grabbed the back of Paul's head and forced him to take the entire length of his dick in his mouth. „Ah shit... That feels good...", Will softly moaned... Paul began bobbing up and down on his lover's oozing dick and when he sensed Will was about to have an orgasm, he stopped and raised his head to look at him: „Oh no... I'm not ready to make you cum... not just yet!", he said to Will, with a sexy grin on his face... Now that Will's dick was well lubed, Paul moved to kneel over Will, straddling his crotch... Sitting on top of his lover's dick and facing him Paul smiled and began to grind against him... Will responded by grabbing Paul's ass cheeks, spreading them... Paul reached behind him and grabbed Will's cock and placed the length of it in between his ass cheeks... Then he pressed it up against his asshole... As Will was moaning, Paul began to slowly lower himself onto his lover's throbbing dick... When the head of Will's cock entered his ass, Paul moaned. It felt so good... Will's dick began to slide in. Paul slowly lowered himself further onto it... all the way... so that his lover's entire cock was now deep inside his ass... Will sat up straight with his dick deep inside Paul's tight ass. He wrapped his strong arms around his lover, pulling him even closer. They began to kiss passionately, with Paul's dick hard pressed against Will's abs... Paul felt Will stir inside of him while kissing. With his right hand, Will reached between their hard-pressed bodies, grabbed Paul's hot dick and began jerking him off... Paul wanted to cry out, feeling all these amazing sensations at once... Will then started moving, fucking Paul... He knew he was hitting that incredibly tender spot at the top end of Paul's velvety passage as he thrust in to the hilt... Will forced his lover to ride up and down on him, by pressing on his shoulders. Since Paul was sitting over him with his legs bent, Will was able to thrust up into him, as well as Paul to drive himself down onto his big cock... They were both moaning with passion as Will's dick kept racing in and out of Paul's tight arse. „Harder...", Paul moaned, his arms around his lover, his mouth on his... Will's rushed breath in his mouth... Paul's entire body was writhing and convulsing as Will kept pounding his dick, fucking him hard at the same time... Suddenly, Paul gasped several times, his muscles tensed, his jaw clenched, and several volleys of his juice shot out of his dick all over Will's fist... Will continued jerking him off and Paul gasped as his orgasm stretched on... He felt like he couldn't stop cumming... Will couldn't keep it in any longer and soon he was cumming deep inside of his lover. Paul felt Will getting rigid and then, he felt the warmth of his lover's cum inside his hot fuck hole. Will's eyes were shut, his beautiful mouth wide open... Paul leaned towards him and kissed him full on the mouth. Will bucked his body up against Paul as hard as he could, holding him in his arms as tightly as possible as he shot volley after volley of his hot cum inside his lover. As Will ejaculated, Paul squeezed his ass muscle tight around his lover's dick and he held on to him tightly until Will was completely spent... „Ahhhhhh", Will sighed as the aftershocks of his orgasm reverberated through his body... „Ah yeah!", Paul moaned, closing his eyes in ecstasy... „That was one hell of a fuck!", Will said to his lover, in a husky, breathless voice. „Sure was...", Paul answered, grinning... Soon their breathing slowed down. They stood like that for five minutes, just savoring every second. Will's dick going soft inside his lover, Paul's swollen but soft cock against Will's body, his arms around his neck and his head on his strong shoulder. „I love you so much Paul...", Will softly said as he ran his hands through his lover's blond hair... Paul looked at Will and, with a lovely smile he answered: „You're mine Will... and I'm yours, till the end of our days..." Later, they went for a swim into the Sea, to clean their bodies... Later on, as they were slowly walking back to the mansion, Paul looked up at a window on the second floor, where lights were shining... It was Ludwig and Pierre's bedroom window... „...Our two brothers are already going to bed... Guess it must be late...", Paul said to Will... „No, it's not that late... but they must be tired...", Will simply answered... Were Ludwig and Pierre tired? Ohhhhhhh noooooo! and they were quite busy, with Ludwig teaching a thing or two to his friend... and not from his schoolbooks!

EIGHTEEN

„You're not serious Pierre, are you?", Ludwig said to his young friend, in a state of shock... „...Why not Ludwig?" „I'm straight... that's why!" And your too young..." „I'm seventeen...", Pierre answered, insulted. „...And you look too much like your brother Paul... I couldn't do it! And besides, it would be like incest..." Pierre raised his eyes to look at Ludwig: „WHAT?", he shouted... „We're not ever related..." „.... Maybe...", Ludwig answered... „Nevertheless, since our two brothers are lovers..." „So what? I mean... If I was a girl, and you were in love with me... would that be a legal obstacle for us to get married, huh?" – „...No." „See! And it's not my fault if I look like Paul so much... You look like your brother Will and I don't make a fuss about that...", Pierre said... „Anyway... you're crazy! You want a straight guy like me to teach you about gay sex! That's totally stupid pal..." „I know you've got experience in that field..." „Oh? „Yeah!...", Pierre answered, grinning. „What do you mean?" „I know that in Paris... you were fooling around with François and Philippe..." „What do you mean?", Ludwig asked, frowning... „I've questioned François and Pierre about that... but they wouldn't answer me. I've tried everything... but they remained as silent as a suitcase..." Ludwig smiled to himself, hearing that. He knew his two friends would never have betrayed him. „... I miss them a lot...", Ludwig finally said, looking at Pierre with sad eyes... „I know Ludwig... Me too.", Pierre sincerely answered. „Yeah..." „Anyway... Since François and Philippe didn't want to answer my questions... well... I did what I had to do and spied on the three of you on the sly...", Pierre finally said, with a big smile on his face. „You did what?" „...I spied on the three of you on the sly. I listened at your bedroom door when I knew the three of you were in there... and I overheard what was going on inside..." „You did not!", Ludwig angrily said... „Sorry pal... but

I had to know...", Pierre answered not really feeling sorry for what he had done... „So?" „Listen Ludwig... I don't really know who was doing what... but I know the three of you were not playing cards, okay?" „... That's none of your business..." „That's true. That's not the reason why I brought the subject Ludwig. (...) You know I'm gay... and I know you're straight. But I also know you have experience with gay sex... while I don't. That's why I'm asking you to teach me..." „Well, you certainly have some experience, since your Mum caught you with your friend, back in New York...", Ludwig answered. „Talk about that! He was giving me head... and Mum came in before I even had time to cum..." „Shit!", Ludwig answered, grinning... „That's too bad..." „Yeah!", Pierre answered with a very sad smile on his face... „Anyway Ludwig, since we left Paris what have you been doing to relieve your needs? Wanking huh? Aren't you tried of that?" „Look at your shorts Ludwig: You have a hardon... and you're oozing! You're as horny as I am" Ludwig looked down at his crotch and indeed, his very hard dick was making a tent in his shorts... and a precum stain was clearly visible at the tip of his big oozing dick! He quickly covered his crotch with his two hands, blushing... „Oh come on Ludwig, don't hide it! And next I suppose you're going to run to the bathroom to wank? Why don't you teach me how to give you a good blow job instead huh?" „...I don't know...", Ludwig answered, a bit apprehensive... But before he could say anything else Pierre undressed so fast, Ludwig didn't have time to realize what was going on... Now Pierre was standing right next to Ludwig's bed, stark naked, with his right fist wrapped around his hard dick... „What the hell are you doing?", Ludwig asked, stunned... „Teach me!", Pierre answered, grinning... Since Ludwig was sitting on the edge of his own bed with his two feet touching the floor, he now had a perfect view of his young friend's dick and balls... as Pierre was standing right in front of him, less than two feet away... Ludwig grinned, looking at Pierre... He could see his young friend had a well toned body, from all the hard work he had been doing on the Plantation... He had broad shoulders, a nice chest and what was starting to look like a six pack... And a nice dick too... „How long is it?", Ludwig asked, grinning... „Eight inches...", Pierre answered, grinning too... „Not as big as yours though, from what I can see in your shorts... Show it to me Ludwig!" „Just a minute pal! We've got to talk first!", Ludwig answered, patting on his bed right beside him... „Sit... and stop wanking, will you?" Pierre smiled at

Ludwig, removed his fist from his hard cock and sat next to him on the bed... „And what do you want to talk about?", Pierre asked, turning his head to look at Ludwig... „A few things..." „Okay... go ahead pal." „First, I want you to know I don't feel comfortable with this whole thing..." „Oh come on Ludwig... we're not babies anymore..." „Maybe... anyway I'm just telling you how I'm feeling. Are you mature enough to understand that?" „Yes Ludwig... I do understand. Sorry." „Good (...) Second, with François and Philippe, we had an agreement..." „Oh?" „Yeah! First, they swore to me they would never tell anyone. Never. Second, they had agreed not to kiss me on the mouth... ever!" „...We could have the same agreement, you and me..." – „There's something else..." „What?" „You know Lisa, don't you?" „Our maid? Sure... What about her?" „Yeah... our maid. And as you know her Mum also works for us... and so does her Dad..." „I know... I've worked with him at the distillery..." „Have you noticed how Lisa is good-looking?" „Hey! I may be gay... but I'm not blind. Sure, she's good-looking... so what?" – „Well...", Ludwig started to say... „I kind of fancy her, if you see what I mean..." – „Ohhhhh.... And how old is she?" „Nineteen..." „I must say Ludwig you have good taste... She's beautiful..." „I know... and I think she likes me...", Ludwig answered, blushing... „Good for you pal! You two would make a beautiful couple..." „Hey... We're not there yet. But if I bring the subject it's to tell you that IF you and me do something tonight... well... there might be no sequel to that... cause if I start going out with her, I'll be faithful to her and then, I don't want you to feel bad and think I've used or manipulated you..." „Look at me Ludwig... All I'm asking you is to teach me a few tricks... I'm not asking you to be my lover! I'm not in love with you and I swear I'll be happy for you if you start going out with Lisa. And that's the end of if. And I'll never think you've used or manipulated me. In fact, I'm the one who is manipulating you..." „...You sure are!", Ludwig answered, laughing... „Now... Show me that big dick of yours, will you?" „My dick huh? You want to see it huh?" „Yeah!", Pierre answered, with a sexy grin on his face... „Well... there it is!" At that Ludwig jumped on his feet, removed his shorts and showed to Pierre his half-hard dick... „Oh shit...", Pierre exclaimed... „And it's not even totally hard yet... How long is it when you're hard?" „Ten inches...", Ludwig proudly answered, playing with his dick... „Oh shit! Is that a dick or what!", Pierre answered... „Not too bad huh?" „Now... What do I do?",

Pierre said looking at Ludwig... „Have you ever given a blowjob to someone before?" „No" „Alright! I'll teach you. I'm going to give you a blowjob first... so you'll see how it's done, okay... Then, you can blow me. You'll learn the difference between a blowjob and a REAL BLOWJOB" „Okay... go head... I'm ready..." Ludwig knelt right in front of Pierre, and gave his throbbing dick a look... He looked at his young friend's nice smooth, hairless balls... smiled... and said to Pierre: „Well pal... I guess I'll have to stop telling you you don't have balls... With what I see here, I mean... nature has been good to you!" Pierre smiled, looking down at Ludwig and answered: „I'm proud of them..." „Un-huh", Ludwig answered, grinning... Then Ludwig wrapped his fist around Pierre's hard prick... squeezing it... „Ohhhhhhh yes!", Pierre cried out... „Like that huh?" „I think I'm going to explode", Pierre replied, whimpering... „Oh no pal, not yet... Shit! I've not even started. First thing you'll have to learn is to control Again Ludwig squeezed his young friend's oozing knob... and he heard Pierre moan and groan... Then he kissed the oozing knob and licked the swollen mushroom cap. Pierre gasped... „...Control pal. Control...", Ludwig said grinning, looking up at Pierre... „Yeah, I'm doing my best you know...", Pierre softly said... Ludwig kept his fist firmly wrapped around his friend's hard dick, and began kissing his balls... Then he started sucking his nut sack... „Oh shit... That feels so good...", Pierre moaned... Then Ludwig went back working on Pierre's swollen knob, tasting his clear nectar... „Hummmm... You taste good dude...", Ludwig said, grinning... Ludwig leaned a bit on his young friend's dick and took it in his mouth... tightening his lips gripping it. „...Ohhh my God Ludwig...", Pierre cried out... Ludwig's left fingers dug into Pierre's blond pubes, and his right hand gripped Pierre's left thigh. All Pierre could think was wanting and needing to get the head of his throbbing dick into Ludwig's throat. It took several tries... but finally Ludwig relaxed his throat muscles, and Pierre's dick interred it... „...Ahhhhh", Pierre shouted, as he felt his dick inter Ludwig's throat... „I think I'm going to cum Ludwig..." When he heard that Ludwig immediately removed his friend's dick from his mouth... „...Too soon pal... Control... When you feel you're about to cum, stop what you're doing and wait for a few seconds okay?" „Okay... I'll try that!", Pierre answered, panting... After a minute or two, Ludwig went back working on his friend's pulsating dick. Tenderly he began sucking on his knob... then he tightened his lips around his hard cock rod started moving his head back and forth... „Stop moving...", Pierre cried out after a few seconds... And Ludwig stopped, grinning, with his friend's cock deep into his mouth... Pierre was learning... and fast! „...It's okay now...", Pierre finally said... „Un-huh...", Ludwig answered... So, he went back, bobbing his head faster and faster on his young friend's hard, oozing dick... and it didn't take long for Pierre to cry out: „Oh shit Ludwig... I can't hold it anymore..." „Un-huh...", Ludwig answered, feeling Pierre's dick pulsating in his mouth... „I'm going to shoot Ludwig... I'm going to... Shit, Shit, Shit...", he suddenly shouted when he felt his dick exploded deep inside Ludwig's hot mouth while being massaged by his friend's expert tongue... Ludwig slowed his pace after a second or two, concentrating only on the head of Pierre's dick, hungrily swallowing Pierre's hot, young cum... including his final trapped was... Pierre let out a loud moan... „Shut up", Ludwig said, letting go of his young friend's dick... „You're going to awake the dead..." – „Oops... Sorry!", Pierre answered, panting... „But it feels so good..." „You loved it huh?" (...) „Damn! (...) Now I know the difference between a blowjob and a REAL BLOWJOB!!!" – „I take it what your friend gave you in New York was a „blowjob" huh? „I guess he didn't know better... and at the time I didn't complain you know..." – „Yeah. I understand... Well dude, it's my turn now...", Ludwig replied, grinning...   Pierre grinned and as he was about to kneel in front of his friend, Ludwig said: „Oh no... You're not going to blow me pal... you're going to fuck me! I want your dick deep inside my ass..." „What?", Pierre exclaimed, stupefied... „Oh come on dude... don't tell me you haven't been dreaming about fucking a guy..." „Well... Yeah! Sure! But I mean... you really want me to fuck you?" „Yeah!", Ludwig answered in a husky voice... „Stretch on your back on my bed..." „Where are you going?", Pierre asked as he looked at Ludwig walking out of their bedroom... „I'm going to get a lubricant...", Ludwig answered, laughing „Wait just a second..." „Oh..." „Never try to fuck a guy without a good lubricant. And if you don't have any, use your saliva..." Ludwig said to Pierre before leaving the bedroom... And a few seconds later and was back with a bottle of lube... Pierre was already laying on his back on Ludwig's bed... His dick was still very hard, even though he had just cummed moments before... „What are you going to do?", he asked Ludwig... „Just watch me... and learn!" Ludwig hopped on his bed and knelt on all fours between Pierre's parted legs but opposite to him, so Pierre could have a direct view of his nice, firm butt... „Do you see my rosebud?", Ludwig asked his young friend, while parting his tight, compact ass cheeks with his two hands... „Sure do...", Pierre answered, grinning... „Now... the lotion... Smear some over your fingers..." „Okay... now what?" „Now with your middle finger start rubbing my hole... Yeah... just like that... Good! (...) Now slowly push your finger inside my hole... Slowly I said... Slowly... Yeah! Just like that. Yeah!" Ludwig moaned... „Now... Start wiggling your finger inside my ass... Ohhhh Yesssss! Just like that... Yeah! Now pal, find my prostate..." – „Your prostate?" „Yes. Do you feel it on the tip of your finger... No! Not there... Not there either... YEAH, there! You found it! Now with the tip of your finger start massaging it... Yeah Ohhhhhhh... Just like that, yes... It feels so good..." Now Pierre was all excited and his hard dick was oozing like a faucet... And so was Ludwig's! „Okay... Now put a second finger in there... Slowly... SLOWLY!!! Yeah... that's it... Remember... always do it slowly." – „Okay!" „That's perfect dude... That feels so good... Now take your time and insert a third finger... Yeah! Just like that... take your time... Ohhhhh Yes! That's good..." „Does it hurt?" „Noooooo. Not if your fingers are well lubed and if you do it slowly... That's it, pal. Don't forget to use your middle finger to massage my walnut..." „Your what?" Ludwig grinned and answered: „My walnut... my prostate you dummy!" „Oh...", Pierre answered, laughing... „Yeah... just like that... You learn fast dude! (...) Now start fucking my hole with your fingers, slowly at first okay?" „Like that?" „Yesssss", Ludwig sighed... „Yessssss...." And after about three minutes Ludwig turned to look at Pierre and said: „Now dude slowly remove your fingers from my ass... remember... SLOWLY... Ohhhhh yes! Just like that!" Once Pierre had removed his fingers from his friend's arse, Ludwig turned to face him and then he straddled him, sitting on his knees... with Pierre's hard, throbbing dick right under his arse crack... Ludwig grabbed the lotion and spread some all over Pierre's dick. Then he lubed his glory hole... Looking at Pierre straight in the eyes Ludwig said: „Now dude, never ever tell anyone you've fuck me, huh? Swear to me!" „I swear I will never tell Ludwig. I swear, believe me!" „Okay", Ludwig answered as he began lowering himself over Pierre's hard dick... He took his young friend's cock into his hand and guided it to his rosebud... „Don't move...", Ludwig said to Pierre „And refrain from slamming your dick into my hole, you hear me? Cause if you do... I'll kill you... Just don't move and let me do the rest, will you?" „Okay okay... Don't worry..." At that Ludwig lowered himself a bit more and the head of Pierre's cock began to penetrate his asshole... Ludwig grunted... „Does it hurt?" Pierre asked his blond haired friend... „(...) No... not really... It's just that I haven't done that since we left Paris, so..." Ludwig paused for a few seconds, then began to slowly lower himself on his young friend's cock with Pierre grabbing his ass cheeks, spreading them some more... „Yeah Pierre... That's it!", Ludwig said, moaning... Pierre was moaning too as the sensation was unbelievable. Ludwig raised himself slightly, then he lowered himself onto Pierre's cock slowly... „Ohhhhhhh", he moaned... „That feels so good..." he moaned... „Really?", Pierre asked, looking at Ludwig... „Shit yeah! (...) Now grab my dick and start wanking it, will you? Smear some lotion all over it... it will be even more pleasant" Pierre did as asked and began jerking him off... slowly... „Yeah! You're a fast learner!" Ludwig said, grinning... Then Ludwig began riding on his friend's hard, oozing dick... faster and faster... forcefully, repeatedly and roughly... using Pierre's hard dick as he wished... As Ludwig was now sitting over Pierre's crotch with his legs bent, Ludwig said to him: „Now dude... start slamming your dick into my ass... don't worry... You can do it as fast and as hard as you want. I'm well adjusted now." After a few thrusts, Pierre began moaning and panting... „Ohhhh Ludwig... I can't believe it... I can't..." Pierre moaned in a husky voice... „Un-huh!", Ludwig answered, sighing... „I know..." Pierre's dick was rubbing Ludwig's love spot with every thrust of his dick... and Ludwig was getting really stimulated, with Pierre wanking his big, oozing dick... He just wanted this to last forever... His dick was leaking so much precum as Pierre was jerking him off... faster and faster... „...Ludwig... I think I'm going to cum... If you don't stop riding my disk like that, I'm going to cum..." „Okay pal... cum inside my ass... cum... cum dude!", Ludwig answered, panting... At that moment, Pierre's cock exploded... his cum shooting deep inside Ludwig's love chute... „Oh God... OH MY GOD! Here I cum Ludwig... I'm shooting... I'm shooting..." he cried out. „Keep wanking me pal... I'm almost there too...", Ludwig answered... Ludwig felt Pierre's hips grinding him as his young friend was cumming deep inside him... „I'm going to shoot...", Ludwig shouted out... as he let his orgasm engulf his body... shooting his hot load down all over his young friend's chest and abs... „Oh shit... Ahhhhhhh", Ludwig moaned...

„Yessssss", Pierre answered, with a big smile on his face... When the spasms subsided, Ludwig collapsed on top of Pierre. He gasped for air and looked into his eyes: „... That was a hell of a fuck dude!" he said, grinning... „Shit Ludwig! I had no idea it would be so good...", Pierre answered, laughing... „Un-hun!", Ludwig answered, grinning... „And there are a few things I still have to teach you..." „Oh yeah?" „What do you know about rimming?" „About what?" „Rimming"... Ludwig answered, laughing... „And you've never been fuck huh?" „Are you kidding... you know perfectly well that I'm still a virgin..." „Yeah! Well... We'll have to take care of that too huh?" „Will it hurt?", Pierre asked, a bit worried... „...A little... at first... but then, you're going to love it... I swear", Ludwig answered, laughing... „Ludwig?" „What?" „...Don't start going out with Lisa before you teach me, will you?" „(...) Okay okay... I'll teach you..." „Thanks. You're a pal!", Pierre said, giving Ludwig a peck on the nose... „Pierre?" „What" „...Never do that again okay?" „Sorry! I forgot..." „Well don't. Only my brother Will can give me pecks... ant that's different..." „I'll remember..." „Fine!"

NINETEEN

And later on, over the following weeks, Ludwig had time to teach Pierre a few more tricks before he started going out with Lisa... It was obvious to Ludwig that Lisa liked him... and of course, he liked her a lot. She was a beautiful young woman, with features that made Ludwig salivate. Since both her parents were mulattos, her skin was rather light colored and she had beautiful hazel eyes... Only problem was, her Dad wasn't too happy to see Ludwig running around his daughter, since to him, Ludwig was a „Béké"... In Martinique only 1% of the total population born on the island is white and they are the direct descendants of the old masters... the slave owners. They are the „Békés"... Even nowadays they still control a significant share of the island's economy and are involved in many different spheres such as agriculture, real estate, tourism and banking. Apart from that, the real problem with many Békés (but not all of them...) is that a lot of them still look at the black inhabitants as inferiors! Of course, they never mingle with them... as they tend to live apart from them. At Le Robert, a village located in the heart of „Béké country", they live in beautiful, secluded houses... and they make sure the roads leading to their plantations are not too well maintained, so that the „others" do not have easy access to them! So, for Lisa's father to consider that Ludwig was a „Béké" was not meant as a compliment! But Ludwig wasn't born in the French West Indies... and he was certainly not a descendant of the old slave owners... And since they had moved to Martinique, Ludwig and the others had always treated the blacks as their equals! They had been working and living with them... and many of their friends were black. To them the color of a person's skin had no significance at all! So why consider Ludwig as if he was a Béké? At first Ludwig didn't understand why Lisa's father didn't seem to like him very much. Then Lisa explained to him the history of the island, and told him about slavery... and of how much her people had suffered... Of course Ludwig had heard about slavery... but never before had he really understood how much the slaves had suffered, how hard work was on the plantations at the time... how it felt to be „own" by someone else... living with the permanent threat of being sold to another slave owner... or worst: Seeing your wife or your children being sold to another slave owner without you being able to do anything against it... Ludwig knew about the big trial that was going on at the time in Nürnberg (Nuremberg...), where high Nazi officials were accused of crimes against Humanity... And he had those crimes in mind when he said to Lisa: „I have no doubt slavery was a crime against Humanity... and that slavery was terribly wrong! But tell me Lisa... Am I responsible for that crime just because I'm white? I have nothing to do with slavery. Hell, I was not even born at the time...So I would be responsible for crimes committed by white people more than a hundred years ago... just because of the color of my skin? Is that what your saying to me? That would be racist, no?" „Yes Ludwig! That would be racist. And I sure don't think you're responsible for what happened here a long time ago... No. That's not what I think Ludwig. And I know you're not a Béké... As for my Dad, well... you know... All the whites he knows are Békés... except for a few Métros... „Métros?" Lisa grinned, then said: „Yeah! The whites who have come from France to work in the administration. They are not Békés... since they were not born on the island... but let me tell you that most of them treat us as bad as the Békés do... Now, you, your brother and all of your friends here on the plantation are different! You've never treated us like that... So, I guess my Dad doesn't know how to react to that... It's all too new to him and I think he's under some apprehension..." „I'll have to talk to him then..." „...Good luck!", Lisa answered, frowning... And indeed, later during that week Ludwig had a talk with Lisa's father... and it wasn't an easy conversation... „...You know we are not Békés, Sir... And since we came to Martinique you had time to learn about us... the way we think... who we are. You've seen the way we act. We are not racists, and you know that! The question is: Are you?", Ludwig asked him. Lisa's Dad looked at Ludwig and for a while... and just stared at him. Obviously he had not expected such a question... and had never given a thought about that! To him, the racists were necessarily the whites looking down at the blacks, and never the other way around... „If you don't like me just because of the color of my skin, well... you have a big problem... since you are a mulatto... You are the offspring of a black parent and a white parent, aren't you? Who was white: Your Dad or your Mum, huh?", Ludwig asked. „...My grandmother was white...", the man answered, looking down at his feet... „...And do you hate her because of the color of her skin? (...) Sir, I love Lisa... and I know she loves me. Eventually we would like to get married. My intentions are good Sir... and you know me: I'm a good man. Please Sir, don't prejudice me..." Lisa's father looked at Ludwig and remained silent for a while... then he said: „....Look Ludwig... give me some time to think about that, okay?" „Yes Sir. I'm sure you'll see the light cause I know you are a good man too..." A few days later, as Ludwig was working at the distillery, Lisa's Dad came to see him. Ludwig turned to look at the man and said: „Oh ... bonjour monsieur..." The man grinned back at Ludwig and after a moment he asked: „....You love her huh?" „With all my heart Sir!" „....She told me she loves you too..." Ludwig smiled... „Well... I won't stop you from marrying her. I know you're a good man Ludwig... and I'm not a racist. It's just that we've suffered so much..." „I know Sir... But let's not dwell on the past... Let's built the future instead huh? I'm not saying we must forget all the bad things that happened in the past... like slavery...no. We must never forget those things, so they don't happen again. All I'm saying is that we are living in the present... and we must built on the common values we share... and love is one of them. And I sure don't give a damn about the color of your skin Sir. And I sure love Lisa's skin color... She is so beautiful!" „She is, isn't she?" Lisa's Dad proudly answered, with a big smile on his face... „Have you talk to your brother Will about marrying Lisa?" „Not yet Sir! I wanted to have your blessing first..." The man looked at Ludwig with a bigger smile on his face. The fact Ludwig had asked for his blessing was very important to him... and a sign of respect! „We'll go along just fine, you and me... I like you Ludwig! Now, talk to your brother...", the man finally said. „I will Sir!", Ludwig answered, with a big smile on his face. That very same night, Ludwig talked to Will... „....Look Will... I'm twenty-one... I know what I'm doing... and I really love Lisa. Deep in my heart, I know she's the one for me..." „But you're so young..." „How old were you when Paul and you began living together huh?" Will looked at his brother with a grin on his face... „Are you sure bro that's what you want?", Will asked his brother with tears in his eyes... "Look at me Will: I have no doubt... I love her and I want to spend the rest of my life with her..." – "...Give me a big hug bro...", Will answered... The two brothers hugged for a while... and both of them were crying... After a while, Will said: "...Let's tell Paul huh?" "Yeah", Ludwig answered, wiping a few tears from his face using his shirt sleeve... The two brothers went to find Paul... and when they found him, they told him everything... "I'm so happy for you Ludwig. She's a find young woman! You two will make a great couple! And do you know what? The wedding could be celebrated here, on the plantation... you two could get married in the Chapel... what do you think?", Paul said to Ludwig... "...I'll have to talk to Lisa about that... but I think it's a great idea...", Ludwig answered, beaming... "...So I guess a new house will have to be built on the plantation huh?", Paul said, grinning... "Do you really think that could be done?", Ludwig asked, full of hope... "Sure bro!", Will answered... "Look, one day you'll have babies... and as much as I love children, I don't intend to be awaken at night by a baby... crying to be fed...", Will said, laughing... "...Me neither!", Paul added, laughing too... "When do you intend to get married?" "We haven't decided yet. How long do you think it will take to have a new house built?" "I don't know... Let me give a call to a contractor I know in Fort-de-France... We'll see..." After Paul had talked to the contractor, he looked at Ludwig and Will and said: "Two months! He says it can be done in two months... and at the same time, he'll do some much needed repairs to the Chapel... the roof is leaking, and the paint on the columns is peeling..." "Not just on the columns...", Will answered, laughing... "Since we moved here, we haven't spent too much time there, have we?" "Yeah well... I'm not a grenouille de bénitier... (a frog, swimming in a Holy-water basin...)", Paul answered, laughing his heart out... "But now, we have a good reason to have that building repaired, before it crumbles..." "Yup!", Ludwig answered, grinning... And a few days later, work began on the plantation and before long, a new Creole house took form at a certain distance from the big mansion... close to the beach. The Chapel was also repaired! "It's beautiful...", Lisa and Ludwig exclaimed when their new house was completed and as they were visiting it with Lisa's parents and all their friends in tow... A few days later, they were married in the newly renovated Chapel by the local priest... with cowers everywhere. All their friends were there... as well as

Lisa's large family members... After the wedding ceremony, they all went back to the mansion where a superb banquet was waiting for them. That's the moment Will and Paul chose to give Ludwig and Lisa their wedding gift... „Here...", Will and Paul said to the newlywed... „Open it..." The newlywed took the envelope and opened it... It was the title-deed of their new house. Will and Paul had subdivided a part of the plantation, and now Lisa and Ludwig were the official owners of the large piece of land upon which their house was now standing... And there was also a check attached to the title-deed... Ludwig looked at the check... then raised his eyes to look at Will and Paul... For a while he remained silent with his eyes full of tears... „...It's way too much...", he finally said... Will and Paul smiled at the newlywed, and Will said: „It's our pleasure bro... Now I hope you'll follow Paul's advice and invest that money..." „...Sure will...", Ludwig answered, beaming... Lisa and Ludwig went to Paris on their honeymoon, where Lisa was introduced not only to Paul's father... but to François and Philippe as well... A month later, when they came back to Martinique, Ludwig told Will and Paul the latest news from Paris... „...Your Dad was very happy to see us...", Ludwig said to Paul... „He's not getting any younger, but he's doing fine. Still working at the Head office... As for François and Philippe... I guess they work hard, studying to become doctors... But they're doing great! And they are planning to come to Martinique next summer... to visit us..." Of course, Paul already knew about that, since in his last letter to Paul, François had written about the trip he and his lover were planning... So, Ludwig and Lisa moved into their new house, and life went on...

A year later, in the summer of 1947, Lutz's brother Hans also got married... in the same Chapel... And another house was built on the plantation for him and his new wife! At the wedding, not only were François and Philippe there... but so was Ludwig, holding his first born child into his arms. His son! What a proud father he was! And beaming with that... and so was Lisa. Three other children would follow that first born child... and Will and Paul couldn't stop laughing, watching them running through the mansion... Although Ludwig, Lisa and their children were living in their own house near the beach... the children were always running to Will and Paul... whom didn't miss a chance to spoil them... even though from time to time, Ludwig was protesting... Eventually, Ludwig's children were joined by Hans', who had four of his own... And of course, Lutz and Franz were worst than Will and Paul, spoiling them... Now that Pierre was attending college at Fort-de-France... Will, Paul, Lutz and Franz felt the mansion was a little empty... and so the children were always welcome... Three years later... in August of 1950... Paul received a cable from his Dad, telling him his mother had died. Paul called his brother Pierre at Fort-de-France to tell him the news... „... What do you want me to say...", Pierre answered... „And I'm not going to Paris, to attend her funeral... if that's what you wanted to ask me. Do you intend to go?" „...No.", Paul answered. „I'm not going either. I just feel sorry for Dad, that's all..." „Look Paul... The new airport at Le Lamentin will be inaugurated in a few weeks... so maybe you and I could then cy to Paris... to see Dad... what do you think?" „Good idea... I'll tell Dad okay?", Paul answered... As they had said, in November of 1950, Paul and Pierre flew to Paris from the new international airport of Fort-de- France, and they went to see their Dad... „You're looking great Dad...", Paul said to his father... It felt very strange to Paul to be back on Avenue Foch... Six years had passed since the last time he had set foot there... „I'm sorry for Mum...", Paul said... „But as you know, we couldn't make it on time for her funeral..." – „Yes, I understand... (...) You know Paul, it wasn't easy living with her the last few years..." „I can imagine...", Paul started to say... „Has she ever inquired after Pierre and me?" From the moment she had learned that Paul... and later Pierre were gay... their Mum had refused to talk to them... since in her mind, they were sinners. She had never accepted the idea that her two sons were gay... and so she had cut all the bridges with them... as if they had never existed... Paul's Dad was not surprised that Paul was asking him that question though. He had always hope his wife would change her mind... and accept the truth. So it is with very sad eyes that he looked at his two sons and said: „...No. She never inquired about you two. I'm so sorry..." „Don't. It's not your fault Dad...", Pierre answered. After a moment of silence, Paul looked at his Dad and said: „Hey Dad... I was thinking... Why don't you come back to Martinique with us... you could spend some time there with us... see where we live and everything... you could cy there with us huh? Say yes Dad... please..." „...Are you serious? Me? Going to Martinique?" – „Why not? Just for a visit... Why not dad?", Pierre added... „Well..." „That's it, Dad! You're coming...", Paul said, with a big smile on his face... The man finally agreed to go and two weeks later the three of them flew to Fort-de-France... where Will, Lutz and Franz were waiting for them at the new Lamentin Airport... „Welcome to Martinique!", Will said to the man, as he was getting off the plane... „Thank you Will... It's so nice to see you again... and you too, Lutz and Franz..." „Welcome Sir", Lutz and Franz answered, shaking hands with Paul's father... Paul's Dad was very pleased to see how well his two sons were doing in Martinique, and was very impressed by the plantation... „I'm so proud of you, sons... So proud!", he said... „And I'm glad I came... But now, I've spend five weeks here... and it's time for me to go back to Paris..." „Sure Dad... But you know you're welcome to stay longer if you want... But I understand you want to go back... although I wish we could keep you here with us...", Paul answered, with a smile on his face... „Well... Thanks. But my life is in Paris..." „We understand Dad..." Paul and Pierre answered. A few days later, they all drove to the Lamentin Airport... and as he bid his sons farewell, the old man said to them: „...Remember that I love you sons... and take good care of one another... I love you! So much!" „We will Dad... and you too, take good care...", they both answered. They were all waving at the old man as he was walking on the tarmac to his plane. They looked at him as he was slowly climbing the stairs leading to the plane. Then, as he reached the top of the stairs he turned to look back at them and waved to them, with a big smile on his face. They waved back to him with tears in their eyes. Then the plane left. That was the last time Paul and Pierre saw their Dad, as a few months later he died of a heart-attack. Paul and Pierre flew to Paris to attend his funeral... and after the funeral, Paul took some time to settle his father's estate. With their sister Catherine, Paul and Pierre were the sole heirs to their father's large fortune. While he was in Paris, Paul received a very good offer from a serious investor who wanted to buy their shares in the company... As they were staying on Avenue Foch, Paul and Pierre had a meeting with their sister... and after good consideration, the three of them agreed to accept the offer and to sell all of their shares... It was also agreed that Catherine would keep the mansion on Avenue Foch... and Paul also agreed that she could go to Bagatelle as often as she wanted to, as long as she would pay to keep the château in good condition... As Paul had inherited Bagatelle from his grandmother, he was the sole owner of the estate, and he didn't want to sell it... since the château had belong to his family for so many years... However, since they had moved to Martinique, nobody was living there, and the maintenance expenses were quite large. Of course that was not a problem for Paul, as he was a very rich man. No... that was not the point! But why keep the château if no one was going there. And since Paul had no intention of ever moving back to France... well... why keep that estate? That was the question! And so, Paul was very happy to see that his sister Catherine wanted to spend some time at the château... for his problem was solved. No need to sell the estate. At least... not for now! The night before they were set to cy back to Martinique, and as the three of them were having supper at the mansion on Avenue Foch, Catherine looked at her two brothers and said: „...I want you to know that I love you guys... and that I don't give a damn about the fact you two are gay... I love you, that's all! And I want you to know it has not been easy for me either to live here with Mum... She was... well... I guess I don't have to explain..." „Yes...", Paul answered with a sad smile on his face. „I can imagine it wasn't easy for you..." „We love you too Catherine", Pierre said... „And I sure hope you will come to visit us in Martinique... I miss you Catherine... Please, come to see us there... „ „I will... I swear..." She answered, smiling at her two brothers. (...) „And before you two leave tomorrow... is there's something in here you would like to keep and bring with you?" „No", Pierre answered... „My memories of the mansion here are not among my best..." „I understand.", she answered with a sad smile on her face... „And you Paul?" „Well... There's dad's desk in the study... I'd like to keep it..." „Sure. I'll have it packed and ship to you, no problem... Anything else?" „No...", Paul answered... „That's all...".

TO BE CONTINUED

In the last part of the trilogy, Jack, the first-person narrator, invites readers to join him on an emotional journey in Martinique. At 15 years old, Jack is grappling with the complexities of self-discovery, especially as he begins to understand and explore his identity as a young gay man. His growing realization and acceptance of his sexuality are central to this part of the story, and his friendship with Paul becomes a crucial source of support in navigating these challenges.

This part of the series delves into the emotional intricacies of friendship, identity, and love, highlighting the transformative power of connection and mutual support. It offers readers a deep, emotional exploration of coming-of-age in a complex, often uncertain world.

Let yourself be taken on an exciting journey filled with unexpected encounters, lived history, and personal discoveries and follow Jack to the island of Martinique:

Olivier Bernard

Crossing Shores
A Journey of Gay Love and Self-Discovery

CROSSING LINES

Set in the turmoil of World War II, the first part of the trilogy *Crossing Lines, Fates and Shores* is a captivating tale of unexpected bonds and forbidden emotions that transcend the brutal barriers of conflict. The story follows Paul De Brion, a young Frenchman who finds himself caught in the occupation of Paris. Arrested for failing to carry his identification, Paul is brought before German officers for questioning. It is here that he meets Wilhelm von Rundstedt, a young, compassionate German officer tasked with translating and overseeing Paul's interrogation.

As the narrative unfolds, Will's demeanor surprises Paul. Far from the harsh, stereotypical portrayal of German soldiers, Will exhibits kindness and humanity. When Paul learns that his beloved grandmother is dying in a nearby hospital, Will takes an unexpected risk by assisting Paul in visiting her, defying orders in a display of empathy. This shared experience deepens their connection, leading to a complex blend of gratitude, trust, and burgeoning feelings.

The story portrays a rich tapestry of historical context, personal growth, and the defiance of prejudice, resulting in a unique story of love that dares to blossom in the most unlikely of circumstances.

Olivier Bernard

Crossing Lines
Gay Love in the Shadows of War